WILD ROSE

Katherine Kingsley

A SIGNET BOOK

NEW AMERICAN LIBRARY

NAL BOOKS ARE AVAILABLE AT QUANTITY DISCOUNTS WHEN USED TO PROMOTE PRODUCTS OR SERVICES. FOR INFORMATION PLEASE WRITE TO PREMIUM MARKETING DIVISION, NEW AMERICAN LIBRARY, 1633 BROADWAY, NEW YORK, NEW YORK 10019.

SIGNET, SIGNET CLASSIC, MENTOR, ONYX, PLUME, MERIDIAN and NAL BOOKS are published by NAL PENGUIN INC., 1633 Broadway, New York, New York 10019

First Printing, January, 1988

1 2 3 4 5 6 7 8 9

PRINTED IN THE UNITED STATES OF AMERICA

Prologue

THE stableyard of the Aylesbury Arms was silent in the pre-dawn, except for the faint rustling of the animals stabled within. The ground was covered with a brittle frost, and the shadowy figure at work on the large carriage parked off to one side stopped occasionally to pull the voluminous cloak more closely together, warding off the heavy chill that hung in the air. A wheel had been carefully loosened with a wrench and now the thickly gloved hands were at work on the shaft that the horses would be attached to only a few hours hence.

Slowly and noiselessly, the saw wore away at the underside of the axle, ensuring that when the wheel fell off, the axle would snap in two. A rooster crowed once as the sky began to lighten to gray and the cloaked figure stopped working, standing back and examining the carriage with satisfaction. Emblazoned on the side was the crest of the Earl of Carlyle.

"Bryonny? Bryonny, wake up!" The knocking came loudly at the door, and Bryonny turned over and buried her head in the pillow with a groan. It couldn't be more than six o'clock in the morning, judging by the light, and it was unbelievably cold in the little room.

"Bryonny, come along. Shake a leg, Papa wants you down for breakfast in twenty minutes. I'm not leaving till you've answered me." Her brother could be amazingly persistent, she thought with a reluctant smile.

5

"Oh, all right, David, I'll be there. But I beg you, will you send someone up with hot water, and to lay a fire?"

His laugh came through the door. "I can't believe you haven't adjusted to the climate yet—it's been two months! But not to fear, I've attended to it. The woman will be along directly."

"Thank you, David. You can go now; I promise I'll be down on time."

"I trust you will; you know how anxious Papa is to get to Hambledon Abbey. He's ordered the carriage for half-past-seven promptly, and it's another good day's journey."

She heard his footsteps retreating, and a moment later another, lighter knock came at the door. It was the chambermaid with the water, and in a matter of minutes she had a fire blazing in the grate. Bryonny refused any offers of help in her toilette, and waited for the girl to leave before she threw the covers back and ran shivering to the fireplace where her clothes were laid out on a chair.

She wasted no time removing her nightdress and struggling into her traveling clothes, for once grateful for the thick petticoat and heavy wool skirts that she'd habitually cursed since arriving on the shores of England. Scrubbing her face with the water that was now lukewarm, she impatiently tied back her long, thick hair, then closed her trunk, grabbed up her pelisse, and tore down the hall and down the stairs into the private parlor where her father and brother were waiting.

Lord Carlyle looked up from his kippers with a smile. "I'm well pleased, my dear. You're only five minutes late this morning."

She kissed his cheek. "It's the cold, Papa. I'd swear I was sixty instead of sixteen with the way my bones feel. It takes them at least half an hour to thaw!" She helped herself from the sideboard, and sat down to eat a heaping breakfast with her usual—unfashionably—healthy appetite.

David looked at her over his teacup with amused

blue eyes. "I do remember that I used to say the same thing ten years ago when I first arrived. I thought Shelbourne the coldest, most inhospitable house in the world. But now on the rare occasions that I return to Jamaica, I find it insufferably hot. It's all a matter of acclimatization."

"I have no intention of staying long enough in England to acclimatize, dear brother," said Bryonny tartly.

Lord Carlyle raised his eyebrows. "Let us not have this argument again, my girl. It's time to transform you from a hoyden into a woman, and you'll stay as long as it takes to have a Season. By that time, I doubt very much you'll have any inclination to return home."

"Papa, I simply don't understand how you could have spent so many years teaching me about the equality of the sexes and then turn around and expect to sell me like a prize cow!" The yellow flecks in the green of her irises stood out as always when she was adamant.

Lord Carlyle shook his head and laughed. "As usual when it comes to this subject, you're thinking with your emotions and not your brain. I've never said that I would force you into an unwanted marriage, Bryonny. I'm only giving you the opportunity to experience another kind of lifestyle, perhaps to fall in love as young people are wont to do, and to marry and raise a family."

"Papa, how is it that *you* left England and married and raised a family on a Caribbean island, and now you're so anxious for David and myself to be condemned to the life you left behind?"

Lord Carlyle and his son exchanged a quick glance, then Lord Carlyle said gently, "Bryonny, you know that David is heir to the earldom and all that it entails. It is his responsibility, one that for my own reasons I preferred to leave to your godfather to look after for me. To be perfectly honest, I had no intention of ever coming back to England, but with your dear mother dead, it seemed that it was only right to bring you over myself and see to a proper introduction to society for you."

"Bah!" said Bryonny succinctly.

David smiled and shook his head, wondering how she would cope with the rigors of society the following spring. Or rather, how society would cope with her. With an inward chuckle at the idea he rose, placing his beaver cap on his fair head.

"I'll just go see to the loading of the carriage, Papa. Bellings is sure to have it waiting."

Bryonny looked out from the carriage window and sighed with impatience. She was thoroughly bored with sitting hour after endless hour, and this was the third tedious day of travel. She shot a look at her father and brother, who were engaged in quiet conversation, and for the hundredth time wondered what trouble had sent them hurtling toward Hambledon Abbey with no warning.

She'd been on the cliffs that afternoon, those sheer golden cliffs of Dorset that she found so fascinating. One could stand looking down on the slate-gray ocean watching the turbulent waves seething below as the wind rushed up, bringing fine sprays of salt up that stung at the eyes. It made her feel like a wild creature, part of the elements that swirled around her. But she had learned how very dangerous those elements could be; unfamiliar with the weather patterns, she hadn't read the signs of a storm moving in. Fortunately, her horse had sensed it and she followed his lead, but not in time to escape the downpour, the freezing rain pounding down on them, chilling through to the bone and made only colder by the howling wind whipping around them. As they rounded the last knoll and Shelbourne Hall came into view, its massive stone exterior even darker with gusting rain, she'd breathed a sigh of relief and it was then that she'd seen the carriage departing from the house. There was no crest on the side to identify the caller, and she'd only just been able to make out the blurred image of a cloaked figure through the rainswept window.

She'd found her father and David closeted away in the small salon. They'd both looked grim and her father instructed her to see to the packing for them all.

They were to leave for Hambledon Abbey the next day. The most she could discover was that there had been a disquieting piece of news, and they needed to consult Lord Hambledon at once on a legal matter.

That had been all, and two days ago they had set off on the journey. Once again, Bryonny squirmed in the seat, longing for the interminable trip to be over. It was late afternoon and the day which, although cold, had been bright, had now darkened ominously. The wind had shifted to the northwest, bringing in heavy storm clouds, and Bryonny hoped they would reach the Abbey before the clouds opened up and rain slowed the carriage's progress.

"How much further, Papa?" she asked anxiously.

"Not too long now, child. I seem to remember that the last turning led to Market Kettering, and that's about half an hour's distance from the Abbey, isn't that right, David?"

"Yes, Papa. Not to worry, Bryonny, you'll be released from your torment shortly."

"Oh, good," she sighed, shifting and rubbing her bottom which had gone quite numb. "What is Lord Hambledon like, David? It seems peculiar having a godfather I've never met, as if I should be obliged to be fond of him. Will I like him, do you think?"

"Oh, yes, I should think so, Bryonny. He's a very kind man, and has been most generous about offering himself as family. Of course, he is family—a second cousin, which may not seem like much, but when you're alone and far from home, it seems like a very great deal. You'll find that he and his son Julian, if he's there, don't stand on ceremony, which should relieve you considerably."

"Oh, it does! Will I like him, too, do you think?"

David paused, then shrugged. "I couldn't say. To tell the truth, we're not that well acquainted. He has a busy life in London, and our paths don't often cross."

"Oh—well, who else lives at the Abbey, then?" Bryonny was consumed with curiosity, for these would be the first people in England she'd met outside of Shelbourne.

"No one other than a small staff. As you know, Lady Hambledon died many years ago and Lord Hambledon doesn't entertain. There's Simms, the butler, Cook, of course, and Mrs. Merk, the housekeeper. You'll find her most amusing, Bryonny. She puts me in mind of a plump little partridge, very busy and always poking around in some corner or another, clucking about—"

A loud noise suddenly sounded like a crack of thunder and there was a terrible jerk as the carriage lurched and then seemed to hurl itself crazily onto its side. Bryonny registered David's shout and the scream of the horses as she found herself flung through the air, and then there was nothing but a spinning void as the world upended itself and disappeared into blackness.

Rain lashed heavily down from the evening sky, packing the ground in a sodden carpet of mud. It splattered the roof and windows of the carriage which had pulled up in front of Hambledon Abbey at a breakneck pace, and stung at the face of the fair-headed man who carefully pulled the unmoving body of a young girl from its depths. He lightly ran up the steps with his burden in his arms, then impatiently banged at the enormous arched door.

After what seemed an eternity it opened and an elderly gentleman, obviously the butler, appeared in the portal. He registered no surprise, but mildly inquired, "Yes, sir?" as he looked the stranger up and down.

"This girl needs help. Will you give me leave to enter?"

"Who shall I say is calling, sir?"

"For God's sake, man—this is no time for questions! Can't you see the girl's badly injured? There are others out there, dead!"

"If you will wait a moment, I'll summon Lord Hambledon, sir."

The man regarded him with disgust. "'And I'm to stand here in the pouring rain while this child dies in my arms? Stand aside at once!"

He spoke in a tone accustomed to command, which made sense to Simms considering that he was dressed in the uniform of the Coldstream Guards, and no less than a captain. But what was he doing descending from Lord Hambledon's carriage, and with the body of a young woman in his arms at that? Simms acted as any sensible butler would in such a situation, and stood away.

"Yes, sir. Please come in. I shall summon his lordship immediately." But before he could move, a figure appeared at his shoulder, tall and slightly stooped with a full head of white hair and an aristocratically long, thin nose.

"There's no need, Simms. Direct the gentleman upstairs immediately and call for Mrs. Merk, then send for the doctor. I think the front bedroom would be best."

"Yes, my lord." Simms hurriedly climbed the stairs in front of the captain and showed him into a large bedroom with an enormous four-poster bed.

The captain carefully laid the girl down, then straightened. "I'll watch her now. Perhaps you'll be so kind as to have the doctor summoned."

"It's been done." A voice, breathless from hurrying, came from the door and the captain turned around to see a small, plump, middle-aged woman with spectacles perched firmly on the end of her nose and a no-nonsense bun planted on the back of her head. She was still tying her white apron over her black dress as she bustled into the room and past the captain and Simms. "My goodness, what do we have here!" she exclaimed as she took in the motionless form of the girl. "Only two minutes back from my day off and look what greets me! Whoever is the poor child?"

"I have no idea," the captain said curtly. "But I suggest you not waste your time on speculation and do what you can for her, immediately."

"Why, yes, of course I shall," she said, bristling, clearly annoyed that a perfect stranger had just put her in her place. But she hurried back to the door and peered down the hall. "Lucy! Bring me hot water, soap, and linens, and be quick about it!" Mrs. Merk turned back to the captain. "His lordship requested you in the library, sir. Simms will show you the way. Lucy and I will watch over the dear thing until the doctor arrives."

The captain nodded his head, and with one last careful look at the girl, he followed Simms out of the room.

"Now, captain, perhaps you'll tell me exactly what you and the girl are doing here in my house?" Lord Hambledon frowned as he poured two brandies from the decanter.

"My lord, I'm afraid there's very little I can tell you about the girl. I was simply riding down the road about three miles from here when I noticed a wheel lying on the side of the road next to a large skid mark. I looked over the embankment; that's how I found them."

"Them?" said Lord Hambledon sharply, turning. A small splash of cognac fell on the carpet.

"Yes, my lord. There was an overturned carriage below, badly splintered. Naturally, I went down to look, in case there were people in need of help . . ."

"Well, go on, man, speak up!" cried Lord Hambledon impatiently.

"They were all dead." He looked away for a moment, and ran a hand through his hair. "All but the girl. She must have been thrown clear along with the coachman. She was lying not far from him. She stirred, and just as I was attending to her, your own coach stopped and your men offered assistance—"

"How many? How many people?"

"Other than their coachman, only two men, my lord; one was younger, the other in his later years."

Lord Hambledon sank into his chair, still holding the two glasses. His face had paled alarmingly. "Dear God . . ."

"My lord?" The captain crossed quickly to his side and gently removed the glasses from his shaking hands, placing them on a table. "Are you unwell? Perhaps I should call the doctor down?"

"No. No, that will not be necessary. You're certain there was no one left alive?"

"Yes, I made quite sure. Do you—do you know these people, my lord?" The captain looked horrified.

"I am terribly afraid that I might." He appeared to have aged in moments, as if the bones beneath the skin had suddenly crumbled. He passed a hand over his eyes, then collected himself with a visible effort as the captain addressed him with concern.

"My lord, are you quite sure you are not in need of a doctor?"

"I've had a bad shock; I shall be better shortly. This is a damnable thing!"

"Who are they, my lord?"

"I was shortly expecting guests, the Earl of Carlyle and his family. They were traveling from Dorset and not due here until tomorrow, but with your description . . ." He gestured wearily toward the door. "Perhaps you would be so good as to have Simms send my coach for—for the others." He leaned back heavily in his chair.

"I believe your men went directly back for them, my lord. I am so terribly sorry. But surely it *cannot* be? Would you not have recognized the girl?"

"No. I've never met Byronny. They lived in Jamaica, you see. Her father only recently brought her to England. But she would be about the right age, and with that auburn hair, I can't imagine who else it could be." He passed his hand over his face. "I cannot believe such a misfortune can have overtaken them."

"It is indeed a terrible thing, my lord." The captain rose and walked over to the window. "I can only be intruding at this difficult time. I'll be on my way now. I don't suppose there's much more I can do."

"No, please; I am greatly in your debt, sir. If it hadn't been for you, we might not have found them for days. Won't you stay the night, at least?"

"Thank you, my lord, but I wouldn't want to impose. In any case, I really must move on. I have to be back with the regiment tomorrow, in London.''

There was a knock on the door and Mrs. Merk entered with a tray of food. "The doctor has left, my lord. He asked me to give his apologies for not speaking to you himself, but we called him away from a difficult birthing in the village and he had to get back immediately.''

"Yes, yes, Mrs. Merk, that's all well and fine, but what did he say about the girl?''

"I'm afraid he wasn't very optimistic, my lord. She has a knock to her head that's caused bad swelling, he said, and is still bleeding, although fortunately all her other cuts stopped some time ago from the look of them. Poor dear, we had to cut off all that pretty hair; such a pity, I thought it.''

"Did he say anything else?'' interrupted Lord Hambledon impatiently.

"Yes, my lord. He said she's far too weak to lose any more blood; I'm to keep a close eye on her. If her condition worsens I'm to call him, but he'll be back to look in on her as soon as he can. He said that all we could do was hope, but that with the rain and the cold, it didn't look very promising. Do we have any idea who the poor thing is or what happened to her?'' Once again she shot the captain a look brimming with curiosity.

"Unfortunately, we do. Thanks to this young man here—good lord, I don't even know your name!''

"It didn't seem quite the time for formal introductions,'' said the captain with a little smile. "I had the advantage of knowing you to be the Marquess of Hambledon from your men. I am Captain Philip Neville.''

"Captain Neville found the carriage. I'm afraid it's very bad news, Mrs. Merk. It seems that Lord Carlyle's carriage went off the road and he and Lord Wycomb were killed. . . It is Lady Bryonny upstairs.''

All the color drained from Mrs. Merk's face until, as he finished, the tray she was holding slipped from her grasp and went crashing to the floor. "Dear heaven!" she gasped, her hands going to her throat, her eyes dilated with shock.

"Mrs. Merk! Here, you must sit down. Captain, the brandy!" He helped the overwrought woman to a chair, and Captain Neville pressed one of the untouched glasses into her trembling hands.

"Here, please take this, ma'am. It will help to calm you," he said kindly.

"Oh, yes, thank you. How kind . . ." She stared at him uncomprehendingly and then her eyes went to the glass in her hand, and she took a tiny sip, gasping as the liquid burned at her throat. Then, with a slight bit of color returned to her cheeks, she looked up at Lord Hambledon. "I beg your pardon, my lord, how very clumsy of me. It was the shock, you see; I—I had no idea. I thought it was a stranger . . . I can scarcely credit it!" Tears welled up in her eyes and flooded over, tracing an uneven path down her soft, lined cheeks. Lord Hambledon offered her his handkerchief and she removed her spectacles and dabbed at her eyes.

"Try not to distress yourself, Mrs. Merk. I know how fond you were of David."

"Thank you, my lord, but I should not be thinking of my own feelings at a time like this. I'm so dreadfully sorry for your bereavement. Please let me assure you that I will take the very best care of the poor, dear thing. I know just what the child will need. Don't worry, we'll pull her through, you'll see."

"Mrs. Merk, I can't think of a better person than you to whom I might leave Lady Bryonny's care. She'll be needing much love and understanding, and you are filled with both."

"Thank you, my lord," said Mrs. Merk, blushing and looking down at her clasped hands. "If you'll excuse me now, I'll summon someone to clean up and replenish the tray. Simms is bringing a bottle of claret from the cellar. Will Captain Neville be staying the night?" She had returned to something approximating her usual efficiency.

"No, I'm afraid he must be on his way tonight."

"Then I'd better be about that food. We can't have a hero leaving on an empty stomach, can we?" She rustled out of the room to go about her business and see to her new charge.

Captain Neville took his leave shortly after, and it was with great sadness that Lord Hambledon indentified the bodies of his cousins brought back in his carriage. He then went into the room where the girl he now knew for certain to be Bryonny Livingston was lying in the four-poster bed.

"My lord." Mrs. Merk rose from the chair. "I'm afraid there has been no change."

Lord Hambledon looked down at Bryonny. Her face was chalky white and a bandage, stained with blood, was wrapped completely around her head. Her chest rose only slightly with her breathing. She looked very young and vulnerable, and only just clinging to life, her lips blue and her skin cold to the touch.

"Poor child," said Lord Hambledon softly, sitting down on the bed. "Leave her with me, Mrs. Merk."

"But my lord, you should be getting your rest. You know you're not well."

"I'm perfectly well, Mrs. Merk, and in any case it's not my health that concerns me. I very much doubt I shall be sleeping tonight. Go now. I'd like to be alone with the child."

"Yes, my lord," said Mrs. Merk disapprovingly, but nevertheless she left the room, shutting the door quietly behind her.

The next two hours went by painfully slowly, the only sounds in the room the crackle of the fire and the ticking of the carriage clock, marking the heavy minutes. Lord Hambledon sat alone with his thoughts, turning the accident over and over in his mind. Death was certainly not new to him, but this tragedy had some very long-reaching consequences.

The silence was broken abruptly by the sound of footsteps pounding up the stairs and faintly, a deep voice saying, "Which room?"

"Your mother's old room, my lord," came Simms's reply from the hall.

Only seconds later, the door burst open and a tall, dark-haired man entered, still wiping the rain from his face.

"Father! What in the name of heaven's happened?" He strode to the bedside and looked down at the small figure bundled there, his hands resting on his hips. "Who the devil is that?" he asked in surprise.

Lord Hambledon regarded his son wryly. As usual, Julian had skipped over the amenities and gone straight to the heart of the matter. At times it made him wonder how Julian was forging himself such a successful career as a diplomat for the Crown.

"Well?" he asked, turning his penetrating gaze on his father. "What in sweet hell is going on here? I was dining out on my way back from that blasted meeting in Stamford when word came that there'd been an accident of some sort with the carriage and the men had been killed! I sent it back hours ago with a note saying I would ride rather than keep them any later, but I saw both the footmen outside just now, thank God. I nearly broke my horse getting back here. So I ask again, who is this?"

"Sit down, Julian," said Lord Hambledon gently, knowing that Julian's curtness was a result of the worry he must have felt at the news.

Julian pulled up a chair and swung himself into it, regarding his father impatiently.

"It wasn't our carriage that met with an accident, Julian. It was Lord Carlyle's. David and his father were killed."

"*What!* Dear God . . ." His eyes, gray as steel, snapped back to the bed. "Then this must be David's sister—Bryonny, isn't it?" He stood and bent over her, regarding her more carefully now, and taking in the stained bandage and skin as white as parchment beneath the cuts and bruises. She was a pretty girl from what he could tell. Her face was heart-shaped, with a high, smooth brow, a nose that was straight and delicate over a full, bow-shaped mouth that turned sweetly up at the corners, and a pointed little chin.

He slowly sat down again. "What did Dr. Walters say? Does he think she'll live?"

"We don't know, Julian. He doesn't seem to think it likely."

"This is a damnable thing! I'm so very sorry, Father. I know how much you were looking forward to this visit, as unexpected as it was."

"Yes . . ." said Lord Hambledon with a frown, looking very like his son. "They weren't meant to come until late next month, you know."

"Yes, I do know. How odd. . . I wonder what could have been so urgent; he ought to have said something in his letter. Now I suppose we'll never know unless Bryonny has some idea."

"That's the least of our worries at the moment."

"Ah, well. I imagine the speed at which they must have been traveling did the damage on these treacherous roads, not to mention the storm. It's certainly not the first time such a thing has happened."

"No, it's not. Bryonny was terribly fortunate that Captain Neville happened to be traveling the same road and saw where the carriage had gone over the embankment."

"Captain Neville? Who the devil's he?"

"A stranger who was kind enough to help. Then the carriage you'd sent home saw his horse and stopped. They brought them here, naturally."

"And where is this heroic captain now?"

"He left soon after. Really, Julian, must you be so sarcastic? He did us a good turn, after all."

"You have to admit it's the stuff of which books are made—gallant captain rescues damsel in distress. But to go back to this situation, now what happens? Suppose the girl does die? I believe she's the last of the Livingston line?"

"Yes, which makes it even more tragic, if that's possible. We simply will have to see that she lives through this. It's a miracle she survived the fall."

"Well, at least she has youth on her side."

"And from what I gather from her father's letters, spirit. That will surely do no harm. Although I have also gathered that her spirit has caused no end of trouble in the past." He tried to smile. "I believe John thought that bringing her to England for a Season might help to take her in hand. No one could have known it would lead to this . . ."

"And that's my next question. Now that the girl's an orphan, where will she go?"

"She will stay here, naturally."

Julian cocked an eyebrow skeptically. "Come now, Father, you can't be serious! Surely she has people back in Jamaica who will look after her?"

"You're forgetting that I'm her godfather, Julian. She is my responsibility now, and one I'm certainly not going to shirk."

He looked at his father incredulously. "My God, you are serious! I can't believe it! You don't know anything about young girls, Father, and in any case, you're far too old to be taking up child-rearing!"

"I can see you think so, Julian," said Lord Hambledon with a dry smile. "However, I'm neither senile nor in my grave yet, and although you may be fully twenty-eight, you're still my son. I'd thank you to remember that."

"I beg your pardon," said Julian, looking not the least bit contrite. "But that doesn't alter the fact that it's an insane notion, to up and take in a child."

"The child is your cousin, Julian. A distant cousin, perhaps, but we're the only family she has."

"Yes . . . Thinking of that, what of the Livingston fortune? I suppose that goes to Bryonny?"

"Yes, it does. Why do you ask?"

"It's yet another point to my argument. That's another burden for you to have to shoulder. It's a tremendous responsibility."

"My dear Julian, you seem to forget that I have been managing the Livingston affairs along with our own for many years now. The only difference is that I shall be managing them for Bryonny rather than her father."

"I suppose that's true. I've always thought Lord Carlyle was incredibly irresponsible taking off for Jamaica and never returning to England, not even to take over Shelbourne when his father died. What was the scandal behind all that anyway, Father? Don't you think I'm old enough now to be told?" Julian grinned, a broad, attractive smile, and it transformed his face, giving it a charming, slightly roguish quality.

"You're old enough to have some scandals of your own behind you, certainly," said his father tartly.

"Oh, come on, Father. I've never done anything terrible enough to be sent packing to a Caribbean island. I think you like to exaggerate my little exploits."

"Your little exploits are keeping you from settling down and starting a family, Julian."

"For God's sake, let's not start on that again," said Julian with irritation. "'Well? What happened?"

"There was an incident at Shelbourne involving a servant, and that's all I'm going to say on the matter."

"It must have been one hell of an incident to keep him away for almost thirty years."

"No, no. That was over almost immediately, simply a matter of poor judgment. No, John quarreled badly with his father. The man was quite a tyrant, and after John was sent off to Jamaica, he met Georgina McGregor, whose father had a plantation and no son, and that was that."

"How ironic that the Carlyle succession should be wiped out because he returned to England after all this time."

"Indeed. And poor Bryonny." Lord Hambledon looked at her sadly. "I don't know how I'm going to tell her."

"If she lives . . ." Julian met his father's eyes, as gray as his own.

"Yes, if she lives."

Chapter One

IT was early morning and Lucy had come quietly into Bryonny's bedroom, carrying a pitcher of hot water. The room was pleasantly furnished with light yellow silk hangings on the four-poster bed and around the casement windows which looked out to the east where the sun was just rising above the orchard tops. It poured through the windows, filling the room with hazy golden light. Embers left from the night glowed warmly in the fireplace, and she crossed over to add some wood and stir the fire into life. A grouping of comfortable chairs covered in pale green and yellow stripes was arranged in front of the fireplace and off against the wall between the two window seats was a long cheval glass that reflected back the sunlight. Crystal bottles and silver-backed hairbrushes lay on top of the dressing table in the corner, and in the other corner stood a beautifully carved armoire. This Lucy opened and took out a shirt and a pair of breeches, then went over to her mistress, fast asleep in the big bed. She began to pull back the hangings, letting in the sun.

Bryonny opened her eyes and blinked, then sat up in bed and rubbed her eyes. Despite the fact that it had been a year since she'd been at the Abbey, she still often woke with a sense of surprise to find herself there. "Good morning, Lucy," she said, stretching. "It looks like a fine day!"

"Good morning, mum," said Lucy, bobbing a curtsy. "A fine day, indeed." Seventeen-year-old Lucy was a sweet and simple girl from Hambledon Village. She was large-boned and buxom with bright blue eyes, pink cheeks, and a button nose. She had a fancy for Dougal down at the stables. She also had a passionate devotion for Bryonny, who had always treated her with kindness. It had been Lucy who had sat with Bryonny during the long, slow months of her recovery, Lucy who had offered her simple words of comfort in her wrenching moments of grief and who had always found ways to make her laugh in spite of her unhappiness, with tales of her rowdy brothers, village life, and the quirks of the inhabitants of the Abbey in which Mrs. Merk played a large part.

"What's the time?" said Bryonny, swinging her legs over the edge of the bed.

"Early yet, my lady, but I knew you wouldn't want to miss a moment of the sun after all the rain we've been having, especially knowing how you've been pining to ride. I brought your hot water."

"Thank you, Lucy, and you're quite right. It's high time Bedlam had some exercise. He's been making enough noise down at the stable to wake the dead, and George has had plenty to say about it!"

Lucy grinned. "Mr. George has plenty to say about everything that I've ever heard, and that stallion of yours is the least of it! But then he's been head groom for a donkey's age and thinks he owns the place and everyone in it."

"I know. But he's as loyal as they come, Lucy, despite his ornery ways. As long as you appreciate a good piece of horseflesh, he's all kindness."

"Yes, my lady, but I haven't forgotten the first time you showed up at the stables and turned your nose up at the pretty mare he had waiting for you, and demanded to ride Lord Richmond's gelding. There were sparks flying between you for days!"

"I do remember," said Bryonny with a laugh. "And who won?"

"Why you, my lady, but then you always have, that I've ever seen."

"It's all a matter of being resonable, Lucy. And

Lord Hambledon has been a wonderful ally. He's never stood in the way of my doing things differently, just for the sake of observing conventions." She pulled her nightdress over her head and reached for the breeches.

"No, my lady, and my mum says it's a wise thing, too. She says the best way to tame a wild thing is to give it its freedom and before you know it, it's eating straight out of your hand—oh, forgive me, my lady!" Lucy's hand flew to her mouth and she blushed deep crimson.

"Don't give it another thought, Lucy," said Bryonny, choking back her laughter. "I daresay your mother's probably right. It's how I broke Bedlam, after all, and they said it couldn't be done."

"Yes, my lady. At least, Mr. Forbes told Dougal that the only person he'd trust to break him would be Lord Richmond, and it was that reason he sold his prize stallion to Lord Hambledon. Mr. Forbes was fit to be tied, said Dougal, when he heard that Lord Richmond had been gone for a year. It had never crossed his mind that the beast was for you."

"What is he like, Lucy?" she asked through the splashing water.

"Oh, he's short and stocky with a big belly like a—"

"Surely not, Lucy! Oh, Lucy! How could Lord Hambledon's son have a pot belly?"

"Oh, no, my lady! I thought you meant Mr. Forbes!" She laughed uproariously at the idea. "Lord Richmond is anything but! He's very tall and dark, and handsome as the devil, and he has the devil's own temper, too, when something doesn't go his way. But I've only been here a year, my mum not wanting me to go into service until I was sixteen, and only met him once."

"Lord Hambledon says he works for the Foreign Office." Bryonny pulled the brush through the cap of auburn curls and made a face at herself in the mirror.

"So it must be, my lady, I couldn't really say. We're not supposed to poke our noses where they don't belong, says Mrs. Merk, and musn't inquire into the affairs of our betters."

"Oh, I see. I didn't mean to lead you astray, Lucy. I'm just curious. I had a letter from him when I first arrived, but it was very formal and polite, welcoming me to the family and all that, and I couldn't tell anything about the man himself. He's been on the Continent, you know, according to his father."

"Oh, my lady, right in the middle of that nasty war! He'll be killed! That man Napoleon will be the death of us all, says my mum."

"I don't believe he's gone to fight, Lucy, but I don't know exactly what he is doing, except that it's government work and very secretive. I'm sure he'll be quite safe. Lord Hambledon didn't seem overly concerned when he told me."

"That's a blessing, my lady, for his lordship worships the ground his son walks on. It would be terrible if he met with any harm."

"I don't think we need be worried. I must admit, I would like to meet him."

"Oh yes, indeed, my lady, for you would be bound to fall head over heels in love." Lucy sighed rapturously.

"That wasn't exactly what I had in mind, Lucy," said Bryonny, laughing again. "I have no intention of falling in love with him or anyone else, for that matter."

"Yes, my lady," said Lucy obediently, and bent to help Bryonny on with her riding boots, so Bryonny missed the all-knowing smile on Lucy's face.

The stables were quiet when Bryonny slipped into Bedlam's stall, and she pulled his snaffle bit off the peg on the wall and slipped it into his mouth, stroking his velvety muzzle and talking softly to him. He gave her only a token protest, then accepted the bit, snorting. He was as eager as she for the ride ahead, and Bryonny led him out into the stableyard and mounted his bare back in a smooth, easy motion. She'd been riding all of her life and was a skilled horsewoman. She preferred to ride without a saddle; it was more natural to her to have nothing between them but the thin cloth of her breeches so that they could each feel the other's slightest movement. Bedlam danced beneath her, then settled down as she gathered the reins in her hands and collected him under her, calming him with her voice.

Guiding him out of the stableyard and using her legs to straighten him when he would sidle off sideways, she took the road that followed in a wide curve around the west wing of the house past the flower gardens, leading into the front driveway which cut between the lawns and the front of the Abbey. There she paused, drinking in the early morning light.

The Abbey was highlighted by the soft light, its old stonework bathed in the colors of the fading dawn. It was a magnificent building that over the centuries had had changes and additions made to it according to the needs of the Ramsay family. Three stories high, it now consisted of a large central building flanked by a pair of wings which extended out and then back to form a courtyard from which the stables were but a short walk. It was an informal household and many of the larger rooms such as the ballroom and drawing rooms hadn't been used in many years, Lord Hambledon preferring to do any rare entertaining in the warm and comfortable library.

Bedlam grew impatient to be off, and gave a soft whinny, shaking his head. "Yes, all right then, Bedlam, we're going," said Bryonny with an amused smile, and turned his head down the long driveway, urging him on with her knees. Choosing the path leading into Three Mile Wood, which stretched to the east in a wide triangle, they turned off the drive and entered the deep quiet of the forest. It was mid-March and the ground had just begun to stir with the first signs of spring, and a rich, loamy scent of earth, wet from the constant rain, pervaded the air. A cuckoo called in the distance, heralding the end of winter, and Bryonny laughed in simple pleasure. She felt at one with the wood, caught in the same process of transition from winter into spring. It had been a difficult year; she would never forget her terrible pain when she had finally regained consciousness after the accident only to learn that her father and brother were dead. It had taken many months for the raw, grating misery to dull, but life had gone on, and she had learned to put her unhappiness to one side and adjust to the fact that this was to be her home from now on. And slowly she had learned to love her Uncle Richard, as he'd insisted she call him. He had been kindness itself, helping her to continue the strong academic education her father had given her and teaching her about the management of the inheritance she had come into in such a tragic fashion. Now her biggest worry was how she was going to survive the dreaded upcoming Season, the one point on which Uncle Richard had refused to budge, citing her father's wishes as reason enough.

Bryonny shook her head, dismissing this thought, and pushed Bedlam into a slow trot. He stretched his neck out, playing with the bit in his mouth, but as soon as he'd settled down again she moved him into a gentle canter. He had smooth, even gaits, and even without a saddle, was beautifully easy to sit. But Byronny knew full well that she couldn't relax her vigilance for a moment. He was still very green.

They went about a mile, and then she turned him around and headed at a brisk walk back the way they had come. She was well pleased but knew that he had a tendency to lose his head when he had missed his exercise. Still, with time and the right handling he would make a wonderful hunter. The next job would be to break him in to a saddle; perhaps she could ask George for one of Julian's boyhood saddles . . . Absorbed in her future plans for him, Bryonny was taken completely by surprise when a loud crack rang out in the stillness and something whistled past her ear. Bedlam shied and then reared in terror and took off with a great leap. Startled by the shot and Bedlam's sudden reaction, Bryonny desperately tried to regain control of her mount, but Bedlam had taken the bit in his teeth and was running blindly toward home. Despite her expertise, Bryonny found herself slipping as Bedlam went tearing around a corner and she was flung off his back.

The next thing she registered was the face of an

attractive, blond-haired man with deep brown eyes
bending over her. He started as she opened her eyes
and sat up.

"Oh, thank goodness! You gave me quite a scare
for a minute. You're not hurt, are you? That must
have been something of a fall you took." He reached
out a hand to help her up.

"No, thank you, I'm fine," replied Bryonny, standing shakily and brushing herself off. "Just a bit embarrassed. But who are you, and how did you find me,
and—and where's my horse?" She looked around in
alarm as she realized that Bedlam was nowhere in
sight. "I don't suppose you're the idiot who fired a
gun in the woods, are you?" she finished suspiciously.

"A gun! No, of course not!"

"Then who are you? And what are you doing on
Lord Hambledon's land, anyway?"

"If you will allow me to answer your questions
before you hurl any more at me . . . I am Philip
Neville. And who might you be, my lad?"

"Your lad?" said Bryonny indignantly. "I am certainly not your lad. I'm Bryonny Livingston and I live
here!" She glared at him, hands on her hips, looking
for all the world like a ruffled cat who had been
dropped from a tree.

"Good Lord!" exclaimed Philip. "You're Lady
Bryonny? I—I beg your pardon, my lady, but you
might see where I made the mistake . . ."

Bryonny followed his gaze and belatedly remembered her garb and her short cap of hair. It was enough
to take the wind out of her sails. "Oh. Well, I suppose
I can see, but I never expected anyone at this hour. I
suppose you came to see my godfather."

He hesitated with a smile. "Well, actually, the truth
of the matter is I came to see you."

"Me? Why on earth would you be coming to see
me? I don't know you," she said firmly.

"No, you don't. But I have actually met you, you
see. I wouldn't expect you to remember."

"Why don't you stop playing at riddles and explain

yourself?" She was thoroughly out of temper by this time.

"I was the person who found you at the—the accident," he finished carefully.

"Oh!" said Bryonny, taken aback. "You're the captain?"

"I am. Lord Hambledon wrote me and invited me to pay you a call, now that your year of mourning is over. I saw a horse come bolting out of the woods—he went in the direction of the stables, by the way. I naturally assumed that someone had been with him, so I followed the path and found you lying on it quite oblivious to your circumstances."

"Oh, dear. You must think I'm forever lying around unconscious in need of rescuing! I suppose I should thank you for coming to my aid once again, but I'm afraid I'm feeling rather cross and miserable and absolutely furious at the irresponsible fool who let fire a shot and frightened my horse. Please accept my apologies for having forgotten my manners so badly, but I might as well warn you that they're not likely to return for at least an hour." Then, remembering Bedlam, she said, "Oh—I must find my horse!" and she turned on her heel and started off down the path leaving Philip to stare after her.

Collecting himself quickly and gathering his own horse, he ran to catch up with her and asked her to describe the incident of the shot more fully. "Did you see anyone, Lady Bryonny, or anything at all that might give you an indication of who could have done such a foolish thing?"

"No, I did not, Captain Neville," answered Bryonny curtly. "I was quite busy at the time trying to control a new, green stallion who was intent on breaking both our necks." Bryonny was not usually so rude, but her pride had been badly injured by allowing herself to lose control of Bedlam. She was deeply concerned that she had destroyed the trust she had built up in him; she was also more shaken by how close she had come to being hit by the bullet than she cared to admit. And she also hated to admit that she had been caught looking and behaving like her father's proverbial hoyden.

The rest of the walk back passed in silence, with both of them thinking their separate thoughts, and they arrived at the stable only to find Bedlam happily munching on oats in the unattended feed room. He gave a contented whinny when he spotted Bryonny, who laughed with delight and half-heartedly scolded him as she led him to his stall, telling him what bad manners it was to eat with his bridle on.

After seeing to Bedlam and Captain Neville's horse, Bryonny led the captain to the house for breakfast. They were met by Mrs. Merk in the front hall.

"Lady Bryonny!" she gasped, and then as Philip appeared in the doorway behind Bryonny, "Captain Neville!" Her voice had risen about an octave, and she snapped her mouth down hard as she stared at them.

"Yes, Mrs. Merk, you're quite correct on both counts. Why don't you show Captain Neville where he can wash up and then give him some breakfast. I'll be down as soon as I'm changed." Bryonny realized with amusement that she was covered in dirt from head to foot and looked nothing like the young lady she was supposed to be. The poor woman must be horrified, thought Bryonny, if the expression on her face was anything to judge by. She took the steps two at a time, calling for Lucy to bring hot water as she tore down the hallway—only to be stopped in her tracks by Lord Hambledon.

"Well, well, what have we here, my dear?" inquired Lord Hambledon tactfully.

"Oh," said Bryonny, looking down at her untidy clothing. "It's been a most peculiar morning, Uncle Richard. I suppose you should go downstairs to the dining room and ask Captain Neville all about it. But I have to warn you, I don't think he's very happy with me. Somehow I have the feeling I wasn't quite what he expected."

"Well, never mind that, I'm sure it can be amended. I suggest the first step would be to get yourself cleaned

up and changed, and then you can join us for breakfast. It would appear that you and Bedlam have been
having a difference of opinion." Lord Hambledon
chuckled. "Yes, indeed, Captain Neville. I'd forgotten
all about him. I did invite him to come up to inspect
the fruits of his labor, didn't I." And off he went to
greet his guest.

Bryonny dashed to her room, quickly cleaned up,
and fidgeted while Lucy helped her dress. "Oh, Lucy,
that will do just fine—really it will. This isn't the
Presentation Ball, you know."

"Now just be a little patient, my lady. The captain is
a handsome gentleman and we want you looking nice
for him. Just another minute and I'll be finished."

"The captain may be a handsome gentleman, Lucy,
but I sincerely doubt that anything you do will change
the impression I've already made on him. There, that's
fine." Bryonny jumped up from the dressing table and
flew out the door before Lucy had a chance to protest.

She entered the dining room at a sedate and ladylike pace, determined to behave properly to the captain, who after all had been kind enough to save her,
and to do her best not to further disillusion him.

"Lady Bryonny!" exclaimed Captain Neville, rising
as she entered. "You look quite transformed!"

"Thank you, captain," replied Bryonny. "I'm sure
the contrast must be alarming."

"Oh, but it's a delightful contrast, I assure you, my
lady. Don't you agree, Lord Hambledon?"

"Yes, indeed," replied Lord Hambledon, eyeing the
captain with interest. "But then, I find all of Lady
Bryonny's contrasts delightful."

"I must tell you what a pleasure it is to find you so
well, my lady, and in such—ah—high spirits. The last
time I was here, we all feared for your life."

"And I must thank you properly for what you did,
Captain Neville. I am deeply aware that I owe my life
to you. Please forgive my earlier incivility; I'm afraid I
was feeling a trifle discomposed."

"Not at all, my lady, I quite understand. Tell me
now, how do you find life at the Abbey?"

"I find it very pleasant, captain. But I'm flattered that you should take an interest in my welfare."

"There's an old Chinese proverb that says he whose life you have saved is forever your responsibility. I was merely taking advantage of the saying to have the pleasure of meeting you."

"That's very kind, but I assure you, you needn't feel that I'm forever your responsibility. Uncle Richard has enough of that as it is."

Lord Hambledon laughed. "It's no burden, Bryonny. How was I ever to know I would have such a comfort in my old age?"

"A comfort, Uncle Richard? Are you sure you wouldn't care to rephrase that?" Her eyes danced at him in amusement.

"Well, perhaps a challenging companion, I should say," said Lord Hambledon with a twinkle.

"That I find more believable." She turned toward Philip. "Uncle Richard is a great diplomat. I have shattered his peace and turned his household upside down and he has been kind enough not to grumble."

"I can't imagine anyone's grumbling at your presence, my lady. I should think you've been a breath of fresh air."

"Aha! Another diplomat in our midst, Bryonny! What do you say to that?"

"I say that I think you're both full of balderdash. Would anyone like some kippers?"

Bryonny found the captain a very pleasant companion and that afternoon she suggested that they ride together, George discreetly following at a distance at Lord Hambledon's quiet suggestion. This time Bryonny was mounted sidesaddle on a quiet mare and for once she made no objections. Philip made a point of drawing Bryonny out on her life in Jamaica.

"It's hard to describe it to you, really, if you've never been to the Caribbean . . ." She spoke for some time, caught up in a description of her old home, but then, realizing that she was rambling, she stopped herself abruptly with a sheepish smile. "I'm sorry, I've been boring you."

"Not at all; it sounds delightful, indeed. But what a different lifestyle it must have been." Philip frowned. "Slavery, for example; I can't imagine such a system. It goes against my grain."

"Oh, yes, it's terrible! But we didn't have slaves, you know. Papa felt very strongly on the subject, and when he took over the plantation from my grandfather, he gave all the slaves their freedom. Of course, most of them stayed on after that. Where else would they find comfortable living quarters and kind treatment—not to mention wages."

"Really? How very progressive of him."

"It caused no end of agitation among the other plantation owners. They firmly believed it would breed dissent among their own slaves, and then when they discovered he was teaching them to read and write—well, you can imagine," she finished on a laugh. "Papa was an educator, you see."

"Surely, there must have been trouble about the matter?"

"At first, I suppose, but it died down. After all, mutual interests had to be protected, and anyway, Papa was an aristocrat."

"And that was enough to excuse him for what surely must have been regarded as tremendous folly?"

"You have no idea how important that is even so far away from home—in fact, it's probably made more a to-do about than over here."

"And how do you feel about that, Lady Bryonny? After all, you're one of the aristocracy yourself."

"I loathed it. Whenever we had to go into Kingston, all the social conventions were observed to the fullest. When Papa told me I had to come to England for a Season I cried for a full week, but I found myself on the boat despite all my efforts."

"It seems cruel of your father to force you into something you didn't want."

"Oh, no, not really. Papa was incapable of intentional cruelty, Captain Neville. He only wanted what was best for me. I suspect he privately dreaded the trip here as much as I did."

"Indeed? Why was that?" Philip regarded her curiously.

"I don't really know, to be honest. He had a distaste for this country, although he never discussed it. Personally, I'm sure it had to do with the weather." Bryonny smiled wryly. "Unfortunately, it appears that I'm to learn to bear it."

"I'm sure Jamaica was paradise on earth, but England has its fine points, too. I think you might like London, Lady Bryonny. It will be quite unlike anything you've ever experienced. It teems with life—of the human variety," he added with a smile, "and from every end of the spectrum. And the theater, and opera, and dances are all amazing spectacles in themselves. I would consider it a privilege if you will allow me to show you around when you come, and that won't be too much longer, I gather."

"No, it won't. I would like that, but you'll have to call me Bryonny, and I shall call you Philip, or I'll die from standing on ceremony! Anyway, as you pointed out, you saved my life. I think that makes us acquaintances enough, don't you?"

Philip laughed in amusement. "Agreed, Bryonny. Now, let me tell you more about my country since you are to live here." He painted her vivid pictures of life in England until she felt that she had been to all the places he had described. She asked a hundred questions, which he was happy to answer, and by the time the afternoon was drawing to a close, she felt that they had become friends.

"Tell me of the future, Bryonny. What do you plan to do with yourself, now? As I understand it you will stay at the Abbey?"

"Yes, and to tell you the truth, it's not such a bad prospect as I had originally thought it. I am becoming more accustomed to England, and I like the countryside. But most importantly, I've grown very fond of my Uncle Richard, who is the only family I have left.

Except my cousin Julian, of course, but I've never met him. At least, not to know about it."

"Oh? Why is that?"

"It's rather like yourself. Apparently he was at the Abbey the night of the accident."

"Was he?" said Philip, looking very surprised. "I didn't see any evidence of him."

"He didn't come in until later. And he's been gone since then. Do you know him, Philip?"

"No, not personally, but Lord Richmond has quite a name for himself about town."

"Really? What sort of name?"

"He's reported to be very stylish, extremely handsome, and a lady-killer. He's also renowned for his skill with the horses and the pistols. Oh, and I've heard he's very active in the House of Lords. I'm afraid I can't tell you much more. I'm a simple army boy, Bryonny, and I don't much run in his circles. I couldn't afford it."

"Why did you go into the army, Philip?"

Philip shrugged. "I was brought up by foster parents, who although fairly well-off, were certainly not what you would call rich. They're dead now, and when I turned twenty-one, I took some of the money my foster father had left me and bought myself a commission in the Coldstream Guards. I thought it was a way of making steady, respectable money to supplement my own small income. It's a good idea if one has no title to gain entrance into society; we officers are welcomed by the *ton* as suitable. I've been in nearly eight years now, and it's not so bad, except that of course one's freedom can be a little limited and you never know when you're going to be sent off into battle. It's not that I mind fighting—it can just be deucedly inconvenient for one's social life!" Philip laughed. "But seriously, it's not a bad lifestyle."

"Oh, Philip, your childhood couldn't have been very easy! At least I had my mother until I was eight, and the rest of my family until recently, and my father and I were very close. But to grow up without your own parents is very sad. What happened to them?"

"They both died. I do thank you for your sympathy, Bryonny," he added at the crestfallen expression on her face, "but as you can see, I survived quite well. My foster parents were kind to me and I grew to care for them very much. Of course, I never ceased to miss my mother—my father I had no memory of—but children adjust after a time. I'm glad you have Lord Hambledon to look after you. He seems like a nice sort of person for—" Philip cut himself off abruptly.

"For a member of the aristocracy, were you going to say? Why, Captain Neville, if I didn't think better of you, I'd say you have a chip on your shoulder when it comes to the subject!"

"It's only that I feel people should be judged on their merits and not their rank in society."

"I couldn't agree with you more, but aren't you practicing a reverse discrimination? We can't help what we're born to, after all, and we can only make the best we can out of circumstances."

"It's true, although some are born to more fortunate circumstances than others. More than once I've seen people abuse power and privilege."

"Naturally, but that has more to do with faultiness of character than rank. You can't condemn an innocent babe just because he carries a crest on his cradle."

"Nor should you condemn him if he doesn't."

"And do you feel condemned, Philip Neville?" asked Bryonny curiously.

He smiled. "I've done the best that I've been able with my own circumstances. Naturally, there have been times when I've wished it to be different; who would not prefer to be brought up by one's natural parents? But I've realized that one can never change the past."

"But the future is yours to make of it what you will."

"And so I intend. But it grows cold and we should head back. I'm expected for dinner with my hosts."

"Oh, what a pity! I was hoping you could dine with us. Will you be back tomorrow? I must confess that it's been nice having someone closer to my own age to converse with."

"I'm complimented, but I'm afraid that I must return to my regiment tomorrow. But did you know Lord Hambledon has invited me back again the next time I am free? I accepted with pleasure, but I hope it's agreeable to you."

"No, he hasn't said anything, but I'm delighted! I've enjoyed your company, Philip, and now I have something to look forward to. And the next time you come, I promise that you shall find me wide awake and on my feet!"

They returned to the house, and Bryonny found that when the captain made his farewells, she was sorry to see him go.

Chapter Two

A day passed, then two, interminable days during which it poured unceasingly with rain, driving Bryonny into a thoroughly bad temper after the brief, wonderful respite of sunshine. She finally threw down the book of Greek history Uncle Richard had given her to study, unable to concentrate. Sighing with frustration, she wandered over to the window, and sighed again, turning away in disgust. Smugly she thought to herself that her low opinion of British weather had more than been proven correct. It was little wonder that people wasted away in this climate and so many children died in infancy. If she'd been born here she, too, would probably have taken one depressed look out of the window and breathed her last.

"Lady Bryonny?" Mrs. Merk stuck her head in the open door. "Am I disturbing you?"

"No, not at all, Mrs. Merk," said Bryonny with resignation, hoping Mrs. Merk hadn't come in for one of her "little chats" that could go on for hours. The woman meant well, she knew, but Bryonny was in no mood to smile and nod. She had already heard about all the staff arrivals and departures at the Abbey, not to mention their activities in between, including Mrs. Merk's own when she had come to look after Julian on the occasion of his mother's death. "He was only five, poor mite, but then my own dear husband and little boy so close to Master Julian's age had been carried off by the fever, so it worked out most auspiciously. I like to think I've been a mother to him and I'm sure he'd tell you the same himself," she'd said with great satisfaction. And now Mrs. Merk had fallen into the habit of clucking over Bryonny as the newest of her brood, mothering that Bryonny didn't need or particularly welcome.

"I thought I'd just take your dresses down to sponge and press, poppet," she said comfortably, opening the armoire and scooping the said items into her arms, and Bryonny breathed a sigh of relief, but then Mrs. Merk went on, dropping the dresses onto the bed and readjusting her spectacles, a bad sign. "That Lucy tries, I know, but she has to be reminded. And there she is visiting her mother again, I just heard from Simms. You'd think she was still a baby the way she goes running home, and without so much as a by-your-leave—"

"I gave her two days off myself, Mrs. Merk," interrupted Bryonny. "I had no need of her and she's been working very hard."

"Oh, I see," said Mrs. Merk, briefly wondering whether she'd been chastised but quickly deciding that dear Lady Bryonny was far too sweet-tempered to attempt such a thing. "Well, in that case I suppose it's all right, but I really do wish—"

"Mrs. Merk, if you'll excuse me, I have things to do," said Bryonny, and promtly fled from the room, down the back stairs and into the safer recesses of Cook's kitchen where Mrs. Merk was sure not to follow. Cook was a mine of information and Bryonny loved to while away the time with her. She always said precisely what she thought, and with complete authority. Not everyone was allowed free access to Cook's domain. She considered herself in equal standing with Mrs. Merk and never hesitated to let the fact be known. Mrs. Merk had learned long ago not to question Cook's authority and the two lived side by side in an unspoken and wary domestic truce, rather like a cat and a dog who must share a common master.

Bryonny had an equal affection for them both; they were as different as night and day and she loved to watch the way they carefully circled each other keeping the peace. Where Mrs. Merk treated Bryonny as an adored but helpless child who must be protected from the cruel world at all cost, Cook treated her as a welcome companion whom she was going to educate in the way of things. That is, the Way of Things According to Cook, thought Bryonny with a smile.

Bryonny settled herself in her usual spot at the table near the enormous brick fireplace with its spit and hooks and ovens, where the noble and portly Cook was at work baking the day's bread.

"It's another one of those awful wet days, Cook, and I shall be stuck inside for all of it, I can tell."

"You sound just like Master Julian when he was a child, deary. He never could bear it when it wasn't perfect sunshine so he could ride those horses of his around all day. He'd get up to the worst kind of mischief and plague us all if he had to be cooped up. I used to dread rainy days as much as he did!"

"Tell me about him, Cook. He's a complete mystery to me, and I must confess, my curiosity about him is overpowering!" She listened contentedly as Cook, delighted to answer Bryonny's questions, briefly touched upon Julian's finer assets and then went on to describe his volatile temper in loving detail, lingering over some of the pranks he had perpetrated in his twenty-nine years, some not so far in the past.

"In my opinion," stated Cook firmly, leaving Bryonny in no doubt that Cook's Opinion was the first and last on the matter, "Master Julian and his father are too much alike for their own good. That's why they are always going on at each other hammer and tong," she continued, rhythmically kneading the dough with large, capable hands. "They both have those exploding tempers and stubborn ways, just you wait and see, deary. There's bound to be an argument not twenty-four hours after he returns home for a visit. And high time it is for that, I might add." She leaned forward confidentially to Bryonny, who was surprised to hear that her Uncle Richard had a temper of any kind. She had certainly never seen any evidence of it.

"The latest round of fighting has been over the marquess wanting to see his son married off and getting him heirs. Master Julian doesn't want any of it; he's been in here any number of times telling me about it. 'Cook,' he says to me, 'I've never met a woman I'd want to marry, and until I do, I'm not getting myself shackled, no matter what my father wants, heirs or no heirs! You'd think one heir would be enough for him!' he says. Not that they don't love each other, mind you; they're as fond of each other as two pins, and his lordship is that proud of Master Julian. He just thinks his son has been gadding about and chasing the skirts long enough, and it's time he settled down. I wouldn't mind seeing it, either. The Abbey's been without a mistress too long as it is."

After this long speech, Cook pushed the loaves of bread into the deep oven, fanned herself vigorously, and settled her bulk comfortably in a chair. Bryonny sat absolutely riveted by the wealth of information that had just come pouring out; it seemed that everyone had a different opinion of Julian Ramsay. She really couldn't wait to meet the man.

The remainder of the day passed slowly, the rain unceasing. Bryonny read throughout the afternoon, but that did nothing to alleviate her boredom. When a break in the rain finally came toward dusk, she grabbed her opportunity, leaped into her breeches, thrust a cap over her hair, and headed for the stables.

Bedlam needed a good, unfettered run. He had started to shy at loud noises and sudden movement, and Bryonny wondered if that wasn't the result of the gunshot incident still a puzzle to everyone. Uncle Richard had been furious and had the wood combed for clues that same day, but in the end it was put down to a poacher who had not expected anyone to be about at that time of the morning. He had cautioned her to be more careful when riding very early or very late, and to keep to the roads and avoid the woods. They'd had trouble with poachers in the past, and Lord Hambledon wanted to be sure there would be no more accidents.

This actually suited Bryonny very well as she had found a wonderful stretch of road which led to the back entrance of the Abbey and was nearly always deserted. It was the perfect place to give Bedlam his head.

The air was still and heavy from the rain, which had left behind a pleasingly clean, crisp smell. The soft light caught the glistening raindrops still clinging to the leaves, and the grass threw off sprays of water around Bedlam's feet as he stepped lightly off the stableyard path to the shortcut through the trees which lined the back road. A fine mist rose from the ground, thickening into fog up ahead as the cool evening air moved in after the warm, wet day.

Bedlam was eager for the exercise and Bryonny could feel his muscles rippling under her as she held him in check. They started out slowly, warming up at a trot, both of them savoring the anticipation of the gallop to come. Bryonny whispered sweet words of encouragement to him and his ears pricked back and forth in response to her soft voice. The mist continued to rise and thicken around them as they made their way to the long road where they could unleash their desires and fly uninhibited, undisturbed. It fell softly upon Bryonny's skin, and clung to her eyelashes and the wisps of hair that curled around her face, causing them to cling to her cheeks. It covered Bedlam's coat, depositing a dewy sheen on the ebony silk. Slowly, Bryonny gathered the reins in her hands as they approached their destination. She could feel the stallion tensing in excitement, and as she pointed him down the stretch, she squeezed ever so lightly with her thighs. His muscles bunched as he leapt into the air, his long neck stretched forward, his powerful legs reaching out and finding their stride. It was heaven; the wind rushed past them inhibiting all sound but the pounding of hooves on dirt.

And then very suddenly, there came out of the mist another sound, a loud clattering immediately behind them, descending rapidly. Before there was time to think, Bryonny pulled Bedlam hard to the right and he reared in alarm and veered, jumping the ditch on the side of the road. Bryonny, once again with no saddle to give her a better grip, flew sideways off his back into the ditch. "Oh, damnation!" she cried, but at least this time she managed to keep his reins in one hand as she fell. Getting up, she looked around her in confusion, trying to work out what had happened. Just down the road she spotted a sleek black phaeton with a fine matched team of bays who were prancing and sidling about as their owner tried to steady them and bring his vehicle to a halt. So this was what had practically run her down—the driver was obviously an incompetent fool!

The man shouted over his shoulder. "You there, are you all right?"

"No thanks to you!" returned Bryonny furiously. She turned back to soothe Bedlam, who was trembling but at least standing still, and when she next looked around, it was to see a tall, cloaked man with dark waving hair and steely gray eyes striding toward her with murder reflected all over his face.

"You *stupid* boy, we could both have been killed!" He was upon her now, spitting out the words from between clenched teeth. A muscle twitched in his cheek as he tried to control his fury to no avail.

Bryonny raised her snapping green eyes to meet his own. "Strange, that was exactly what I was going to say to you! Surely you must realize that it wasn't my fault. You were behind me, and if you hadn't been driving so fast and recklessly, you would have seen me before you almost ran me over!"

"Absolute nonsense!" he retorted. "If you don't know how to control the beast, you shouldn't be riding him! And what you're doing on Forbes's prize stallion is beyond me—I should report you for that, not to mention your impertinence. You should thank your lucky stars you're in one piece! You deserve to have had your neck broken!" And with that he spun on his heel and went storming back to his phaeton.

"What! Why you unspeakable wretch!" shouted Bryonny. "Not only have you no manners, you can't even drive a team! And as for Mr. Forbes—" But he was gone and her last words were lost in the wind.

Bryonny slowly walked Bedlam on foot back to the stables giving him a chance to calm down. The near accident had given them both a shaking up and Bryonny muttered to herself the entire way back, saying every now and then, "Isn't that right, Bedlam?" She managed to run through every curse she'd ever heard and made up others to suit the occasion. Feeling better, she tied Bedlam to the mounting post and called for George, intending to tell him the entire story. But George was not about, so she asked Dougal to look after Bedlam, and realizing how late it was, dashed through the courtyard and into the house, running up the back stairs to seek refuge in her bedroom and change for dinner.

Bryonny took her time washing and dressing in order to recover her temper and equilibrium. She didn't think this was a story Uncle Richard should hear about, as he might start to think that Bedlam was too dangerous to ride, and she didn't want him to notice anything amiss. She looked at herself in the mirror as she dried her face. Her eyes were sparkling like emeralds, the yellow flecks pronounced, and her cheeks were flushed. She looked the very picture of good health, although in fact her high color was more a result of temper than exertion. Going to the armoire, she saw that Mrs. Merk had not yet returned her dresses. With a shrug she picked up the old muslin she'd been wearing earlier. It was not really suitable for dinner, and it certainly was not fashionable, but she had little choice. Tugging it on, she quickly checked her appearance in the mirror. She looked all of thirteen, she thought to herself with a rueful smile, and her cropped hair certainly didn't help the picture. She'd brought the dress with her from Jamaica and the bust was now too tight and flattened her chest out, and the hem was too short and rode above her ankles. Still, they dined alone, and she doubted if Uncle Richard would notice. It would have to do.

She dashed down the front stairs and stopped short

when she heard the murmur of voices coming from the open library door. Simms was standing at attention in the entrance hall and with a sinking heart she asked him, "Who is it, Simms? Not a dinner guest, I hope?"

"The Earl of Richmond has arrived, my lady," replied Simms in a solemn voice, but looking very pleased beneath his formal exterior.

"Lord Richmond! Oh, no!" gasped Bryonny, looking down at her dress in dismay and turning to flee. But it was too late. Lord Hambledon had heard her and appeared at the library door, a big smile on his face.

"Bryonny, my dear, you'll never guess who is here! Do come in and meet your cousin Julian." He ushered her into the library.

Bryonny's heart seemed to stop for a split second as she took in the tall man lounging against the mantelpiece. Surprised gray eyes met startled green ones, and her breath caught in disbelief as Julian's mouth tightened in recognition. Neither spoke a word, and the silence deepened in the room.

"Julian! Your manners!" said Lord Hambledon in sharp surprise at Julian's behavior.

Julian turned languidly toward his father and responded, "I beg your pardon, sir. I'm afraid I left my manners along with my temper back on the road when an irresponsible—stableboy—lost control of his horse and nearly killed us both." And turning back to Bryonny, he made a casual leg. "Lady Bryonny, may I tell you what a *pleasure* it is to meet you at last? Allow me to welcome you personally to the family and once again express my condolences at your loss." His eyes were about as warm and welcoming as a steel trap.

"Thank you, Lord Richmond," answered Bryonny, dropping a little curtsy in his direction. "It is indeed a great pleasure to finally make your acquaintance. I can't tell you how much I've been looking forward to this moment. It is indeed fortunate that you weren't injured in the incident you mentioned or perhaps I would never have had this delightful opportunity. I do hope the poor stableboy you nearly ran down wasn't harmed."

"No less than he asked for and not as much as he deserved," retorted Julian coolly, with a glint in his eye.

"Oh dear, surely you don't mean you *wished* him to come to harm?" said Bryonny, looking prettily dismayed.

"Oh, I think a good thrashing would have sufficed." He aimed a menacing look at her.

"I see," said Bryonny, restraining a strong desire to punch the man. "I'm sure the unfortunate lad would have enjoyed giving you a good thrashing as well, but given your size, it wouldn't exactly have been a fair match, would it have?"

Julian was looking at Bryonny balefully, and the tension was palpable in the air, but before he had a chance to respond to this last barb, Simms announced dinner. Lord Hambledon gave Bryonny his arm and she sailed out of the room with a look of complete disdain on her face, leaving a scowling Julian to follow behind.

Dinner was an interesting affair, the sparks flying throughout, and Lord Hambledon enjoyed himself immensely. It had not taken much bandinage to figure out that Bryonny was the errant stableboy who had incurred Julian's wrath and that she considered him equally responsible. He continued to thrust subtle barbs at her, but they did not have the expected effect of making her blush in confusion, and it obviously irritated him that he couldn't seem to rattle her; instead, her sharp wit, finely honed beneath her youthful exterior, came flashing out, parrying Julian's own. Lord Hambledon doubted that Julian had ever encountered anyone quite like her. "Now the fun begins," he chuckled to himself.

"I beg your pardon, Father?" asked his son politely.

"Oh, nothing, my boy, nothing at all. Don't allow me to interrupt your brilliant conversation." By this time the conversation had moved on to politics, in which Bryonny was well versed. She and Lord Hambledon had spent many a contented evening debating different political topics and he had taught her a good deal about current issues. Laying the bait, he innocently asked Julian his opinion on the effect that February's Regency bill, which had given control to the Prince of Wales over his ailing father, George III, would have over the progress of the war with France.

There followed a interesting discussion, which quickly grew heated as Bryonny, unable to restrain herself, jumped in with both feet. "How can you take that attitude, Lord Richmond? If the Prince of Wales had the gumption to replace that weakling, Perceval, with a prime minister who knew how to run a government, we wouldn't be in the trouble we are now! He's made it very clear that he knows nothing about running a war."

"What, a little Whig in our midst?" drawled Julian infuriatingly. "It's no wonder the Whigs are in so much trouble if they all think like you. Perceval's nowhere near as incompetent as you make him out to be. At least he has the good sense to supply weapons and food to the army and let Wellington get on with fighting Napoleon. Mark my words, Wellington knows what he's doing; he just needs a little more time. This Peninsular War is a difficult matter. But then I wouldn't expect you to understand. In any case, children are meant to be seen and not heard."

Bryonny finally lost her carefully kept composure. "You're impossible!" she shouted in frustration. "Just because I'm younger than you and a female, you think I have no right to my own opinion! And I'm not a child to be spoken to in such a manner!"

"My dear girl," interrupted Julian, "hasn't anyone ever told you that women shouldn't discuss politics? They only succeed in making themselves sound like fools and bore their listeners in the process."

"You are a typically arrogant and overbearing male," she said in cold fury. "You just can't bear to be challenged by a woman; you find yourself threatened and have to resort to nasty set-downs. Coward!" Her eyes were kaleidoscopes of green and yellow, snapping in vexation, the color high in her cheeks, her pointed little chin thrust forward in challenge.

Julian had lost his cool, sophisticated composure. His gray eyes, narrowed in battle, were blazing and he leaned forward over the table to meet Bryonny's glare.

"You call *me* arrogant, girl? From the first moment of our unfortunate meeting you have insinuated that you are superior to me in all matters! May I remind you that I have had a great many more years of experience in the world—and a civilized world, at that—and a university education over you? Or don't you think that counts for anything?"

"That's unfair and well you know it; I never said I was superior, and I only meant that women can be the equal of men in many things and probably superior in others if they were only given the opportunity. You have to admit it's an absurd idea to assume that women are born simple-minded. Our only problem is not having been trained to anything but how to catch a husband and then having to while away the rest of our days lounging on a sofa somewhere planning the next social activity! Well, I for one, have no intention of living my life like that, nor do I care to be treated as if that were the limit of my capability. If you're so determined to prove me inferior to you, that's exactly what you'll have to do—prove it! I grant you that you have more experience in the world than I, but that doesn't make you naturally superior, nor do I know what use you've put that time to. For all I know, you've frittered it away on wine, women, and song."

"Why you impudent little—"

"And as for your precious degree, has it even crossed your mind that I might have liked to go to university myself? But instead I've had to rely on my father and books for my education. No, wait; I haven't finished. There's one last thing. You imply that I'm an uncivilized savage because I've grown up in Jamaica. If you'd had the same benefit, I doubt that you would think 'civilized' man quite so wonderful. The horrors they perpetrate upon their slaves would turn your blood cold. I have seen more civility, not to mention humanity, from the Jamaican people than ever exhibited by the British, and I'm not referring to social graces! So—if you're so educated, I would think that you'd believe in a fair trial. The day that I behave like a simpering, feather brained miss is the day that you'll have the right to treat me like one! Until that day, you have no right to do so!"

Lord Hambledon applauded Bryonny saying, "Bravo, my dear, well spoken! What do you have to say to that, Julian, eh? You have to admit she has a point. You've always been one to champion fairness."

"Hmm," murmured Julian, looking at Bryonny speculatively. "If you are so eager to prove your case, Lady Bryonny, then who am I to stop you? Please do feel free to show me just exactly how equal you are!"

Lord Hambledon let out a great guffaw of laughter. "Watch out, my boy, you may be taking on more than you realize. You don't want to have to eat crow, do you?"

"'No fear of that, Father. This chit needs to be taught a lesson before she's foisted on the polite world, and I consider it my sacred duty to see that she learns it."

"We'll see who has a lesson to learn, my lord," countered Bryonny. "What do you have in mind as the first challenge?"

"I was considering that. It seems logical to me that we should begin at the beginning. You challenged my ability as a horseman; we shall have a race. As I don't suppose you drive, it will have to be on horseback and we'll determine who is the better rider. You have the right to refuse if you wish."

"Never! I accept the challenge. My horse against yours, tomorrow morning at eight, if the weather holds. We'll meet at the stables and race the back road. Agreed?"

"Done!" said Julian with satisfaction. "I must confess, I'm amazed you didn't challenge me to pistols at dawn, dear cousin. Now if you'll both excuse me, I'm tired from my journey and would like to retire." He rose from the table.

"Good night," Lord Hambledon said to Julian's retreating back. Making sure his son was still within earshot, he addressed Bryonny. "Now, my dear, shall I call Simms to bring the brandy and cigars?"

Julian halted abruptly and turned to stare at them in disbelief, and they both burst into laughter.

"Not tonight, I think, dear Uncle Richard. I think I'll also retire to rest up for the race tomorrow. Will you be watching?"

"This I wouldn't miss for the world, Bryonny, not for the world," Lord Hambledon smiled. "But I'm not going to put any money on the outcome. This one is too close to call."

Julian shook his head and went upstairs without another word.

The next morning dawned cool and bright, one of the first of real spring. Bryonny leapt out of bed, threw herself into her shirt, breeches, and boots, and flew downstairs to tell Cook what had transpired the night before while she ate her breakfast.

"You'll never guess what happened last night, Cook," she shouted as she ran down toward the kitchen. "You were absolutly right, he's mean as sin, got the filthiest temper ever, and he's totally pig-headed to boot—" She ground to an astonished halt at the kitchen door to see a horrified Cook and an amused Julian, who was looking at her benignly, one eyebrow raised.

"Good morning," he said pleasantly. "That wasn't me you were referring to so delicately just now, was it?"

Bryonny regarded him scornfully. "You know perfectly well it was, and you deserved to hear every word because it's all true."

"Well do go on, dear cousin, don't let me stop you now! Just think how instructive your comments could be."

"What, and swell your big head even more by having yourself the center of attention? I don't think so, thank you," retorted Bryonny. "I haven't any more time to waste talking to or about you. May I have my breakfast now please, Cook? I have an appointment to keep with a horse and a snake."

At that insult, Julian rose to his feet. He was clad in a white linen shirt and a beautifully cut coat, the rich brown cloth stretching smoothly over his broad shoulders and tapering in at his slim waist. His buff-colored breeches were skin-tight over long, well-muscled thighs and his Hessian boots had been polished to a high gleam. The whole effect was finished off by a simple but elegantly tied neckcloth. Bryonny was unaware that she was staring.

"Is something amiss, ma'am, or are you so fond of men's clothing that you require the address of my tailor?"

Bryonny blushed hotly. "N-no," she stammered, "I was—I . . ."

"Now you leave the poor girl alone, Master Julian, and let her eat her breakfast in peace. It's a sharp tongue you have on you this morning, and no way to talk to a lady," announced Cook.

"Ha!" snorted Julian. "I wouldn't call her a lady! And you heard the way she spoke to me, Cook; I think I've been a model of restraint. Haven't I the right to defend myself?" Julian had a big smile on his face as he regarded the woman fondly.

"Never you mind that. Now off with you, go on, out of my kitchen till you can mind your manners around Lady Bryonny," scolded Cook.

"Why is it that you address her as 'Lady Bryonny' and all any of you call me is 'Master Julian'? Good heavens, you'd think I was still five years old! I get no respect around here, Cook. You'd never know from the lot of you that I'm a respectable earl, and the rest of the world has been calling me 'my lord' since I was born. All right, all right, I'm going, dear lady, but I do think it's very unfair the way everyone in this household is taking the chit's part over mine. I was here first, you know." And with a wicked grin that flashed strong white teeth, he gave Cook an affectionate squeeze around her ample waist and strode out the door, turning in the direction of the stables without a backward glance at Bryonny.

Her eyes followed after him. "He's a most confusing man, Cook," she said slowly.

"Aye, that he can be, child, but speaking plainly, I'd say you've gotten under his skin. He's usually better-mannered than that, and you were none too polite yourself. Suppose you tell me about it?"

Bryonny proceeded to lightly recount the story from its beginning on the back road to the end of the evening, sparing Julian nothing, and in fact making him out to be Satan himself, and had Cook shaking with mirth, tears pouring down her plump cheeks. "The two of you certainly got off to a fine start. I might have known! Never mind, ducks, he'll come around. You're like two suspicious dogs sniffing at each other, if I do say. Now, how you managed to provoke Master Julian into calling a horse race—that's a ripe one, that is!" She wiped her eyes with her apron.

"Well, this upstart stableboy is going to show him, just you wait and see, Cook. The high and mighty earl is going to get a run for his money."

"That may be, but you'd better watch yourself. It seems to me that no matter what the outcome, there are going to be some tempers flaring around here. Sometimes it doesn't pay to take a man down a peg or two, especially not one like Master Julian, who carries a lot of pride. It's in the Ramsay blood, you know. But in case, I wouldn't count on winning this race, child. Master Julian's been astride a horse since he was in leading strings, and he's well known around these parts for his skill. So you take a word of advice and don't go getting yourself all worked up."

"Oh, don't worry about me if I lose, Cook; at least it will have been fair. That's what makes me upset. Julian doesn't even know me, but he just assumes I'm an empty-headed feather brain who doesn't know my appointed place in his world. I only want to be given the chance to show him what I'm made of!"

"That's all well and fine, pet, but what you're made of may be something that Master Julian is unaccustomed to and finds hard to swallow."

"Let's just hope that I'm an acquired taste, Cook," said Bryonny with a laugh.

"I surely hope so too, or this household is going to be on its ear every time the two of you are together, from the look of things. The truth of the matter is that he's a fine man and a kind one, even if his temper is a trifle hot and he's used to getting his own way. You might give him a little room to show what he's made of too, you know, if you can get beyond your differences. Now off you go to your race, there's a good girl, and let me get on with my work."

Bryonny got up from the table and paused to give Cook a kiss on her soft cheek. "Thank you for your advice, Cook. I shall try to remember it, I promise. Wish me luck!" She was just leaving the kitchen when there came a terrific bellow from the direction of the stable. "Oh, dear," said Bryonny, throwing Cook a worried look, and she went in pursuit.

"Well, well," said Cook to herself, shaking her head. "Well, well."

Chapter Three

JULIAN was pacing furiously up and down the stableyard, where George was holding Bedlam on one side, and Dougal was holding Julian's enormous chestnut gelding Brimstone on the other. "What's this I'm to understand from George about Mr. Forbes's stallion belonging to you!" he thundered at Bryonny as she approached. "Forbes would never sell, most certainly not to a chit like you!"

"Ah, but he did, didn't he, cousin? The evidence is right in front of you."

"Good God, what would you want with a beast like him? Forbes, one of the best horsemen in the county, could hardly manage him! Last night I thought I'd been mistaken about the animal's identity, especially after I realized yours. No wonder you couldn't control the animal! See here, you can't possibly ride him in a race against Brimstone. You'll be killed!"

"Why don't we just see? I'm sure that would make you very happy, anyway; I'd be out of your hair then, wouldn't I, and you'd have won your wager as well. Or does that depend on whether I'm killed before or after the race?" asked Bryonny sweetly.

"I'm serious, Bryonny. It wouldn't be gentlemanly of me to race you on that monster, nor would it be intelligent. And since you prize your intelligence so highly, why don't you exhibit some right now? You're taking this battle between us too far."

"Would you prefer I ride Brimstone, then? I don't

53

think it would be fair to either of you to put you on Bedlam; he's used to a light hand and a small weight, but if it would soothe your conscience, or perhaps your injured pride, I'd be willing."

"Oh, for God's sake, Bryonny!" cried Julian in total frustration.

George had been watching this exchange with great satisfaction. He understood Master Julian's concern well, as he had once been in precisely the same spot, and he was looking forward to the conclusion with happy anticipation. He had expected a scene like this when Master Julian had asked him to bridle Lady Bryonny's mount for a little race. He was prepared when she walked over to him and took Bedlam's reins from his hand.

"Bryonny, I forbid you!" commanded Julian angrily as she lightly jumped onto Bedlam's back.

"I beg your pardon, my lord—you do what?" She turned Bedlam's head and urged him into a fast walk. "I don't think it's your place to forbid me anything. That right belongs solely to your father," she called coldly over her shoulder and broke into a gentle canter, heading toward the race site.

"I swear I'll kill that blasted girl if her horse doesn't do it first!" Julian roared, grabbing Brimstone from a gaping Dougal and leaping on his back.

"Yes, my lord," replied George respectfully, turning away to hide the wide smile on his face as he watched the man kick the sidling, uncooperative horse into a fast canter. As soon as they were out of sight, he strolled down the road to the back gate where Lord Hambledon was already positioned and related the scene, to Lord Hambledon's vast amusement.

Julian finally caught up with Bryonny as she reached the entrance to the back road. Bryonny was sitting calmly astride with an indifferent expression on her face.

"Are you ready now, my lord?"

"Bryonny, I'd like to murder you for this—but if you're so almighty determined to save me the trouble, then let's have at it." They lined up their horses side

by side, both animals snorting and prancing in anticipation of the race ahead.

"Ready now!" cried Julian, and they were off, pounding down the stretch, the wind blowing back raven and
auburn hair, chestnut and ebony manes. They were
both far up on their knees, hands moving back and
forth on their horses' necks in rhythm with their strides
as the great beasts stretched and plunged, reaching out
to their fullest.

"Fly now, Bedlam, my beauty," sang out Bryonny,
her words lost in the rushing wind. "Let's show the
brute what we can do!" She was in a state of complete
happiness, all anger forgotten as they galloped neck to
neck toward the back gates of the Abbey, her small
lithe form contrasting the long, sleekly muscled frame
of her adversary. The wind stung her cheeks and Bedlam's mane whipped in her face, which was pressed
down close to his outstretched neck. Bedlam had never
been raced against another horse and his blood responded instinctively to the challenge. Faster and faster
he lunged, his hooves only barely seeming to touch the
ground as he leapt forward, stretched to his limit.
Bryonny could see that they had suddenly pulled into
the lead, and just as suddenly she realized that she no
longer had complete control over Bedlam or the race.
Terrified of what might happen, she eased back on his
tender mouth and dropped herself down onto his back,
subtly bringing him back under her command. She
could feel Bedlam hesitate for a fraction of a second,
pulling against the bit, but the pressure on his mouth
was enough. He collected his stride and slowed his
pace and Bryonny breathed again.

And suddenly, there were the open gates just ahead
of them and the figures of Lord Hambledon and George
standing well off to one side as the horses came crashing through together, mouths foaming and coats steam-
ing. Swerving in opposite directions, the riders checked
their horses and brought them to a walk.

Bryonny was laughing from sheer joy and relief.
"Oh, Bedlam, you magnificent beast, what a challenge
you are!" She stroked his soaking neck and slipping

off his back handed him over to the waiting George to
be cooled down.

"Well done, m'lady," said George, beaming at her.
"You rode a fine race."

"Thank you, George. It was a good race, wasn't it!
Extra oats for Bedlam today! He should be proud of
himself; he's come a long way." She looked over to
where Julian was talking with his father and was amazed
to see him smiling at her. He walked over to her, his
hand outstretched, and taking her small hand in his,
he bowed over it.

"I owe you an apology, Bryonny. You are indeed a
fine horsewoman, and you've done a good job with
Bedlam, as you've so aptly named him. A draw,
wouldn't you say?"

"I think that's fair," replied Bryonny, looking into
his gray eyes and feeling an absurd warmth suffuse
her.

"Ha!" laughed Lord Hambledon. "I told you that
you were taking on more than you realized, Julian. It
was nose to nose, Bryonny, nose to nose!"

"That's very gratifying, but I think I had the advantage, to be fair," Bryonny's hand was still in Julian's,
and her eyes had not moved from his. "After all, I've
been working with Bedlam daily, and I'm sure it's
been a long time since Julian has ridden Brimstone.
Also, I'm a much lighter burden."

"That's very kind of you, I'm sure, cousin," said
Julian coldly, dropping her hand abruptly, "but I assure you I don't need a handicap created for me." He
glowered at her.

"That's not what I meant! I was only trying to say
that you would probably have won if you'd had my
advantages. Why are you always so quick to take
offense? I've never come across anyone whose pride
was so easily damaged!"

"My dear girl, if you didn't spend so much time
trying to prove you are better than a man, you might
behave more appropriately like the female you were
born, and then you would understand where my pride
enters into it. Look at you! You even dress like a man,

for God's sake! If you'd concentrate your energies on turning yourself into a woman, not that I can imagine the result, you'd find my treatment of you far different. I was, after all, brought up to be polite and respectful to females. You, however, make it very difficult when you insist upon behaving like a shrew whose sole ambition in life is to trample down masculinity so that you can wear the breeches!" He stood glaring at her, hands on his hips and feet planted wide apart, eyeing her garb with obvious distaste.

"You are totally impossible! Last night you promised not to judge me on my sex, and here you are harping on about it again. I think you're just upset because you didn't win the race by a mile after all the fuss you made!"

"No, Bryonny, I think I'm upset because you didn't fall off and break your neck as you so richly deserved!" And with that parting comment he turned his back and went storming off to the house.

"I don't think your son and I have developed a very cousinly relationship, Uncle Richard," said Bryonny to him as they slowly walked back to the house, taking the long route around the west wing to the front entrance.

"I certainly wouldn't call it that, Bryonny, I quite agree. Exactly what I would call it, I couldn't say. I think I might have a little talk with him."

"I'm sorry, Uncle Richard. I know that I haven't been behaving very well either, but he does goad me into it."

"I suggest, my dear, that for the rest of Julian's stay, which after all, is only until tomorrow, you put down your fists as best you can and try to be anti-inflammatory. In other words, try to be as much of a conventional young woman as you can without sacrificing your personality or principles. Perhaps you might retire your, er, breeches, until he's gone, now that you've proven your point. Don't misunderstand me," he interjected, seeing the crestfallen expression on Bryonny's face. "I don't mean I disapprove of you or your behavior in any way. I simply feel for the sake of peace in the house, you might try an armed truce. I'll suggest the same to Julian. You know, Bryonny, he's really a very pleasant and considerate man when he's not exercising his temper, hard as that may be for you to believe just now."

"I wouldn't believe it at all if I hadn't heard the same thing from so many people," sighed Bryonny. "I beg your pardon, Uncle Richard, I'm being very rude about your son. I'm sure he's terribly nice with everyone else. There must be something about me that sets him off."

"Yes, now you just give him a chance to show you his true character by trying not to anger him, tempting as that may be. He's a very proud man, you know, and not accustomed to being challenged by one so small—or so adept, I might add."

"I'll do my best, Uncle Richard. But I'm not going to be an object of his ridicule. If he starts insulting me, I'm going to defend myself." They had entered the front hall, and Lord Hambledon gave Bryonny a reassuring pat on the shoulder as he turned to enter his study and she went upstairs to wash and change.

She paused in surprise as she reached the top of the stairs, hoping she was unobserved by Julian and Mrs. Merk who were enjoying an affectionate greeting outside Julian's bedroom.

"Oh, we've missed you, Master Julian, that we have. You really shouldn't have stayed away so long! You know, I could have sworn it was you only two days ago when I saw what looked to be your carriage, very early in the morning. It was on the main road but it didn't turn in at the gates and I was that disappointed. But then that was the same day as all the excitement and it blew the thought of you clear out of my mind, if you can believe that!"

"What excitement was that, Mrs. Merk? It must have been quite something to make you forget me!" said Julian with a smile.

"Why, Lady Bryonny's near shooting, and the dear captain arriving in time to rescue her once again!"

"I should have known it would have something to

do with her," muttered Julian. "Come, sit in my room and tell me all about it while I wash up."

"Bah!" Bryonny said to herself as she slipped into her room as soon as the door had closed behind them. "Now I'm bound to hear about this, too." She decided to stay out of Julian's way until dinnertime.

Late that afternoon Lord Hambledon did have the promised talk with his son, who, although not happy about it, promised to curb his temper and his tongue.

"She doesn't make it easy, you know, Father. It isn't just the fact that we got off to a bad start—she keeps needling at me and it's almost impossible not to react. I wonder you allow her to get away with her wild behavior. How on earth do you think you're going to get her through a Season? It starts only next month, for heaven's sake!"

"Oh, don't be such a prig, Julian," said Lord Hambledon in annoyance, perfectly well aware that this was not the issue. "You could be a great deal more charitable toward her, you know; she's suffered a terrible loss. Personally, I find her refreshing; she says exactly what's on her mind without any of the simpering airs and graces one usually has to put up with. But aside from all that, Bryonny is trying hard to make a new life for herself and I intend to make it as happy for her as possible. And I fully expect you to help me in that endeavor, including introducing her around London next month."

"Ah, you are cruel, Father. I can see I have no choice but to bow to your wishes, but you can be sure that as happy as you make Bryonny's life, mine will be made equally miserable. You have to know she's not going to be ready for a Season, not to mention a husband! Good Lord, what man in his right mind would have her?"

"'She'll be a great deal more ready than you realize, my dear boy. Your problem is not going to be finding her suitors, but keeping them in check—especially the fortune hunters when they get wind of her inheritance. I don't think she has any idea what she's in for."

"That inheritance is enormous. God only knows what the chit will do with it if she gets her hands on it. We'd better find a responsible husband for her or all hell is bound to break loose."

"It's clear you don't know your cousin at all, Julian. I don't know why you've taken such a dislike to the girl. You had no objections to David."

"She's nothing like David, little that I knew him. He was pleasant and polite, certainly unassuming, unlike his sister. She doesn't even *look* like a Livingston with that coloring of hers, and God spare us her temper! Give me the Livingston blue eyes and blond hair any day, and manners to match. The girl's an undisciplined hellion!"

"Listen to me, Julian, the girl you so easily call a hellion is, in fact, very sensitive and intelligent. But far more important, you and I are her only remaining relatives and if I should die, her guardianship passes to you. I would expect you to treat her as I do, with love and respect."

"Oh, dear God, that would be all that I need. But tell me, Father, with such a large fortune, who is her heir? Has she made a will up?"

"Yes, of course I've seen to that, Julian. As you and I are her only remaining relatives, we stand for now as her heirs."

"Oh, marvelous, Father! The perfect motive for murder. Just think, I could kill off two birds with one stone. Be permanently rid of Bryonny, and increase my fortune twofold! What an intriguing thought."

"Julian, don't even joke about such a thing! And if you'd calm that stubborn temper of yours long enough to take a good look at Bryonny, you would find the warmth and gentleness that you seem to think is missing, although unassuming she'll never be. She has too much spirit and imagination for that. But I guarantee you that you will never find such a woman among your London set. You'd have to search far and wide to find another the likes of Bryonny. I'm not surprised you haven't found someone to marry yet with the sort of woman you seem to think suitable. Bring me home someone you can be proud of, who isn't afraid to stand up to you and speak her mind!"

"Oh, not this again, I beg you, Father. Now you sound as if you want me to marry the blessed Bryonny, which would only happen over my dead body! If ever there were a marriage made in hell, that would be it! If I marry, and I have told you repeatedly that I don't intend to for a good, long time, it will be to a woman who knows her place and her manners, not to a small firebrand with an overinflated sense of her own importance!" Julian's voice had been getting louder and louder as he lost the last tenuous hold on his temper, and he ended in a shout.

"Julian," sighed Lord Hambledon in exasperation, "calm down and stop being ridiculous. I am not asking you to do anything except be kind. You'd think the girl was your mortal enemy or something equally absurd, the way you've been treating her, instead of your suddenly orphaned cousin who has only you to turn to as her family."

"Second cousin, Father, and I think it's a little late for anything beyond forced civility. I do promise that I'll try for that, anyway, for the rest of my stay, and will attempt to keep it in mind in future. I don't know if my nerves can take any more haranguing from you or that she-devil! I will say that I feel practically forced out of my own home by the two of you!" Julian finished with feeling. "Now enough of that. You've extracted my promise of good behavior. To change the subject, what's all this Mrs. Merk has been telling me about gunshots and captains!"

Lord Hambledon explained the whole story, and his conclusion about the poacher.

Julian was silent for a long moment, apparently absorbed in the letter holder on his father's desk. Then he said, "My, my, life certainly has become exciting around here since little Bryonny's arrival. And she's already found an attentive suitor. I find it hard to credit."

"You are an impossible child, but I confess that I'm glad to have you home again."

Julian looked up then and smiled. "Thank you, sir. You are admirably loyal despite the provocation I always manage to give you. Shall we retire next door for a game of chess? I'm still smarting from the sound defeat you gave me last year."

Their disagreement forgotten, they moved amiably into the library.

"Oh, Lucy, I'm so glad you're back!" cried Bryonny. "Lord Richard's come home!"

"I heard from Mrs. Merk, my lady. Isn't it exciting?"

"Exciting?" Bryonny grimaced. "Not in the way you mean, Lucy. The man's a tyrant!"

"I heard downstairs that there had been some disagreement between you, but it's only natural, my lady. Don't you worry yourself over it. Come now, it's time to dress for dinner. We'll have you looking beautiful in no time."

"Beautiful I can't expect, but ladylike would help. Lord Richmond has a searing tongue on him when he chooses to. Oh, Lucy, what will I wear?"

"I think the new silk would be nice, my lady," offered Lucy.

"Yes, you're quite right, Lucy." Bryonny sat down in agitation and Lucy dashed out to prepare the bath water.

They made a special effort over her appearance that night. Lucy shook out the dress, never before worn, but nevertheless sponged and pressed by Mrs. Merk; it was a delicate sea-green, the color reminding her of the shallow water which lay over and around the coral reefs in Jamaica. The material fell softly from a high waist in subtle folds that seemed to change color as she moved. The sleeves were small and capped and the low neckline scooped. On her small feet she wore a pair of simple silk sandals of the same soft green. For once she sat still as Lucy brushed her hair until it glistened, twisting the soft curls around her fingers and then threading a ribbon through them. In fact, the short style suited Bryonny. It emphasized her long and graceful neck, and although when her face was dirty

and she was wearing her breeches the short curls con-
tributed to the look of an urchin, tonight there was no
doubt that she was a young woman. Finishing, Lucy
clasped a simple gold rope about her mistress's throat
and stood back to admire the effect she had created.

"Oh, my lady," exclaimed Lucy in delight, "you are
a picture! I don't know when I've ever seen anything
so pretty!"

"Thank you, Lucy, but I fear you exaggerate." She
examined herself critically in the cheval glass. She had
changed over the last year, she knew. She was taller
and more curved than she had been, but still her
reflection gave her a surprise. She had not expected to
look so—well, so different as she did in her new dress,
in fact quite passable, she assessed.

"Lucy, you've done a wonderful job! I hardly recognize myself. Don't let me keep you any longer, I think
I'm as ready as I'll ever be."

Lucy had drawn her own conclusions as to the
goings-on between Lord Richmond and Lady Bryonny.
She was a straightforward country girl and as far as
she saw it, the only important thing between a man
and a woman was the irresistible calling of their physical natures. "Don't you worry, my lady, you'll be the
most beautiful thing he's ever laid eyes on. There's
magic about you tonight, and if his blood doesn't stir
and his heart pound in his chest, then he's no man!"

"Oh, Lucy," laughed Bryonny, "whatever does go
on in that head of yours! Believe me, Lord Richmond's blood will never stir with anything other than
fury at the sight of me. The last thing I want is his
heart pounding! Now, off with you before you get
even more carried away."

Bryonny held her head high as she descended the
long, wide stairs. Quietly, she entered the library to
find Julian with his back to her, gazing out the arched
window and sipping a sherry. He was lost in thought
and completely unaware of her presence. Somehow he
seemed very different as he stood there, not aloof or
threatening, but peaceful, almost vulnerable. She felt
a strange sensation, as if the world had stopped just

then and the two of them were suspended in a timeless moment.

Bryonny did not move or speak, caught up in the tranquil silence which seemed to throb like a living thing. He presented a handsome picture; his evening clothes were simply but impeccably cut, showing off a tall, lean, and well-shaped figure. His long-tailed coat emphasized his broad shoulders and narrow waist; small, stiff points rose from the collar of his shirt, over which his thick black hair curled at the back. The waistcoat was simple but his neckcloth ornately tied. Breeches stretched creaselessly over long, powerful thighs and his calves were encased in silk stockings. She had forgotten what an imposing figure he was. He emanated the powerful grace of an animal—and like an animal, he seemed to suddenly sense the presence of someone in the room.

Spinning around, he was caught off guard, and as their eyes met and held, Bryonny could hear a sudden sharp intake of breath.

"I'm sorry to have alarmed you, my lord. Perhaps I should have retreated and fetched Simms to announce me in sonorous tones." There was a mischievous sparkle in her dancing eyes.

He said nothing, looking at her with an expression she couldn't fathom. The silence swelled between them and Bryonny found her cheeks coloring under his gaze.

"Have I intruded upon a private moment?" she asked softly.

Julian smiled wryly. "No, not at all, Bryonny. My thoughts were elsewhere and I was just taken aback for a moment by your unexpected appearance. Allow me to compliment you on your choice of dress this evening."

"Why, thank you, dear cousin. I'm so happy that my appearance finally agrees with your discerning taste—and may I add that you're looking particularly dashing? That is, if it's not too presumptuous of me."

He bowed at her with a grin. "Not at all. Men appreciate compliments equally as much as the, ah, gentler sex, but are rarely given them. Now, do you think that since we have finished extolling each other's fine dress, if not virtues, I might pour you a glass of sherry?"

"Yes, please, that would be very kind. Wouldn't Uncle Richard be proud of us, Julian? Just think of it; we've managed to get through a full minute of conversation with nary a ruffled feather."

"Yes, indeed." He cocked his eyebrow at her in amusement as he handed a glass to her. "I gather you have been sworn to a truce as well?"

"Yes . . . To a truce and my very best behavior, I fear." She gave a low, throaty chuckle, feeling suddenly and unexpectedly very much at ease.

"In that case, perhaps you should sit down. You must be feeling faint with the strain." He settled them both on the sofa near the fire.

"You are too considerate and kind, cousin. I must admit I was feeling a little weak. But come, let us decide on a safe conversational topic. Surely there must be one or two we can find?"

Bryonny and Julian carried on through dinner much in the same vein, but when they retired to the library afterward, Julian became subtly withdrawn, his manners subdued. He left the conversation to Bryonny and his father, preferring to watch and listen.

"But here, Julian, Uncle Richard has found the perfect subject for us to discuss," Bryonny finally said with a grin, attempting to bring him into their conversation. "Wordsworth has such a nicely neutral eloquence, and 'Intimations of Immortality' is such an optimistic topic, don't you agree? Julian?" she repeated when he didn't respond.

Julian's eyes shot up to hers, and then he looked away. "Oh— I beg your pardon, Bryonny; my thoughts were far away. Wordsworth, did you say?"

"It was of no importance." Bryonny said, feeling slightly hurt by his response. He had said nothing offensive, but there was a coolness in his attitude that hadn't been there before. Was it due to her, something she'd said or done? Giving a little sigh, she dismissed him as impossibly moody and continued her conversation with Lord Hambledon.

Julian stood and stretched his long legs. "I think I'll retire now, with your permission." He glanced briefly at Bryonny.

"Good night, Julian. It was a pleasant evening." She gave him a polite little smile, but her eyes had darkened and the laughter had gone out of them.

He turned abruptly and went upstairs, feeling more disturbed than he had in years. Not the least bit sleepy, he removed his jacket and waistcoat, tugged off his neckcloth, and poured himself a glass of brandy from the decanter on his writing desk. He then settled himself on the windowseat, pushed open the casement window, and drank in the sweet fragrance of the night, warm for so early in the year. The moon was full and low and hung suspended above the treetops, a silver orb outlining the dark branches and casting a shimmering glow over the garden lawn.

Julian drew in a deep breath and released it in a heavy sigh, leaning his head back against the cool stone that framed the window. The moon shifted and its clear light softened for a moment as a cloud drifted across its face like a veil. His long, graceful fingers played with the glass in his hand, twisting the stem round and round as he watched the amber liquid swirl in undulating waves, his clear gray eyes narrowed in thought.

The moon was high in the sky when he shook his head and ran a hand over his face. He leaned over to close the casement window against the night and the eerie spell it had cast over him. Removing the rest of his clothes, he slid his tall, naked body under the cool linen sheets and clasped his hands behind his head. Here was trouble to be sure, trouble he hadn't anticipated in this manner. And unfortunately, there was only one solution for it. But damnably, the solution was more dangerous than the problem. It appeared that Bryonny Livingston was pricking at the conscience he swore he didn't have.

On that thought, he closed his eyes, but sleep eluded him and he tossed and turned throughout the night.

Julian breakfasted with his father the next morning. Together, they planned to go over the estate business and do a round of the Abbey properties, checking on the condition of the tenant farms.

"I appreciate your help in these matters, Julian. I'm finding it more strenuous to keep up with things these days. Old age setting in, you know, and bringing with it aching bones and longing for sleep, although I shouldn't complain, as there'll be plenty of that soon enough, I reckon." He was quiet for a moment, then he chuckled. "Speaking of sleep, you don't look as if you had much of it last night."

"No, actually, I didn't, although I can't think why. I must get up to London directly, Father, much as I would like to stay. I've been away overlong as it is."

"I quite understand, my boy. I have an idea, though. If you could manage to get away for a few days soon, I thought I would have a little house party for Bryonny. It might be nice for her to have a small taste of society before we throw her in."

"It's a good idea, Father. I doubt that she has any inkling of what it's actually going to be like. Whom are you planning to invite!"

"I thought Captain Neville. He stopped by recently to pay his respects and Bryonny found him to be very pleasant. Can you think of someone to make it a foursome—perhaps a nice young woman who can be a companion for Bryonny?"

Julian laughed. "Come now, Father. What nice young woman would accompany me without fearing for her reputation?"

"It's high time you changed your reputation, Julian. I was hoping your year away would knock some sense into your head."

"Oh, indeed, sir? But you know," he said slowly, the idea growing on him, "there is someone who crosses my mind as suitable, although I shall have to ascertain

if she is still unattached. Do you remember Henry
Falsworth's eldest daughter, Cynthia?''

"I believe I do. But didn't she marry that Freddy
Ashford some years ago?"

"Yes, she did, but he died. He wasn't a young
man."

"Ah yes, I remember hearing about that. No sons to
carry on his name, poor man. Left her a healthy
fortune, too. I gather her father married her off to
Ashford in exchange for the money to pay off his
gambling debts."

"I must say, Father, for one who lives such a reclu-
sive life, you certainly know the gossip," said Julian
with amusement.

"I keep my ear to the ground. So, Cynthia Ashford,
is it? As I recall she's quite a beauty."

"That she is. I saw her briefly when she'd come
back into society and she had an enormous crowd of
followers. But if she is still unattached, I don't think
she'd be adverse to the invitation. I don't want you
getting any ideas into your head if I bring her, but she
would be someone for Bryonny to model herself after
if she's to succeed in London. This would simply be to
accommodate your gathering."

"Certainly. It's very obliging of you, Julian. I wouldn't
want to pry into your personal affairs." Lord Hambledon
looked at his son humorously over his spectacles. "I'll
wait until I meet the young lady myself. I'm sure she'll
be perfect for my purpose."

Julian shook his head at his father in exasperation
and addressed himself to finishing his toast while he
contemplated the thought of the lovely Cynthia Ashford.
Yes, the idea appealed to him more by the minute. As
soon as he reached London, he would arrange to meet
up with her for a little diversion—if she was still
available.

A beauty of the first stare, she had seemed very
amenable to him when he had last seen her. The game
of pursuing her would be amusing; he was quite certain that she took lovers, and with the fortune her late
husband had left her there was no need for her to

consider marriage, so he'd be safe on that score. He wondered how long it would take him to bring the seduction to a close. She'd had suitors aplenty and probably knew the game as well as he. Cynthia, with her hair the color of wheat, her eyes a clear blue, and her elegant, sophisticated composure was perfect for him. Yes, Cynthia would suit admirably in all respects.

The rest of the day was taken up with business, and Julian didn't see Bryonny until it was time for him to leave. He'd said his good-byes to Mrs. Merk, who couldn't tell him where Bryonny was, but when he went to the kitchen to bid farewell to Cook, she directed him outside. He found Bryonny working out in the walled garden that stretched off the east wing from the kitchen, where all the herbs and vegetables for the house were grown. Entering through the path off the courtyard, he quietly opened the door. She was on her knees in front of a frame full of seedlings, her face smudged with dirt. Her dress was old and well-worn and covered by an apron, but the signs of patching were visible. He could just make out snatches of a song she was humming to herself. She looked young and pretty and very innocent, a simple maiden working in her garden.

"Julian! You startled me! What are you doing standing there looking like a cat about to pounce on his prey?" She leaned back on her heels, looking up at him with a smile, her green eyes squinting against the brightness of the sun over his shoulder.

"It appears it's my turn to apologize for coming on you unawares. I only came to say good-bye, not to eat you." He flashed her a grin.

"I'd say that was a very wise decision on your part. I somehow doubt you'd find me very tasty."

"Oh, I don't know; I've made meals of worse." He wickedly cocked an eyebrow at her. "Some other time, perhaps. I must be on my way."

Bryonny stood up and looked at her dirty hands ruefully. "I won't offer you my hand, but I wish you a safe journey, Julian."

"Thank you. I'm sure you're delighted to see my back, but sadly I am to return shortly should you miss me too much."

"How delightful, dear cousin. I shall spend the time practicing my manners and ladylike grace for you so that you may be proud of me."

"That is something I can honestly say I would look forward to with pleasure. Now I must be off before it gets any later." He turned to go, then hesitated for a moment, and turned back. "Bryonny . . . I've been remiss in welcoming you properly to the family. Allow me to do it now." And leaning forward, he kissed her lightly on her cheek, then pulled away abruptly. "Good-bye . . ." he started to say, but stopped, astonished, when she burst into peals of laughter.

"Oh, Julian, don't glare at me like that, you look so indignant! Here," she chortled, taking a handkerchief out of her apron pocket and wiping a smudge of dirt from his face. "I'm afraid I'm quite contagious! That will teach you to go around kissing kitchen maids." And she burst into another peal of laughter.

"Dear heaven, girl!" he said, jerking his head away. "When will you learn! You do nothing for a man's dignity but offend it!"

"You only see it that way because your precious dignity is so easy to offend, Julian. Would you have thanked me to let you go walking off streaked with mud? Goodness, what would the servants have thought? I can just hear Mrs. Merk now: 'There goes that Master Julian, rolling around in the dirt again, and goodness only knows who with—"

"Enough, Bryonny! I'm sure you find yourself very amusing, but I fail to see the humor or the taste in your jokes. One would think you'd been brought up in the gutter with the way you behave."

"That was unnecessary, Julian," she said quietly. "And I'm sorry you took offense where none was intended. Good-bye." She turned her back on him and went back to her seedlings.

Julian shot a poisonous look at her, muttered "damnable brat" under his breath, and took himself off, thereby missing the tears that had spilled over and were running down Bryonny's cheeks. His phaeton was waiting for him outside the front steps, his father standing along side of it.

"Good-bye, Father," he said, pushing his anger aside and embracing his father warmly. "I'll look forward to seeing you in April."

"So shall I, my boy. I'll be waiting to hear about Mrs. Ashford."

"Yes, Father, I'll let you know as soon as I can." He grinned. "Let's hope I haven't lost my powers of persuasion. And for God's sake don't let that miserable child run you into the ground. I'll see you soon." He climbed up into the seat and picked up the reins.

Lord Hambledon watched his son depart with a wry smile. "Julian, my boy, your wandering days are over." He walked up the steps to the house with a smile of pleasant anticipation. He had no way of knowing that the gathering he was planning would prove to be his undoing.

Chapter Four

APRIL came unusually warm that year, awakening all the vitality and sweetness the countryside had to give after the onslaught of rain. Spring had well and truly arrived; daffodils and jonquils carpeted the lawns in front of the Abbey and ran unchecked throughout the woods. The lake beyond the lawns stretched clear and blue, interrupted only by the green dots of lily pads which thickly hugged the shoreline and wandered haphazardly out into the vast crystal expanse. It was populated by a regal pair of swans and a handful of ducks who filled the air with their contented quacking and who were drowned out in the evenings by the baritones of frogs who croaked out a symphony from their lily pads, glorying in the fading light and giving voice to the splendor of the season.

Bryonny was at work in the kitchen garden, pleased that the soil she had so carefully prepared and planted was now just beginning to burgeon forth with a wide assortment of vegetables. The sun streaming down on her back and the steady drone of the bees at work in the orchard brought a lazy contentment as she rhythmically hoed the earth. The delicious smell of freshly baked bread drifted enticingly out from the open kitchen window, and in the distant pasture Bedlam whickered and snorted as he pranced around the grass in play. Bryonny was only dimly aware of the sounds and smells around her for her thoughts were preoccupied with the guests who were expected to arrive sometime in the early evening. She had only a few hours left before they descended on her, and she viewed the prospect with a mixture of anticipation and dread. In fact, the only pleasant prospect that she could come up with was seeing Philip again, but even that was overwhelmed by the thought of having to face Julian.

With a twinge she remembered the last time she had seen Julian, inside these very walls. Since then he had often been in her thoughts and even her dreams, which she found completely infuriating. He came into her mind at the most unexpected moments; a gesture made by his father which so echoed his own, or a certain tone of voice her Uncle Richard used along with a raise of his eyebrow would evoke a sudden sharp remembrance of the son. He was an enigma to her, at one moment so thoughtlessly hurtful and at other moments revealing an unexpected warmth and tenderness, as when he had spoken kindly to her and kissed her. And yet in the next moment he had cut her to the quick for no good reason that she could see. That she was a thorn in his side was obvious, but it made little sense to her, and she very much doubted it ever would. And then there was this Cynthia Ashford to consider, and Julian's relationship with her. Uncle Richard had said little on the subject save that she was an acquaintance of Julian's. She couldn't help but wonder what sort of a woman she was. That would tell much about the man.

Sighing, she looked up at the sun, which had dipped a little lower on its westward arc. She'd done enough gardening for one day and would reward herself with a good ride before the onslaught. Perhaps that would shake these troublesome thoughts from her head.

At that moment Cynthia Ashford was rattling toward Hambledon Abbey ensconced in Julian's town carriage along with her dresser, Marie Dupris, an impoverished gentlewoman whose status rested in that netherland between companion and servant and who was very well aware of her position in the world.

Julian rode beside on a horse he had recently pur-
chased. Cynthia sat quietly in the carriage, her eyes
closed and a small smile on her sculptured lips.

"Madame?" Marie's voice jolted Cynthia out of her
thoughts. "I thought you might desire to freshen up
before we arrive. Here, I have some eau de toilette
and a handkerchief ready."

"Thank you, Marie. May I have my mirror, please?"
She dabbed the handkerchief at her throat and wrists.
"No matter how well made these carriages, one still
can't help but become dusty."

"But Lord Richmond does know how to travel in
style, does he not? My father once had a carriage like
this before the Revolution—"

"Yes, dear. Now don't forget, I want you to keep
well out of the way. And remember, I don't want you
mingling with the servants."

"Certainly not, madame. I wouldn't think of such a
thing. Oh dear, I do hope the visit goes well. I must
confess to nerves." Marie knew perfectly well that her
fortune would rise or fall according to her mistress's
position and was as intent on securing Cynthia's future
as Cynthia was.

"Nonsense, Marie. We've discussed the situation
quite thoroughly and I can't see there's anything for
you to feel apprehensive about." Satisfied, she put the
mirror down and leaned forward, admiring Julian's
broad, upright back through the window. "It's time
Lord Richmond took a wife; he's played long enough,
all of London says so."

"*Oui, madame,* and they also say he's the best catch
on the marriage market, heir to all that money."

"Exactly, Marie. Exactly."

Bryonny had just dismounted from Bedlam when
she suddenly heard the clopping of a horse's hooves
on the packed dirt of the road coming round the
corner to the stableyard. "Oh, dear Lord in heaven!"
she softly exclaimed. "It couldn't be yet, it's far too
early!" She thought it to be Philip, expecting Julian to

arrive in a carriage, and her heart sank twice as far when she turned and saw Julian dismounting from a beautiful dappled-gray stallion.

"Hello there, George! Do come out from wherever you're hiding and see the new piece of horseflesh I've just . . ." his voice trailed off midsentence as he spotted Bryonny trying to slip unseen with Bedlam around the far corner of the building.

His amused eyes traveled up and down, taking in her breeches and boots and cap covering her hair. "Well, well, little cousin, some things never change. How delightful to see you again! Come, don't you have a greeting for me, Bryonny? Surely you've missed me and are glad for my return?"

"Not particularly on either count," said Bryonny, approaching him nonchalantly. "I hadn't expected you so early or I would have been decked out in ribbons and plumes for your illustrious arrival. Pray tell, where is your carriage and your friend from the big city? Did they arrive with you?"

"Yes indeed. The carriage is around at the front and Mrs. Ashford is at present engaged in changing into what most women wear when they intend to go riding. Aren't you concerned that your fine captain will find you looking like that?"

"He isn't my fine captain, and no, I really couldn't care. In any case, if he did find me looking like 'this,' as you so articulately put it, he would have the good manners to keep his opinion to himself."

George had emerged from the stable and had overheard this barbed exchange. "Not five minutes and they're already at each other," he said glumly to himself. "I just don't understand it; two of the friendliest people you could ever hope to meet, and the kindest, and they behave like mortal enemies to each other. Very strange, indeed," he finished, shaking his head.

"Ah, there you are, George," called Julian, ignoring Bryonny and her last barbed remark. "Come and see what I've just bought myself. Fine bloodline; I'll wager even you'll be impressed when you see it. I'm going to sell him again for a killing." And he drew

George off into the stable to show him the thorough-bred and his impeccable lineage.

Bryonny was longing to go after them to see the stallion more closely and examine his papers, but she was too proud to follow uninvited, especially after Julian's scathing comments. Still, she had to admire the fine animal. He was exceptionally well formed with a beautifully shaped head and an alert, intelligent expression, from what she had seen. She busied her-self with wiping down Bedlam and putting him away in his stall with a bucket of oats, while she occupied her mind with black thoughts about her insufferable cousin. She heard his carriage being brought in and unhitched and the horses put away, and was grateful that she and Bedlam were in the other end of the stable. She didn't feel the least like being sociable, and in any case, Julian's men were probably just as insufferable as he was if his high-handed attitude had rubbed off on them.

George and Julian reemerged from the stable with a pair of horses saddled up. One was a large gelding with an even temper, and the other the docile mare which George had once tried to foist on Bryonny. She ignored them, gathering up her bucket and sponges in the yard.

"Master Julian, would you mind holding Jasmine here for just a moment? I think I hear that stallion of yours kicking at his door and I want to make sure of the lock. I'm short-handed today and those men of yours are still busy with your carriage." George handed the reins to Julian and hurried back inside again.

Bryonny was watching these proceedings out of the corner of her eye and was determined to make no offer to help when she saw a very attractive woman appear from around the corner dressed in a deep blue velvet riding habit, her flaxen hair topped by a high-crowned hat with a single ostrich plume curling down from it. So this, then, must be Julian's Mrs. Ashford. She quickly picked up her bucket and turned away.

"Lord Richmond!" Cynthia cried. "Here I am! It didn't take long, so I thought I'd save you the bother of coming for me." She stopped abruptly as she came to a wide, deep puddle of mud that stretched across the path. "Oh, dear." she said in dismay. "Could you give the horses to the stableboy and come help me over this?"

Julian was vastly entertained by Cynthia's mistaken assumption. "Here, boy," he called, striding by Bryonny and throwing her the reins of both horses, enjoying her outraged expression. He picked Cynthia up and set her down on the other side of the muddy water.

"Oh, thank you, my lord. You've saved my dress from certain ruin!"

"My pleasure, my dear," he replied, milking this situation for all it was worth. Taking the reins of the gelding from a glowering Bryonny, he mounted and waited to see what she would do. So did George, who had just returned and was about to cross over and take the mare when Cynthia walked over to Bryonny and spoke, and he froze in astonishment.

"Oh, what a pretty little horse she is; I'm sure we'll get along famously. Here, boy, help me up!" She looked at Bryonny, who was standing there speechless. Julian was clearly finding it difficult to hold in his mirth.

Bryonny was in an impossible position. If she enlightened Cynthia as to her identity, she would appear a fool, and Julian would laugh himself silly over her predicament. She would not give him the satisfaction. She did as she had been told, although she had no idea how to mount a lady on a sidesaddle. She bent her clasped hands to Cynthia's daintily booted foot and lifted upward with a strong heave. The next thing she knew, Cynthia was flying through the air, her knee missing the pommel altogether. Her skirts tangled around her as she was vaulted over the other side of the little mare to land in an undignified and dusty heap on the ground.

There was a long pause of stunned silence in the stableyard before reaction set in. Cynthia's mouth opened and she gasped, but no sound emerged.

Bryonny was horrified. She had not meant to throw Cynthia to the ground, but had calculated that it would take a great deal of strength to get her into the saddle. Cynthia was obviously not a very experienced horsewoman if she had not been able to correct the thrust. She blushed scarlet in shame, knowing that she was in terrible trouble.

Angrily dismounting, Julian stormed toward Bryonny. He came up behind her, grabbed her harshly by the arm, and spun her around to meet his furious black glare.

"You idiotic, pigeon-brained fool!" he shouted. "Can't you get anything right?" Her green eyes met his full on and did not flicker. The heat of her arm under his fingers burned into him and he crushed it harder in his vise like grip. "Go on, get out of my sight before I do something I'll regret!" And so saying, he threw her away from him with such force that she stumbled and fell to the ground. He moved toward her, then stopped abruptly.

Bryonny picked herself up and turned to him with composure, unshed tears of pain and hurt surprise glistening in her eyes. "I beg your pardon, m'lord," she said in a strong rural accent. "I meant no harm. I be askin' your forgiveness, and . . . and the lady's." The expression on her face and the thrust of her pointed little chin, whose message Julian had learned, belied her words.

"It's lucky for you there was no worse harm done," replied Julian, knowing she would take his double meaning. "Now back to your duties. George will have to see to your punishment later." He watched her as she turned and walked away, taking the mare with her, her shoulders squared and her small back stiff.

"Lord Richmond! Please, could you help me up?" asked Cynthia plaintively.

Julian had forgotten her, his attention completely concentrated on Bryonny from the moment he had dismounted. He went quickly to Cynthia's side and helped her up from her awkward position, saying solicitously, "I beg your pardon, ma'am. I can't think how I could have been so rude; I'm afraid I was so overcome by my anger toward the boy that I could think of nothing else. Please accept my most humble apologies for not tending to you first."

"Yes, of course. Of course you were angry." She brushed off her dress, refraining from saying anything else. She knew by reputation that Julian loathed women prone to hysterics.

"I shall speak to the head groom about the boy, Mrs. Ashford. As for your dress, Mrs. Merk will see that it is cleaned. I'm sorry that this should have happened. Please, allow me to escort you back to the house."

"Oh, yes, thank you," said Cynthia weakly, leaning heavily on his arm. "I'm afraid I was a little shaken by the episode. It gave me quite a fright and I think I'd like to lie down."

"But you are not hurt in any way?"

"Just my dignity." Cynthia gave a shaky laugh.

"Perhaps Mademoiselle Dupris will order a soothing tisane for you. They're a specialty of Mrs. Merk's and I know she would be delighted to make you one." He wanted nothing more than to turn the distraught Cynthia over to her abigail and do his best to forget about the entire incident.

As soon as Julian had seen Cynthia delivered into Mademoiselle Dupris' possessive custody, he took himself off to find his father and have a peaceful conversation in the style of men. He made no mention of the stableyard confrontation, hoping that it would somehow be forgotten.

Bryonny waited until Julian had removed Cynthia and then fetched the gelding from where it had strayed. She found George pulled back in the shadow of the stabel eaves, and when questioned, he told her that he had witnessed the entire episode but had decided that it was wisest not to get involved.

"Oh, George," said Bryonny miserably, "I really didn't mean for it to happen, and I certainly am not looking forward to the consequences, but since it did happen, I can't say I'm sorry, at least not about the refined Mrs. Ashford. But oh, George, now Julian is more angry with me than ever, and will never, never forgive me, and I have to live with the two of them throughout this awful house party, and I solemnly promised Uncle Richard that I'd be civil. Now look what I've done! I've gone and ruined everything." She sat down hard on the mounting block, despair exuding almost tangibly from her.

"Now, now, m'lady," said George kindly, wanting to sit her on his lap like a hurt child, but instead removing the reins of the horse from between her tightly clenched fists and pretending not to notice the tears that now poured hotly down her cheeks. "I reckon it's not as bad as all that. It's true that it might have been wiser not to have attempted the hoax, for Master Julian did seem sorely vexed, but I know you didn't really mean to throw the lady over like that. Still, what's done is done. But if it's any comfort to you, I don't think there will be any worse consequences. He's as responsible as you for letting it happen and I reckon he knows it. And besides that, I saw his face when she'd just landed like a partridge come to earth, and I could swear he was grinning, unlikely as it may sound."

"Really, George? Was he really?" exclaimed Bryonny, her face lighting up and the tears forgotten in her curiosity and surprise. "But then, why did he become so angry and treat me so roughly? He bruised my arm, you know, and knocked me down! I swear there was hatred if not murder in his eyes." She rubbed her arm painfully.

"Well," said George thoughtfully, mulling this question over. He was not a hasty man and seldom ventured an opinion without first giving it a bit of time to settle. This was particularly difficult for him, given the complexity of the two people involved, but he felt Lady Bryonny was in need of some kind of answer to soothe her mind. "Could be—I'm not saying 'tis, mind you, for it has me a bit puzzled, too—but could be he was embarrassed at having his lady friend shown up and was angry at himself for having encouraged it. In my opinion it was a funny sight when you come right down to it, not accounting for the right and wrong of it."

"Oh, it *was* that, wasn't it!" chortled Bryonny, her worries forgotten for a moment as she reveled in the memory. "I don't know that I can like her, George, even though I'd made up my mind to try. The minute she came sailing into the stableyard as if for all the world she owned it, I took a disliking to her. And it was revolting the way she simpered at Julian! It astounds me that he can stomach it, but there's no accounting for taste. At least it explains why I irritate him so if that's the manner in which he expects me to behave!"

"It's not my place to say, m'lady, but I reckon you have something there. But if I was you, I wouldn't go changing myself to her type, Master Julian's opinion or no. We all like you just the way you are, and I'm sure Master Julian will come to like you, too, even if you do get a little high-spirited from time to time and spark his temper. He just needs some time to get accustomed to your way of doing things. Just remember, he's mostly bark and very little bite. Been that way since he was a young 'un and things didn't go according to his liking. So don't you go getting yourself all worked up when it's just as likely he'll calm down and no more will come of it. If I was you—and I'm just as glad I'm not in your shoes—I'd be more worried about the lady recognizing you when you put your skirts on, begging your pardon. There, now I've said too much already. You just run along and let me get on with the horses."

This had been a very long speech for the normally taciturn little man, but he'd felt it worthwhile. He couldn't bear to see his dear Lady Bryonny so upset, and he hoped that his judgment of Master Julian would prove to be correct.

Chapter Five

PHILIP arrived early that evening, and after changing, went to the library where he comfortably settled himself, drinking a glass of sherry and feeling considerably more relaxed. Adjusting the line of his coat, his fingers brushed across the outline of the paper he had slipped inside, to keep it safe from prying eyes. He hesitated, then pulled the paper out, rebuttoning his crimson red uniform jacket with the gold-encrusted collar. His brow furrowed as he once again read the contents, and he sighed. He had a tremendous problem on his hands, and no clear idea how to handle it; as far as he could see, once Bryonny left for London and the Season, all chance was lost. She'd be married in no time, no doubt to someone of high rank. It seemed to him that this was his last opportunity to further his cause, but he still hadn't decided whether to speak to Lord Hambledon. Nevertheless, if he did, then this paper would be his bargaining power. On this his entire future could well depend.

Suddenly he became aware of light footsteps crossing the hall and coming toward the door and his heart jerked. Looking quickly around, his eyes fell upon a slim volume of Hegel lying on the Louis XIV writing table nearby. He grabbed it up and pushed the paper inside, turning casually as Bryonny entered the room.

"Philip, how nice to see you! I'm so sorry that no one was available to greet you; I hope you haven't been waiting long. I trust you've made yourself comfortable?"

"Yes, thank you, Bryonny, I have been very well looked after." Philip placed the book back down on the table and hoped he looked composed, which he certainly didn't feel. He took Bryonny's hand and, bending over it, he kissed her fingers lightly. "You have grown even more beautiful since I last was here. Your life must be agreeing with you excessively to have put such roses in your cheeks and the sparkle in your eyes." He drew her down onto the sofa.

"Well, well, Captain Neville," said Lord Hambledon as he entered. "I see you have arrived. Welcome once again. How nice to have you back with us! Bryonny, my dear, you are looking splendid. May I pour you a sherry?"

"Thank you, Uncle Richard, and yes, sherry would be lovely."

"Have you seen your cousin yet?"

"No . . . Mrs. Merk told me he and Mrs. Ashford arrived some three hours ago, but thought it would be best if I stayed out of Julian's way for fear of inadvertently invoking his wrath."

"Nonsense, Bryonny. I thought the two of you had worked all of that out the last time he was here."

"Not exactly—but it doesn't signify," she said quickly as Lord Hambledon frowned. "I'm afraid that you can't put the two of us within ten miles of each other without setting off sparks of one kind or another."

"Ah," said Lord Hambledon. "Yes, I can understand. Julian can be unpredictable, I know. Well, just try to be politic, but not too politic, if you take my meaning. You know full well what that incites!" He chuckled.

Philip had been standing off to one side, listening to all of this with great interest. He was very surprised to hear that Bryonny did not get along with her dashing cousin. The way he'd heard it, women found him irresistible; most of female society was after the man. And it sounded as if the dislike were mutual. It might well work to his advantage.

"Now tell me, captain, what news from the front? I hear Wellington's last maneuver was bringing him toward Badajoz with Massena in retreat. Do you think we might have another victory to equal the brilliant action of Barrossa?"

Bryonny wandered away from the discussion, her mind occupied with Julian and Cynthia and what would transpire when they finally made an appearance. She was extremely nervous at the prospect.

"Father," announced Julian from the doorway, "may I present Mrs. Cynthia Ashford to you?" He led her forward and Lord Hambledon bowed over her hand, murmuring the usual politenesses, and then introduced them both to Philip, who was standing to one side watching carefully.

"And where is Bryonny, Father?"

"Just behind you, cousin," she answered quietly, and startled, he spun around to face her. She had been standing half in shadow by the bookshelves on the other side of the door so he hadn't seen her when they entered. Now she came forward into the full light, shimmering in gold as if she'd just stepped out of the setting sun.

Julian paused for a fraction of a second and then made a graceful leg, saying languidly, "Why, Bryonny, how very pleasant to see you again. You are well, I trust?"

Bryonny had caught an unguarded, although unreadable, expression in his eyes before they had so quickly shuttered, and it perplexed her. But she did understand the subtle thrust of his question and replied in the same casual tone.

"I'm very well, thank you." She eyed him with caution, waiting for him to introduce Cynthia, who had come to his side and taken his arm. He seemed to be oblivious of her.

"Ah, yes," he said, suddenly becoming aware of the pressure on his sleeve. "Mrs. Cynthia Ashford, may I present my cousin, Lady Bryonny Livingston?"

Cynthia was looking at Bryonny with a puzzled expression on her face. There was something familiar . . .

Bryonny, her heart in her throat, stepped quickly

into the breach. "I am so happy to make your acquaintance, Mrs. Ashford."

"I am pleased to make your acquaintance as well, Lady Bryonny. Lord Richmond has told me so much about you."

"Has he indeed?" replied Bryonny with interest. She strongly suspected that he had told her very little about his wayward cousin. "I can't imagine what there would be to tell. We live such a quiet, uneventful life out here in the country. I would venture to say that nothing exciting ever seems to happen, nothing like your life in London, I would imagine. Life at the Abbey is sadly without incident." A peculiar strangled sound came from Julian, and Cynthia looked at him in surprise, only to find him gazing distractedly around the room and clearing his throat. Her attention returned to the girl before her.

"Yes, Lady Bryonny, it is true that you will find your life very different when you come up to London. Of course, country girls unused to our city ways often find themselves overwhelmed at first when introduced to Polite Society, but one becomes accustomed in time. I'm sure I found it so myself."

"Oh, that I would never believe, Mrs. Ashford," said Julian graciously.

"Perhaps not, Lord Richmond, but then you did not know me when I was in my first Season. Did I understand that you are to have your come-out this year, my dear?"

"Yes, Mrs. Ashford. I shall be coming to London in just a fortnight."

"Then I expect you will be needing someone to look out for you. I would be happy to help you learn."

"How very kind, Mrs. Ashford," murmured Julian. "I'm sure Lady Bryonny is most appreciative for the offer of your guidance."

"Yes, how very kind, Mrs. Ashford," echoed Bryonny sweetly, wanting to kick Julian in the shins. "Lord Richmond has already been so helpful to me."

"I'm sure he has, my dear. And you would be wise

to listen to his advice; he is very well regarded, you know." She smiled at Julian.

It was too much. She should have expected Julian to produce such a namby-pamby creature after all his barbs. And now he had the nerve to stand there and look at her smugly. "Oh, yes," she said to Cynthia. "I can imagine how very well regarded Lord Richmond is, although he would never think of telling me such a thing himself. He is far too modest a man."

"Modesty, my dear Bryonny," Julian shot back, "is a quality I find sadly lacking in some of my younger acquaintances. Perhaps it is acquired with maturity."

"Do you think, Julian? I don't know that is necessarily so. Why, I have met people of much greater age and experience than myself who are terrible windbags and think a great deal of their own opinions."

"That might well be because their opinions are based on something concrete and you are simply too young to understand them."

"Oh, yes, I suppose you're quite right. I know I'm a dreadful simpleton when it comes right down to it. And I often have to be reminded to respect my elders. It's one of my more appalling faults, of which I have a great many. But then, I have no need to worry about that with you. You have always been so charming to me, so careful of my more tender feelings." She met his eyes evenly and found amusement there.

"Hmm . . . Tender feelings, did you say?"

"Very tender feelings, indeed." She couldn't help but smile.

"I confess myself profoundly interested to hear it."

"How very gratifying, my lord. And kind, of course."

Cynthia, slightly perplexed by this exchange, felt as if somehow the advantage had been taken from her and stepped in to regain control of the conversation. "I understand you were raised in Jamaica, Lady Bryonny? How fascinating. You must tell me all about it . . ."

Bryonny drew a deep breath and plunged into small talk.

*   *   *

Cynthia became distracted when she realized Julian was no longer at her side and looked around to where he had joined the other men. She tried to catch his eye but it was focused elsewhere, and following his gaze, she found it fixed on Bryonny. His gray eyes were impenetrable but the intense concentration in them was unmistakable. If it weren't so absurd, she would almost have thought he was angry—no, not angry, something else she couldn't make out . . . Annoyed, she dismissed the effort to fathom his thoughts and decided that it was time to get his mind back where it belonged.

"I beg your pardon, I've just recalled a personal message I was charged to deliver to Lord Richmond by a mutual friend. If you'll excuse me?"

"Most certainly," said Bryonny graciously, vastly relieved to be dismissed. Turning back to look after Cynthia with an amused smile, Bryonny was caught in the full force of Julian's gaze. His eyes were clear, and steadily leveled on her in a highly disconcerting manner. She found herself pulled into them, and was thrown into confusion, her heart tightening in her chest and a heat suddenly suffusing her face. Then mercifully Julian released her, looking away as Cynthia distracted him, and Bryonny, left feeling inexplicably shaken, tried to recover her equilibrium. She was grateful that she did not have time to consider what had just passed between them, for Simms arrived at the door and announced that dinner was served.

During the first course of turtle soup, conversation remained fairly calm and consisted of the usual social chatter. Bryonny kept her eyes on her plate. Julian was seated next to her and she found his near presence very disturbing. Her appetite had fled and she had to force herself to eat; it was a task keeping her hand steady.

Then Philip said, "I trust you are enjoying the Abbey, Mrs. Ashford? I always find it so charming."

"Why yes, Captain Neville, what little I've seen of it

I find absolutely lovely. Unfortunately, I have been mostly in my room since I arrived."

"I hope the journey was not too fatiguing, Mrs. Ashford? It is a fairly long one," said Philip solicitously.

"Oh, not at all, captain. Lord Richmond's carriage is very comfortable. No, I met with a small accident at the stable upon arriving, and thought it best to remove myself until I'd recovered."

At this comment, both Bryonny's and Julian's eyes shot up and they exchanged a quick glance.

"Mrs. Ashford!" Lord Hambledon exclaimed. "Julian, how is it I have not heard of such an unfortunate event?"

"I didn't want to worry you with it, Father, as no harm was done."

"But you must tell me what happened," he insisted.

"It was nothing, I assure you, Lord Hambledon," said Cynthia. "I was being assisted in mounting my horse by a stableboy who was a trifle overly enthusiastic in his task. He managed to catapult me over the horse and onto the ground. I was only a bit shaken, that is all."

"How dreadful!" said Lord Hambledon. "I can't think of how such a thing could occur! Who was the boy, Julian? Surely not Dougal?"

"No, not Dougal. It was the same one who nearly killed me last month, Father. We really must do something about him."

Lord Hambledon suddenly began to choke. He held his napkin up to his mouth, his face averted and his eyes tearing. Julian carefully examined his fingernails while Philip leapt to Lord Hambledon's side. "My lord?"

It took him a moment to recover, but then he was able to say, "I'm fine, just fine, thank you, captain. It was only a little soup going down the wrong way. It seems as if you're forever coming to our rescue. Please, do sit down. Really, I'm perfectly well." He cleared his throat and when he had composed himself and the conversation had safely resumed, he exchanged a long look with Julian, who met his eyes and smiled, but Bryonny uncharacteristically blushed and looked away.

During the second course of fish and a blanquette of veal, Cynthia took over, relating various anecdotes from last year's Season. Bryonny listened in a removed fashion, not particularly amused or interested despite the fact that she was soon to be thrown to these very lions. She noticed that Julian was very quiet, uncharacteristically so. And so he remained through most of dinner, even through Philip's discussion of the Peninsular War, a subject in which she knew Julian was extremely well versed. She drew a scandalized look from Cynthia when she joined in the discussion, hoping to draw Julian in, if only out of sheer annoyance. But he didn't take her bait. It wasn't until the last course of sweets and savories, when Lord Hambledon, who had watched Julian carefully and with a good deal of interest, finally introduced the subject of philosophy, knowing it was irresistible to Bryonny and to Julian as well, that he finally came out of his self-imposed silence.

". . . But given your last point, Uncle Richard, don't you think it would be fair to say that Hegel is the modern-day's Aristotle?" said Bryonny.

"In what way, my dear?"

"In that they both attempt to look at the whole of the universe. Most other philosophers I've read only seem to examine fragments of it."

"What makes you single out Hegel as a philosopher worthy of comparison to Aristotle?" said Julian. "Why not his mentor, Kant, for example?"

Lord Hambledon withdrew from the arena, well pleased.

"In Hegel's last work—" Bryonny attempted to answer but was interrupted by Julian once again.

"You've read *Phenomenology of Mind*?" he asked incredulously. "By God, I'm amazed. That's no easy piece. What did you make of it?"

"I don't know if I can be very clear; I find parts of his work very confusing. The way he describes the rise from simple consciousness to absolute knowledge is fascinating, but I wonder how much his personal views on religion influence some of his ideas—ethical spirit is a good example."

"I believe his religious convictions have played a very important role in the development of his philosophy. For example . . ."

Bryonny found that Julian brought a new interpretation to the work, and somehow managed to simplify the areas which she had found so difficult. She warmed to her subject, asking questions, bringing in other aspects that interested her. Julian's strong hands gracefully carved the air as he described an image. He didn't need to belabor his explanations; she grasped his meaning quickly, and she found that he seemed to anticipate her thoughts almost before she had a chance to articulate them.

"But Julian, when you compare the Platonic Archetype to—"

"Lady Bryonny, don't you think it's time we retired from the table and left the men to their port and conversation?" Cynthia interrupted softly and waited for Bryonny to rise from the table.

Bryonny had no choice if she were not to be rude to Cynthia. She looked at Julian regretfully, but as she started to push back her chair he touched her hand and in an undertone said, "One moment, Bryonny. Your arm—I noticed the bruise. I had no idea I'd hurt you so—I hope you can find it in yourself to forgive me."

Bryonny smiled at him and said very softly, "There is nothing to forgive, Julian. I daresay I deserved it and more. Don't trouble yourself over it; in fact, it is I who owes you an apology." She rose from the table, excusing herself, and led Cynthia from the room, but she felt Julian's eyes on her back as she went.

"Lady Bryonny, my dear, I hope you won't take it wrong of me, but as I know you are not accustomed to the ways of Polite Society perhaps you won't mind if I point out some errors you have made." She closed the library door behind her.

"But of course! Please tell me what I have done that has upset you, Mrs. Ashford?"

"You see, my dear, men are not accustomed to such forwardness from a young lady. I know that you have had no experience and no one to guide you, which is unfortunate. Lord Hambledon simply cannot be expected to know how to bring up a young girl. If you'll allow me, perhaps I can help."

"Indeed, I'd be so grateful."

"Now to start with, you should have given the signal to leave the table much earlier, and not left it to me. But far worse than that was the way you dominated the conversation—and the subject, Lady Bryonny! You simply must not involve yourself in men's discussions. They take it quite amiss and can only lose respect for a woman who behaves like a bluestocking, discussing subjects such as, such as . . ."

"Hegel?" put in Bryonny helpfully.

"Yes. You see, you showed yourself to be presumptuous and sadly lacking the more sensitive and gentle nature that a young woman is meant to possess. You'll never find a man willing to marry you if you carry on in such a way. Men wish for women to limit their discussion to society, children, and fashion. That is why we retire from the table, to allow the gentlemen a chance to pursue their own interests, those of a more worldly nature."

Cynthia's eyes lit upon the offensive volume on the writing table. She swept it up and paced the room, gesturing with it at Bryonny. Neither noticed the slip of paper that fluttered out and came to rest under the wing-backed chair. "It's time someone took you in hand, my dear, before you cause embarrassment to Lord Hambledon or Lord Richmond, or most certainly to yourself. Unfortunately, society is not very forgiving, and one's first impression tends to last. I only speak to you like this because I would like to see you do well for yourself and your family. I would advise you to spend your time reading the fashion plates or *La Belle Assemblée* instead of filling your head with this nonsense."

"I expect you're quite right," said Bryonny, taking the book from her, concerned that Cynthia would break its spine with the way she was flapping it around. "I'm afraid in this predominately male household we are unaccustomed to such things." She placed the book down on the table next to the door.

"In London, you will find them readily available to you. You know, my dear, femininity and fine manners can take you a long way."

"I'm afraid that I really am an ignorant country girl as you pointed out, Mrs. Ashford. It's so kind of you to apprise me of my mistakes. You see, I lost my mother when I was fairly young, and have had no one to teach me. And with my Jamaican background—well, you can imagine. I certainly don't want to make a fool out of myself when I go to London, and ruin my chances of making a match."

"Yes, exactly, dear," said Cynthia, clearly mollified that it had been so easy to show Bryonny the error of her ways. "I'm so pleased that you have the sense to listen to your elders and accept correction. You should have seen the look on Captain Neville's face, first when you interrupted his discussion, but then when you started in with Lord Richmond, he looked absolutely horrified. I wouldn't be surprised at all if you haven't completely ruined your chances with him."

"Oh dear, do you think so?" cried Bryonny distressfully. "I did so want to make a good impression."

"Well, perhaps he will pass over it if you make a big effort to try to behave like a young lady."

"Oh, I do hope so!" There was a knock on the door. "Come in," called Bryonny with relief, and Lord Hambledon entered, followed by Philip and Julian.

"Goodness, whatever have you two been discussing that required a closed door?" asked Lord Hambledon curiously, looking at Bryonny.

"Mrs. Ashford has been very kindly advising me how I might make a good impression when I have my Season, Uncle Richard."

"Oh? How very—interesting, my dear," he said with dancing eyes.

"Oh, yes indeed, it's been most illuminating."

Julian threw her a suspicious glance. "You must tell me what she advised, Bryonny," he said dryly. "Perhaps I can add to the list of suggestions."

"Oh, would you, Julian? That would be so good of you! Just think, you could teach me everything I need to know from the gentleman's point of view!" She smiled sweetly, delighted at Julian's thoroughly disconcerted expression. Philip had turned away with a smothered laugh, Lord Hambledon set down the brandy decanter a trifle hard, and Cynthia looked merely taken aback.

"Lord Richmond," she said hurriedly, "I wondered if you would take me for a turn around the garden. It's such a beautiful night and the moon is so bright."

"Yes, of course, Mrs. Ashford, it would be my pleasure. If you'll excuse us?" He took her arm and led her out the door which opened from the library directly onto the garden.

Julian and Cynthia returned a half-hour later to find Bryonny, Philip, and Lord Hambledon involved in a lengthy discussion concerning thoroughbred bloodlines. Cynthia's pretty mouth curved in a little smile as she listened with only half an ear, mulling over her conversation with Julian outside. Nothing much had been said of any importance, but she had sensed a certain— promise—beneath his words. It wouldn't surprise her in the least if he paid a visit to her room later in the evening, not that she had any intention of succumbing to him so easily. But it boded well for the future. She knew that he was rumored to be a man of great appetite and she would see to it that he became very hungry indeed—hungry enough to offer marriage before she capitulated. After a few minutes of general conversation in the library, Cynthia excused herself, pleading exhaustion, and took herself upstairs. Julian stayed on for a while, leaning against the mantelpiece and listening to the conversation, but then he, too, excused himself and went off to his room.

Bryonny was disappointed when Julian left. She'd hoped that once Cynthia had disappeared he would relax and participate in the conversation. But he had stood silently by the fire, his expression remote, his eyes cool. She thought with an inner laugh that this must be the strange effect eating dinner habitually had on him. But shortly after his departure, she found her attention straying and decided it was time to retire. She rose.

"If you gentlemen will excuse me, I think I'll go to bed. No, please don't get up. I'm going to quietly disappear with my book and you shall carry on your story, Uncle Richard. I don't mean to be rude, but I've heard it before and it does take some time in the telling." She kissed Lord Hambledon affectionately on top of his head, receiving a squeeze of her hand in return.

"Good night, Philip." She retrieved her book and slipped out of the room and the voices faded behind her.

Twenty minutes later, a knock came at her door. She opened it almost immediately, startled to see Philip standing there. She'd loosed her hair and was wearing only a nightshift and a shawl around her shoulders. "Why, Philip! You're the last person I expected to see!" She frowned and drew her shawl more closely around her.

"Goodness, Bryonny, don't look at me with such suspicion! I only came to ask you if I could borrow your Hegel. I'd been reading it earlier, and found your discussion at dinner so interesting that I thought I'd like to read further. I meant to ask you after dinner but it slipped my mind and then I found it was gone, so I assumed you must have taken it. Do you mind, or are you too engrossed yourself? It is rather presumptuous of me, really."

Bryonny relaxed. "Don't be silly, Philip, I'd be happy to lend it to you. I was only going over some points that Julian had mentioned, but I'll enjoy hearing what you think. Wait, I'll just get it." She quickly retrieved the book and handed it to him.

"Thank you, Bryonny," said Philip. "It's most gen-

erous of you. Forgive my intrusion; I look forward to
seeing you in the morning. Good night."

He retired to his room, locking the door behind
him. He sat on his bed and opened the book, leafing
through the pages. Suddenly he turned it upside down
and shook it furiously, but nothing fell out. Nothing.
The book was empty. He slowly placed it down beside
him. Bryonny must have found his letter. But if so,
why did she say nothing? If she had read it, she would
have known it to be his and most certainly would have
commented, given how much it concerned her! And
then he remembered the look on her face when she
opened the door and her quick relief when he took the
book and left. With a heavy frown, he realized that
there was nothing more he could do that night. Her
reaction in the morning would tell him what he needed
to know.

Lord Hambledon, left to himself in the library, decided to enjoy the peace and quiet. The day had been
highly satisfactory. As he had intended, Julian's society woman couldn't hold a candle to Bryonny, and
Julian's peculiar behavior throughout the evening had
confirmed his highest hopes. He well knew he hadn't
much time left to him, and this situation could relieve
all his worries.

"I deserve a good smoke for this day's work, and
hang the good doctor's orders. If I'm going to die,
then I'm going to enjoy my pleasures while I can." He
found his pipe and tobacco in the special mahogany
box where he kept them and with a contented grunt,
he sat down in his wing chair to go through his favorite
ritual. His hands had begun to tremble more in the
last few weeks despite the laudanum Dr. Walters had
left for him, and it caused him no end of irritation
when the half-filled pipe slipped from between his
fingers and fell to the floor, scattering tobacco over
the Oriental carpet.

"Oh, blast the clumsiness of an old man!" he muttered as he leaned over to retrieve the pipe. His fingers searched the floor around his feet but came up

empty, which necessitated his leaning over even further causing a sharp pain in his chest. "Ah, curses," he groaned, one hand going to his heart, but the other still stubbornly searching the floor for his pipe, which he was determined to smoke in spite of everything. His fingers finally closed around the pipestem poking out from under the skirted chair where it had slid. As he withdrew it, a piece of paper it had caught came sliding out as well. He brought both the objects up onto his lap and searched his pocket for his spectacles, curiosity compelling him to read the thing. Placing the spectacles on his aquiline nose, he began to peruse the writing. His brow snapped down hard as the meaning of it sank in, and he read it a second and a third time with total concentration.

"My God! What can the man be *thinking?*" he whispered, lowering the letter to his lap. "Philip Neville, of all people! I would never have thought it possible! But surely he can't intend speaking to Bryonny? He must be planning on coming to me. Yes, yes, that must be it." He sat for some minutes thinking the situation through with great care. "I shall have to deal with this tomorrow. Just how am I going to go about it?" Pain forgotten, pipe forgotten, Lord Hambledon got shakily to his feet. He crossed the library and went through the connecting door into his study, locking the letter safely away in his safe, and then climbed slowly up to bed. He wondered how long it would take the captain to realize it was missing.

Julian had stripped down to shirt and breeches and was restlessly pacing his room, a glass of brandy in his hand. He walked over to the window and looked out over the garden, resting his foot on the windowseat. The moon had risen higher in the sky and its glow made the night seem a living thing. He stayed like that for a long moment, then frowning, he turned away and ran a hand through his hair. He downed the contents of his glass in one quick toss and abruptly left the room.

*   *   *

Cynthia heard a knock at her door and her heart jumped in anticipation. It was as she'd thought. She arranged her transparent robe carefully and then called, "Come in?" The door flew open and Julian stood there. "My lord! This is a surprise!"

"I hope I'm not disturbing you. But please, you must call me Julian; after all, we are friends, are we not?"

"Why yes, Julian, I feel that we are." She smiled at him slowly, her lips parting in invitation.

"Indeed, ma'am, I am pleased." Julian stepped toward her and drew her into his arms, his legs astride as he pulled her soft, rounded body full length against his. Cynthia allowed herself to relax against him just a little, then disengaged herself.

"My lord!" she said breathlessly. "What can you be thinking?"

Julian looked at her strangely. "I beg your pardon, Cynthia. I had not thought you were adverse to my attentions."

"But I'm not, Julian. Indeed, I am flattered. But I cannot think it is appropriate for you to be in my bedchamber at this late hour." She gave a maidenly blush. "I had not thought . . ."

"You had not thought what, exactly?"

"I had not thought you took me so lightly, my lord."

He frowned. "My dear Cynthia, I do not take you lightly. If I gave you offense, I am most humbly sorry."

Cynthia smiled. "I take no offense, Julian. Your attentions were merely unexpected. Here, in your father's house, I cannot help but feel . . ."

"Yes, you're quite right, of course," said Julian smoothly. "I'm afraid I lost my head when confronted by your considerable charms; I hope you can forget my presumption. I'll bid you good night, then. I shan't see you tomorrow until dinner, for I shall be rising early and then be off for the day, but I'm sure that Lady Bryonny and Captain Neville will entertain you."

"Good night, Julian." Cynthia collected herself quickly, but as the door closed softly behind him, she spun around and sat down hard on her bed, her brow uncharacteristically knotted with worry.

Julian went to his own room only long enough to collect the decanter of brandy and a glass, and then took himself down to the dark and deserted library, lit only by the glow of the fire still burning in the grate.

He settled himself in his father's wing chair, and there, deep in the shadows, he watched the fire leap and crackle as he nursed his frustration with the strong spirits.

Going to Cynthia had been a terrible idea; he knew far better than to rush his fences like that. For all he knew, he had thrown away all chance of a pleasant conclusion to the flirtation, although at the moment he couldn't really care. And therein lay the larger problem.

His eyebrows pulled sharply together and he let his breath out in a long hiss of agitation. What had happened to cool logic, self-control? Self-control—that was a joke. He was suddenly hot, and unbuttoned his shirt to the waist, pulling it impatiently out from his breeches. He took another long draught of the brandy and settled back in the chair again, stretching his legs out toward the fire.

Not very much later a small noise from the door interrupted his thoughts and he looked up in surprise. For a moment he thought the drink had fogged his mind more than he'd realized, but it was indeed Bryonny who had entered the room clad only in a thin nightshift, and a shawl around her shoulders. He couldn't quite believe she was real, this creature of the night. She went to the shelves on the other side of the door, withdrew a book, and wandered over to warm herself in front of the fire, dropping her shawl on the sofa. She was obviously completely unaware of his presence.

He sat absolutely still in the shadows, his long legs crossed at the ankles only inches away from her, his eyes drinking in the beautiful profile turned in his direction. Every last detail was silhouetted by the soft glow of the firelight through the fine material. He could see the outline of her firm, rounded breasts as they rose and fell with her soft breathing; could see the contour of her gently sloping abdomen and the graceful curve of her buttocks. Her long, slender thighs, which he had only previously seen clad in breeches, now looked very different indeed. And still he did not move.

Bryonny stared into the flames, her thoughts on Julian as they had been all night, keeping her from sleep. Life was complicated enough without bringing him into it, but in it he was, and she had even less of an idea than before what to make of him.

It was bad enough that he could hold her emotions in the palm of his hand; but even worse, he exerted a physical control over her as well; when he'd locked his eyes with her before dinner, she'd felt as if she'd been stripped naked and he could see into her very soul. It had sent a heat and trembling through her body that had lasted halfway through dinner, and sitting next to him so conscious of his presence hadn't helped to still it. And what was so unfair was that despite how easily he seemed to be able to read her, she hadn't the faintest idea of what he was thinking.

Banishing Julian from her thoughts with determination, she retrieved her book from the mantelpiece, intending to curl up in a chair. But even as she turned, she found herself tripping and falling over a pair of outstretched legs. She gasped in surprise as strong arms went around her waist and pulled her down and she found Julian's face only inches from hers. She stared at him in shock.

His eyes were dark, almost black, and burned unwaveringly into her own with an unfamiliar, intense expression. He said nothing to her, not a word, just looked at her with his curious, glittering eyes, and she was caught up and bound in his gaze, her heart beating faster, the pulse at the side of her throat leaping, her skin growing hot with confusion.

Julian slid his arms further around her, bringing her closer into his lap, one arm going around her shoulders and the other slipping up to the back of her head, his fingers entwining themselves in her hair. Her eyes did not—could not—move from his, and she found her breath coming fast and uneven as he took her face in his hands, and slowly, so very slowly, he bent his head toward hers. The touch of his mouth on hers sent a wave of heated pleasure through her and she shuddered, melting against him, her arms slipping around his neck as he deepened his kiss, opening her mouth and slowly exploring it with his tongue.

And then she pulled sharply away from him, horrified with what she was doing. "No, Julian, no!" she gasped, jumping to her feet and turning her back to him, thoroughly shaken and trying desperately to compose herself.

Julian, too, stood abruptly, running his hand through his hair in distraction. He was opening his mouth to speak when Bryonny spun around.

Control forgotten, her rage flowed over. She spat her words into the dark, her fists tightly clenched at her sides. "How dare you! I'm not a piece of goods for you to toy with as you please, although it's apparent from your behavior that such treatment is your habit! I should have known you well enough to realize that you'd use any woman to indulge your whims, with no care to what her feelings might be! Well, go and use your precious Mrs. Ashford for your selfish needs, but in future, stay away from me!"

Julian looked at her for a long moment, then smiled dangerously, his eyes narrowed. "My, my, Bryonny, such indignation. Don't you think you should reassess the situation? After all, I did not invite you into my lap, you know. And if you don't want to be kissed, then you really ought not run around half-naked in the middle of the night. You can hardly blame me for mistaking your intentions. Or were you looking for someone else?"

He could hear the sharp intake of Bryonny's breath and then she brought her hand across his cheek. The slap echoed in the silence. Seconds passed like an eternity and the tension, heavy and sharp, hung between them in the air. Finally he spoke. "Don't you think it's past your bedtime?"

"My bedtime is no concern of yours, now or ever."

"Then I suggest you keep it to yourself if you wish it to stay that way."

Bryonny turned abruptly and walked from the room. He called after her, his voice cold, "Didn't you forget something?" He held up the book that had slipped forgotten to the floor.

"No, my lord," she replied. "It is you, I think, who forgot something." She turned and left the room.

Julian waited until he heard the faint sound of her door closing. Then, suddenly exhausted, he left the room and made his way to bed, softly closing the door after him.

Just as softly, Cynthia closed her own door after Julian's, her eyes bright with anger, her mind churning.

Chapter Six

BRYONNY awoke with a pounding headache and pushed herself up in bed, feeling strangely disoriented and wondering why she felt so terrible. But then treacherous memory came flooding back with all its embarrassment.

How could she have let such a thing happen? What on earth had possessed her to allow Julian to kiss her, to . . . oh, Lord. She blushed hotly as she remembered and slipped back down into the bed, pulling the covers over her head and squeezing her eyes tightly shut as if she could block out her humiliation. She couldn't face him today; how could she? A knock came at the door bringing her back out from under the bedclothes.

Lucy entered the room with a pitcher of hot water. She took in Bryonny's forlorn expression, pale face, and red-rimmed eyes and immediately assumed that Bryonny was in the midst of some lovesick throes. Her busy mind remembered that Lord Richmond had been in a filthy temper this morning, but then again, the captain had looked none to happy either.

"Are you feeling poorly, my lady? I didn't wake you earlier thinking you might be tired, but it's already noon. You're looking a trifle pale, if you don't mind my saying."

"I'm fine, really, Lucy; as you say, just a bit tired and I have a terrible headache."

"Oh, dear. Shall I have Mrs. Merk make you up one of her powders?"

"No, thank you, Lucy." Bryonny wished she would go.

"Shall I bring you some tea then, or something to eat?"

"No, really, I'm not hungry. Stop fussing, Lucy, I'm just tired. All I need is peace and quiet."

"Yes, my lady," said Lucy, taking the hint and nodding wisely to herself. She left the room to spend the rest of the day at her chores in happy speculation.

Bryonny slipped out of bed and dressed with a heavy heart, taking no pleasure in the new sprigged muslin she had liked so much when she'd had it made. She took a good, long look at herself in the mirror. Her eyes looked better after she had pressed a cold cloth to them, but she was still pale. Fresh air and exercise would put some color back in her cheeks, and also give her a way to avoid Julian. She didn't particularly want to see the others, either. The idea of having to deal with Cynthia was more than she could bear, and she'd probably bite poor Philip's head off.

"Lady Bryonny?" Mrs. Merk's voice called from outside the door. "Are you in there?"

"Yes, come in, Mrs. Merk," said Bryonny with a sigh. She wasn't in the mood for Mrs. Merk's platitudes, either.

The door opened and Mrs. Merk darted through, her little brown eyes peering around the room as if expecting to find the cause of Bryonny's problem somewhere in the corner. "Lucy told me you had a headache, poor lamb, and I've brought you a tisane. Now don't you shake your head at me and give me one of your stubborn looks. I know what's good for you and you just drink this down right now while I watch. That's better. Now why don't you tell me what's wrong, my poppet."

"Nothing, Mrs. Merk, I'm as healthy as a mule. I'm sure it's just all the excitement. I'll feel right as rain in no time at all, thanks to your potion."

"If you say so, my lady," said Mrs. Merk, managing to look as if she were extremely offended but determined not to show it. "Poor Captain Neville waited all

morning for you to go riding with him, but he finally
gave up and went off on his own."

"Oh," said Bryonny, feeling guilty that she had
ignored him but wanting very much to know where
Julian might be lurking. "Where are the others?"

"Mrs. Ashford is still in her room with that French-
woman of hers taking a late breakfast and asking not
to be disturbed, Lord Hambledon has been in his
study all morning and he doesn't want to be disturbed
either, and Master Julian went off to the stables early
and hasn't been back, although he said to expect him
for lunch. This is a very strange party, if I do say, with
everyone closeted away or off on his own." Mrs. Merk
sniffed indignantly. "Well, now that I know you're not
ill, I'll be off about my business."

"Yes, don't let me keep you. Thank you for your
concern and the tisane."

The door shut and Bryonny was left in blessed peace
again. She was very pleased to hear that Julian was
not around, but if she was going to miss him she'd
have to hurry, as lunchtime was already upon them.
She slipped down the back stairs and out into the
courtyard, crossing it to the wide path that led between the side of the stables and the kitchen garden.
Hugging the garden wall, she dashed around its corner, her heart pounding in panic as she heard Julian's
faint voice calling to George. She'd left just in time.
She crept into the cover of the orchard and drew a
deep breath of relief.

It was a glorious day, warm and sunny, and the air
was alive with the trilling of birds and the droning of
bees moving from the blossoms to their nearby hives.
A light breeze rustled through the trees, sending a
cascade of white petals to the ground, but Bryonny,
wandering across the orchard, felt too melancholy to
appreciate its light, airy atmosphere, and slipped instead into the cool, deep quiet of Three Mile Wood.

Bryonny felt at peace in here, comforted and protected by the ancient trees. After a while she found
that her black misery was slowly dissipating, and her
sunny nature beginning to reassert itself. Even Julian's

detestable behavior and the pain he had caused her was not going to keep her down, she determined. He was a ruthless and selfish man who took what he pleased, and it was her own stupidity that had allowed him to take advantage of her, her own loss of control that had caused her to become aroused. And that was all there was to it. She was not going to spend her life running away from Julian or waste her tears on his black heart. She would simply put it aside as if it had never happened and go back to their guarded civility. He had his Cynthia and he could keep her.

With a lighter step she brought herself to the other side of the wood and left its dappled sunlight, mossy scent, and hushed silence.

She stepped out into a meadow, the warm afternoon sun beating down on the sweet vernal grass carpeted with wildflowers, releasing its rich, fragrant scent. Drinking in a deep breath of the soft air, Bryonny turned her face up to the sun. It was a long way back to the house by foot, and her stomach was grumbling with hunger; soon it would be teatime. With that enticing thought, she turned to the northwest, where a series of hills and valleys ran in a large arc, circumventing the woods. A winding stream cut through the valleys, bubbling over stones and down under trees until it found its way through the wood, under a footbridge, and finally fed into the lake. Bryonny felt much better for the exercise by the time she had descended the last sun-soaked hill and crossed over the courtyard and into the kitchen.

"Oh, Cook, you're just the person I wanted to see!" cried Bryonny happily. "I'm famished; have you anything I can eat?"

"Why, child, there you are! You haven't eaten all day and I was worrying about you. Here, have a poppy cake, that should hold you until the other things come out of the oven. Where have you been? Master Julian was in here at lunchtime looking for you and—"

"He was?" interrupted Bryonny in surprise. "Did he say what he wanted?"

"No, just that he was looking and couldn't find you.

That Captain Neville was asking after you, too, and seemed quite agitated. What have you been up to, deary, getting the gentlemen all worked up and you disappearing?"

"Oh nothing, really. I just needed some time to myself." Her voice was muffled by the poppy cake she was devouring.

"Well, if you have some time on your hands and one of the gentlemen doesn't chase you down first, here are the stale crusts for the ducks. Do you mind taking them down to the lake for me, lovey? They'll be expecting their dinner, and I have my hands full. There's another poppy cake in it for you."

"Of course, I don't mind, you know I love to feed them. And I'd love another cake, thank you, Cook. You know they're my favorite." She scooped one up from the tray with one hand, picking up the bag of crusts with the other. Leaving by the back door, she sang out over her shoulder, "Did you know the swans hatched three babes? I only discovered them two days ago. The mother keeps them hidden in the reeds on the other end of the lake."

She took the path around the west wing, past the flower garden, and crossed the lawn down to the lake, the deepening golden light soft on its smooth surface. The shore was shaded into black depths where maples, elms, and willows hung over, casting down their dark shadows down into the water. The lily pads with their large green bases floated placidly on the surface, their treacherous trailing roots concealed from sight.

Calling the ducks over from the far side, Bryonny walked slowly along the grassy bank where clumps of sweet-smelling, sunny-headed daffodils grew. The banks were steep and sloped sharply down to meet the water, which was very deep even at the shoreline. She ducked under the low-hung branch of a maple tree to get as close to the edge as possible. Humming softly to herself as she waited, she watched the ducks approach, quacking their greedy excitement. There was no sign of the swans.

Without warning the branch behind her swung out

with tremendous force and hit her hard on the back of
the head. Bryonny only registered a blinding pain as
she was catapulted forward into the lake. The water
was dark and icy and brought her to her senses as she
hit it, sinking far down into its depths. Bryonny was an
excellent swimmer, but she was no match for this
situation. Dazed and weakened by the blow to her
head, and weighted down by her heavy, wet skirts, she
pulled herself up to the surface but found it difficult to
stay afloat. The more she struggled and tried to kick
her way to safety, the more she entangled herself in
the roots of the lily pads, which had twisted themselves around her skirts and ankles.

"Help!" she cried in real alarm, trying to keep her
head above water. "Oh, somebody, please, help me!"
She thought she saw a quick movement on the bank
above her, but nobody came. She felt the water closing over her head again.

Lord Hambledon heard faint cries through the open
window of his study. He had seen Bryonny go down
to the lake, and the sound seemed to be coming from
there. He hurried out and across the lawn, but his
chest grabbed him badly and he had to slow his pace.
He arrived panting at the water's edge only to find
Bryonny gasping for breath, sinking time and again
below the surface.

Frantically he looked around, knowing he was not
capable of rescuing Bryonny himself. The nearest help
would be at the stables, but that would be too far, and
too late; then mercifully his eye caught Julian coming
out of Three Mile Wood. He waved his arms wildly
and shouted, praying that Julian would see him, and
was immensely relieved to see his son respond. Kicking his horse into a canter, Julian jumped the stone
fence that separated him from the lawn and was at his
father's side within moments. He rapidly dismounted,
taking in the situation at a glance. Pausing only to
discard his closely cut jacket, with no time to pull off
his tight boots, he dove into the deep water and swam

quickly to Bryonny, pulling her up by the shoulders as she thrashed.

"Bryonny! Bryonny, listen to me. Don't struggle, I have you now." It took a concentrated effort, but he finally managed to free her from the roots and with his father's shaky help he pulled her up onto the soft grass. She was a bedraggled sight, and shaking from the cold and shock.

"Oh, my dear Bryonny, you gave us such a scare! Thank God you're safe! You're not hurt, are you?" Lord Hambledon asked in deep concern.

Bryonny was coughing up water, but she managed to shake her head. Julian wrapped his jacket around her and sat down on the ground next to her, putting his arm around her and leaning her forward, to better help her get the water up. Once she had recovered, she pulled away from Julian and looked up at him coldly.

"Really, Bryonny, here I've gone and risked life and limb for you, not to mention ruined a perfectly good pair of boots, and you go and look at me like that! Where's your gratitude, girl?" he spoke lightly, trying to coax a smile from her.

"Gratitude!" Bryonny spat, Julian's words thawing her blood, anger making it flow once again and bringing her out of numb shock. "How *dare* you!"

"Well, really, Bryonny, if you're going to go diving into the lake for whatever reason without having the good sense to remove your skirts first or avoid the lily pads, and then attempt to drown yourself, the least you could do is have the good manners to thank your rescuer!"

"Dive, indeed! I was pushed, as you well know! How dare you have the effrontery to pretend to rescue me and then ask for my undying gratitude, you—you unscrupulous wretch!"

"Pushed! What's this, Julian?" asked Lord Hambledon in bewilderment. "She might have been killed!"

"Unfortunately, Father, the pleasure wasn't mine!" snapped Julian. "As you saw, I was returning from the errands you sent me on. How could you think such a thing of me, Father? And as for you, Bryonny, suppose you explain just how you did get into the lake? You may have run wild in Jamaica and jumped into the ocean whenever it pleased you, but I think this sort of behavior in England is a bit ridiculous."

"Despite all the other things of which you've accused me, Julian, surely you don't think I'm such a fool as to decide to go for a little dip among the lily pads fully clothed, do you? I was hit—look, here's the lump!" She touched her hand to the back of her head and winced with pain. Her hand came away with a streak of blood on it. "And the only person I can think of with any reason to hurt me is you!"

At her words, Lord Hambledon's eyes suddenly narrowed. "Julian, I don't like the look of that at all. Please take Bryonny up to the house and put her to bed. I'll have Mrs. Merk take a look at her and call the doctor if she thinks it necessary. And for heaven's sake be careful with her; we don't want any more accidents. There's been enough trouble, and I intend to have Bryonny living here for a very long time!" He turned and started back toward the house.

Julian looked after his father for a long moment, and then remembering the task at hand, he scooped a protesting Bryonny up in his arms and followed after his father, leaving Brimstone to graze with happy abandon on the lush green grass. She was still too shaken to walk, but not at all happy at being carried by the man who had practically killed her. "Your father is gone, Julian, so there's no longer any need to pretend. I just don't understand why you had to resort to such nastiness. If you had an argument with me, you might have thought to speak it to my face rather than stoop to such an underhanded trick."

"Bryonny, I don't know what I must say to you to convince you that I didn't push you in, if indeed you were pushed at all." He felt her body tighten in his arms, and quickly added, "Isn't it possible that a branch swung back at you after you brushed by it?"

"I might almost believe you if I hadn't thought I saw someone moving up on the bank in the trees when I was calling for help. And it *was* a branch that hit me, at least I think so, but it didn't move on its own, and I'd been standing there for some time. As I said before, you're the only person I can think of with any desire to hurt me, as you have proved over and over!"

"Bryonny, for God's sake be reasonable! I swear I don't wish you any harm. And as for last night . . ." By this time they had reached Bryonny's room and he laid her down on the bed. "Look, before I go any further, let me get you out of these wet clothes before you catch your death of cold. You're shaking all over."

"Never!" she cried in alarm. "Keep your hands off me!"

"Oh, really, Bryonny, now is not the time for maidenly protests. Stop looking so indignant and help me get you out of this."

"Don't you dare lay a finger on me, Julian Ramsay, or I swear I'll scream the house down! You've done enough harm already! I'll wait for Mrs. Merk." She shrank back against the pillows feeling sick and weak, but fully ready to defend herself.

"Father might be hours trying to dredge up Mrs. Merk from some obscure corner of this house. Be reasonable, girl. After all, you are in no condition to be raped, and as I like my women dry, warm, and willing, you're quite safe." He spoke with his back to her as he rummaged in the chest at the end of her bed in search of a blanket.

"Oh, and I'm supposed to believe that after your performance last night? I wouldn't put it past you to have engineered this little incident just so that you could play the hero and tear the clothes off me in victory."

Julian turned around with the blanket in hand and gave a short laugh. "Ha! You certainly have a high opinion of yourself, my dear, if you think I lust after you so much that I felt I had to throw myself into that blasted lake, destroy my clothes, and catch my death of cold just so that I could ogle your little, blue, goose-pimpled body! Good God, give me some credit!"

He looked highly amused as Bryonny glowered at him and reached toward her with the blanket.

"Julian, for heaven's sake, leave me be! You know I'm not strong enough to fend you off! Please, I'm exhausted!" She put out her arms to hold him at bay.

"Yes, speaking of being exhausted, Bryonny, Mrs. Merk told me that you spent all morning in your room. You weren't avoiding me by any chance, were you?"

"I didn't sleep well last night, not that it's any business of yours."

"True enough, I was just wondering. I'm sorry you didn't sleep well. Not bad dreams, I hope."

"That, Julian, depends entirely on whose point of view you're looking from. They centered on a serpent."

"I see," said Julian, smiling wickedly. "Well, my dear Bryonny, that's understandable. After all, if you're going to dally in the garden of Eden, what else can you expect?"

"Oh, Julian, you're such a cad," said Bryonny wearily.

"So you've told me and I daresay it's true. But wasn't it Eve who offered the apple to Adam? Surely you can't blame him for taking a bite." His eyes danced.

Bryonny sat up too quickly, and her head spun. Slowly she lay back again, Julian supporting her.

"I'm sorry, Bryonny," he said softly. "I was forgetting your injury. Seriously, you must believe me when I tell you that I didn't bash you over the head and then throw you into the lake. I have no reason to want to see you hurt or dead, for that matter, which you could well have been. As for my supposed motive, and God only knows what you've concocted, if I'd been able to find you today, my intention was to apologize for what happened last night. I'd had too much to drink, and I'm sorry I took advantage and upset you. So will you forgive me for being what you so succinctly referred to as a cad?"

"Julian, right now I'd forgive you anything if you'd just leave me in peace. I feel tired enough to sleep forever—and I'm sure *that* would make you very happy." She closed her eyes.

"Good, I'll take that as an acceptance. Now stop being so silly and let me get your clothes off. Look, I'll shut my eyes if that will make you feel any better, but I assure you, despite what you may have been told, you will not lose your virginity by appearing naked before a member of the opposite sex!"

"No—Julian!" Bryonny cried as he reached toward her. "I'll do it myself," she whispered weakly.

"Oh, most certainly, ma'am," said Julian, turning her and beginning to undo her buttons. "First you accuse me of trying to drown you, and next I'll be hearing that I'm responsible for your pneumonia. I'd rather not take the chance. These dresses were not designed to be removed when wet—come, stay still so I don't tear the material, not that I think it can be salvaged anyway. Look, here's a blanket ready to put around you."

He was about to slip the dress down over her shoulders when the door flew open and Mrs. Merk entered in a terrible fluster. She stopped dead in her tracks. "Master Julian!" She took in the scene before her with horror. "I beg your pardon, I've come to see to Lady Bryonny. Lord Hambledon sent me."

"Yes, good, Mrs. Merk, I'm glad my father was able to find you. I think she needs some looking after. I'll leave you to it. I think you might call Dr. Walters just to be on the safe side."

"Yes, Master Julian," said Mrs. Merk curtly.

"There's no need to look at me so severely, as if I'd compromised the girl; I didn't want her to freeze to death, so I started to change her clothes. Very sensible, I thought. As you can see, so far she's survived the assault on her modesty. I need to change into dry things myself." Julian stood and left the room, frowning deeply as he left, and Mrs. Merk looked after him in questioning surprise.

Lord Hambledon was waiting for Philip Neville in his study. He'd sent a curious Mrs. Merk to summon

him after she'd given a report on Bryonny's condition,
saying she thought Bryonny would be all right although Dr. Walters had been sent for as a precaution.
There were a great many things he didn't like about
this situation, and although he had been agonizing all
day how best to deal with it, he now thought it wisest
to meet it head on. A knock sounded and he gathered
up the pile of Livingston papers he'd been going through
and locked them in his drawer.

"Come in!" he called, feeling very weary and not at
all sure he was up to this interview. "Ah, Captain
Neville. So glad you could oblige me with this little
chat. Please sit down."

"My lord, I must admit I was surprised by the
request. What is it you want to discuss with me in
private?"

"I'm just getting to that. You see, last night I found
a letter under my chair in the library. What it was
doing there is another matter, but it obviously belongs
to you. Needless to say, I'm extremely distressed."
Lord Hambledon held the paper up.

Philip's face was impassive. "I see. I wondered where
it had disappeared to."

"Is that so, captain? And were you planning on
asking around for it?"

"No, my lord. I reckoned it would turn up sooner or
later. To tell the truth, I was more concerned about
who found it. I'm glad it was you."

"And why is that, captain? You surprise me."

"Do I? I admit that I would have chosen my own
time, but sooner or later I would have spoken with
you. But if you don't mind, I would like my property
back."

"Not so fast, young man. I'm not that big a fool,
although it's apparent that a fool is what you've taken
me for." Lord Hambledon slipped the letter into his
pocket. "This will remain in my safekeeping, thank
you. Now that I know why you're here, let me warn
you; if you try anything—*anything* at all—with Bryonny,
I am going to create tremendous trouble for you, and I
imagine you'd agree that I'd have no problem. I think

you know *exactly* what I mean! I've had dealings with fortune hunters before!"

"Is that what you think me, my lord? A fortune hunter? I believe not."

"However you choose to see your position is of no importance to me. Nobody is going to toy with Bryonny while I live and breathe!"

"You mistake me, my lord. I think my position and my intentions must be perfectly clear to you, and if you're not prepared to be reasonable, then I feel I must address Bryonny herself on the issue."

"You most certainly will not!" said Lord Hambledon coldly. "You seem to forget that not only am I Bryonny's guardian, but I am also a solicitor. Bryonny will be protected from you, of that I can assure you! And furthermore—" Lord Hambledon was interrupted by a pounding at the study door.

"Father, I know you're in there, and I must speak to you at once!"

"Oh, come in, for God's sake, Julian, and stop that terrible noise," he called in annoyance. The door opened to reveal Julian with a face as black as thunder. "Can't you see I'm busy, boy?"

"I'm sorry to interrupt, sir, but what I have to say won't wait. Will you excuse us for a few minutes, captain? I assure you, this won't take long."

"Certainly, Lord Richmond. Please don't hurry on my account." Philip calmly stood.

Lord Hambledon considered throwing his impetuous son out of the room and continuing his confrontation with the captain, but to do that would draw Julian's attention to the importance of the meeting. "We'll continue this shortly, captain. If you'll excuse us? You might wait in the library."

"Yes, of course, my lord." Philip left the room and closed the door softly after him. Moments later there was a strange echo effect as if another door had been shut.

"What was that?" asked Julian, puzzled. "It sounded like the connecting door to the library. If Neville's in there, I don't want what I have to say to you overheard."

"My, you're jumpy, Julian. I'm sure it wasn't latched properly and the wind blew it shut. What exactly is it that you have to say that requires such cloak and dagger secrecy and called for interrupting me? It must be extremely urgent."

"Yes, it is, Father, but first, what were you discussing so heatedly with the captain behind closed doors? He wasn't asking for Bryonny's hand already, was he?"

"A more unsuitable match could not exist. But I don't wish to discuss my conversation with the captain."

"No, I can't imagine you'd give your permission, Father. You've made it very clear that you intend to marry her yourself!"

Lord Hambledon looked totally stupefied for a moment as he tried to absorb the meaning of this completely unexpected remark. Then, as comprehension dawned, he put his head in his hands. It seemed that in less than twenty-four hours the whole world had gone quite mad.

"I can see why you'd be embarrassed, Father. It's a preposterous idea, and well you know it."

"Why don't you tell me, my dear boy, how you put these pieces together?" He looked at his son neutrally, trying hard to contain his amusement.

"Oh, come, Father, you've made it as plain as can be, and why I didn't see it before, I can't think."

"Can you be a touch more specific, Julian?"

"You've taken Bryonny's part against mine from the day she arrived here, and although you claim to be giving her a Season, you say you intend to have her here for a very long time. Not the words of a man who intends to see her married away to someone else. Admit it, Father, you're infatuated with the girl!"

"Tell me, Julian, would your objection to my marrying Bryonny simply be that you don't want her as a stepmother?"

"That horrifying idea hadn't even crossed my mind! Bryonny's far too young for you, Father. She needs someone who can give her a full life, lovemaking, children, all those things; and you need someone of your own age and sort, not a wildcat who will drive you to an early grave!"

"Oh, and you think I'm such an old man that I can't manage? How insulting, my dear child!" Lord Hambledon twinkled. "In any case, my grave is my own affair, and I shall go to it in my own time and way and I intend to enjoy myself in the process. How could you possibly object to that?"

"But that's exactly my point, Father. You're so many years apart, you would leave her a helpless young widow. If you truly cared for her, you wouldn't even contemplate such an idea!"

"What I am contemplating, my hot-headed son, is seeing to her Season. I think the girl should be allowed to choose whom she marries, and I have no intention of forcing her into anything with anybody. I do feel that she would be happiest with someone who understands her intellect and her need for freedom, and who will not take advantage of her circumstance. Personally, I think a Ramsay is perfect for the job." He smiled benignly.

"And if you persist in this insane notion, you'll be the laughingstock of society!" Julian stood in a state of furious frustration. "I will not stand by and watch you humiliate yourself, Father." He stalked to the door and wrenched it open, then turned back. "I warn you, I'll do anything I must to stop you from this idiocy!" He stormed out of the room and out of the house, leaving Mrs. Merk staring after him on the stairs, and Captain Neville, who was awaiting the conclusion of his interview, looking out of the library door in astonishment.

Lord Hambledon breathed a deep sigh and shook his head. That Julian had come up with such a cock-eyed idea was too good to be true, but there were times when he wanted to knock the boy over the head to make him see reason. He supposed he'd better go after the lad and put his mind at ease before he did something stupid in his rage. Captain Neville would just have to wait, but it would be best if he put the blasted letter away somewhere where it would not be accidentally or intentionally found. He considered where he might conceal it; even the safe could conceivably be broken into. Thinking hard, he turned to the bookshelves and took down a volume from his set of law books, and slipped the paper between the pages. No one would be likely to look there for it. Satisfied, he left and crossed the hall.

"Captain Neville, I shall be back shortly. I suggest you rethink your situation very carefully in my absence, or you might find yourself in an untenable position. Mrs. Merk, I expect you to see to it that Lady Bryonny has no visitors."

"Yes, my lord," said Mrs. Merk, throwing a worried look at the captain, and then she hurried upstairs.

Lord Hambledon walked out of the house. Thinking that Julian most probably had headed for the stables, he followed in that direction as quickly as he was able, hoping he would catch him in time. The boy rode himself hard when he was in a temper, and dusk was closing in.

Lord Hambledon reached the stables but there was no sign of Julian. He went in search of George. "Ah, George! Did Master Julian happen to come roaring through here?"

"He did, my lord, in a fearful temper, he was. He took out that new gray stallion not five minutes ago and headed up back for the fields, it looked like."

"Thank you, George. I'll have a little wander in that direction and see if I can spot him. He'll probably come back the same way. I doubt his temper will last long; it never does."

"No, my lord, that's true enough. Just be careful he doesn't run you down in this light."

"If he ran me down, George, it wouldn't be because of the light. He's very angry with me at the moment."

"So I managed to understand. As you say, it won't last long, and he'll be back with apologies before you know it."

"Yes, quite. Well, I can use the exercise, so I think I'll have myself a little amble. Thank you, George."

Lord Hambledon wandered off, taking the same path Bryonny had earlier in the day, but turning northeast up the hill.

The sun was dipping low in the sky, painting the hills and fields with blacks and golds, the sky a wash of red and purple deepening to indigo. The faint bleating of lambs settling down with their mothers for the night carried toward Lord Hambledon. As he reached the crest of the hill he stopped and strained his eyes for the sight of Julian but could make out nothing in the growing dusk. Still, he was glad for the walk, for the fresh air felt wonderful and cleared his head. It was a good thing, for he would need all his wits about him to deal with Philip Neville and dispatch the wily fox. At least he had run him to ground . . .

Lord Hambledon never knew what hit him. He crumpled to the ground and lay unmoving, the blood from his head seeping into the meadow grass. He did not feel the hands that pushed him so that he rolled down the hill, coming to rest in a still heap under the spreading branches of an ancient oak, nor did he hear the singing of the stream that flowed beside him. A robin trilled once, high above him, and then fell into silence as the last of the light faded into darkness.

Chapter Seven

IT was full dark when Julian returned to the stables, and the sky was swimming with a myriad of stars. He felt tired and drained, all fury gone. "Hullo, George. Would you mind putting up my horse? I rode him hard and should really do it myself, but I fear I'm going to be late for dinner."

"My pleasure, Master Julian. How did he go?"

"Like the wind, George. He's as fine a beast as his papers say."

"That's good to hear, especially for the price you paid. Did your father find you?"

"My father?" Julian looked very surprised. "No, whyever should he? I left him in his study and I've been gone this whole time, as you know."

"He came by looking for you and went up the way of the hills. He didn't really expect to catch you, but said he'd like a walk anyway. I reckon he must have returned to the house long since."

"I see; well, he didn't come my way. Thank you, George. I'll see you in the morning."

"Good night, my lord." George led the gray away to its stall.

Julian was surprised when the doctor opened Bryonny's door in response to his knock. "Dr. Walters, I'm glad to see you've come. I hope I'm not interrupting; I hadn't realized you were here. How is the patient?"

"Come in and see for yourself, Julian. I've finished my examination, and I'm delighted to say all is well. She's a lucky young lady, thanks to you."

Julian cautiously approached the bed, seeing that Bryonny was looking much better but very well aware that she was regarding him with an expression that could be described, at best, as cool.

"My, if it's not the knight in shining armor. To what do I owe the honor of this visit?"

"Oh, my lady, stands before you a broken man. I came with my white charger with full intention of carrying you off into the sunset, but then I was forced to reconsider, realizing that you would be deeply offended by the gesture and would insist on riding your own charger in any case. So instead I thought I'd merely inquire after your health." Julian raised an eyebrow at her.

"My health, my lord, is flourishing, so Dr. Walters tells me. I feel quite recovered, you'll be desolate to hear."

"Actually, I feel quite gratified. It would have been such a bore to have gone to all the trouble of saving you from a watery grave to have had you expire in a warm, dry bed. You do look a little more human, I must say." He flashed her a grin.

"How very kind of you. Oughtn't you be downstairs heaping charm on your guests instead of wasting it on me?"

"You're quite right. I'm sure they're pining for my company; as a matter of fact, I know they are. Actually, I hate to disappoint you, but I came upstairs in search of my father and as he wasn't in his room, I thought I'd find him in here."

"Do you mean he's not downstairs? Julian, that's very odd; I can't believe he would abandon his guests, and I haven't seen him since he left the lake."

Dr. Walters had been standing by the door listening to the two of them with quiet amusement but now he stepped forward in concern. "Julian, was your father feeling well today?"

"Well? Yes, I suppose so, although he was upset by Bryonny's accident."

"And whose fault was that, Julian?"

"Oh, enough, Bryonny," he snapped. "I went out for a ride and George tells me that Father came after me and walked up into the hills where I'd gone. That's what doesn't seem right. He should have been back before dark. I just now asked Mrs. Merk if she'd seen him and she told me she'd thought he'd been resting in his room, so it sounds very much as if he hasn't returned after all."

"Julian," said Dr. Walters slowly, "I think we must go out and look for him. It's breaking his confidence to tell you this, and I don't want to add to your worry, but he hasn't been well for some time, and I greatly fear he may have collapsed."

Bryonny looked at Dr. Walters in shock. "Not well?"

"Just what do you mean by unwell, doctor?" asked Julian sharply.

"I don't want to say any more than that. It's for your father to tell you himself if he so chooses. But I feel we must consider the possibility that he is still out there and needs help."

Bryonny reached for Julian's arm. "We must go at once! The moon is starting to rise and we should be able to see well enough. If he's in trouble, we mustn't delay."

"I quite agree, but you're not going anywhere, dear girl. I'll rouse George and the stableboys; it's help enough. You stay right here until we return, and try not to worry. All will be well." Julian spoke quietly but Bryonny knew he would stand no argument.

"Oh, Julian, please, I must help. I'm recovered, truly I am."

"No, Julian's quite right," said Dr. Walters emphatically. "You may feel better, but you're still in no condition to be out riding around in the damp. We'll tell you as soon as we know anything." The two men turned and left the room, Julian stopping only to give a flustered and pale Mrs. Merk instructions to have the guests shown into dinner with his apologies for his absence and a hastily concocted excuse.

*   *   *

Bryonny waited just long enough to be sure that the men had time to saddle up, and then slipped out of bed and into her breeches. Her head ached badly and she still felt a little weak, but she could not remain inactive while Uncle Richard was missing. She crept out into the night and crossed to the stables which, though ablaze with light, were deserted. Quickly she bridled Bedlam, whispered to him to keep herself calm, hoping that he wouldn't sense her fear, and mounting his bare back, she guided him out toward the hills. The moon lit their way, brushing the grass with silvery light as it rose from behind the woods. In the distance she could hear the men calling, their voices faint as they fanned out into the fields. Bryonny paused on the crest of the hill and then decided to follow the lower path, reasoning that she would be out of sight and also that it was an area that was not being searched. She rode down the slope to the stream, a shimmering ribbon that sent its gurgling laughter into the stillness, impervious to the gravity hanging over the night. Dread brushed over her with icy fingers, cluching at her heart and weakening her limbs. She felt as if she were caught in a dream from which she could not escape, which had no bearing on reality, no pattern or logic to it.

"Oh, Bedlam, I know we shall return home and find him safe and sound and laughing at us for our foolishness," she whispered, willing it to be so. And then her heart gave a great, painful jerk in her chest as Bedlam shied away from the shapeless black mass a few yards in front of them. It lay half hidden in a deep shaft of shadow cast by the old oak tree. Bryonny's immediate impulse was to turn and flee, as one would run from any unfaceable terror, in complete, unthinking panic. But she fought it down and dismounted, her hands shaking, her heart in her throat. Slowly she walked toward the oak.

She could see that he had rolled down the slope of the hill as the grass that covered his clothes attested. The blood from the wound in his head, which had ceased to flow long before, had stained his white hair dark and dried in black rivulets down his neck. There was no mistaking the fact that he was dead. Bryonny stood unmoving, unthinking, for a long moment that stretched like an eternity. Then, as the truth of it slowly sank in, she raised her voice in a long keening cry of denial. Calling, "Julian . . ." she dropped to the ground, cradling Lord Hambledon's head in her lap, the tears pouring hot and unchecked down her cheeks and falling onto his cold face as she called his son's name over and over into the deep silence.

Julian heard the fragments of his name carried to him on the wind. He pulled his horse around hard and tore off back across the fields. He rode with a terrible apprehension, directly toward Bryonny's voice. Coming to the rise of the hill, he looked down and saw Bedlam below. He threw himself off his horse and took the slope with long strides, coming to an abrupt halt in front of the tree, his blood turning to ice as shock washed over him.

"Oh, dear God." Bryonny was rocking over his still and bloodied father, holding him in her arms as if he were a hurt child.

"J-Julian . . ." She lifted her face to him and spoke with effort as if trying to catch her breath. "Oh, Julian, he's dead. There was nothing I could do. I'm sorry, I'm so sorry." Her voice caught in her throat.

Julian dropped on his knees next to her. Very carefully he examined his father, and saw the truth for himself. He lifted him from her lap and gently laid him on the ground, covering him with his coat. He turned to Bryonny and helped her to her feet, silently leading her away from the dreadful scene to a flat stone by the stream where he sat her down. He removed his neckcloth and dipped it in the water and cleaned her hands of his father's blood. Finally, he spoke, his voice low and thick.

"Bryonny. It's over now. You mustn't upset yourself so; there was nothing you could have done, nothing anyone could have done for him. It happened hours ago. But it should not have been you who found him. I blame myself for that—Oh, God! I blame myself for everything! He should never have come up here." He took a deep, shuddering breath, his dark head bowed.

Bryonny reached out and touched his hair, her heart breaking for him. "Julian—Julian, you mustn't fault yourself, you cannot. It was an accident. He must have fallen and struck his head. It could have happened at any time, and Dr. Walters said he was ill and might have collapsed."

"Yes, of course, you're right." Julian lifted his face and Bryonny could see it white and strained in the reflection of the moon. He stood.

"I must call the men. You stay here; will you be all right?"

"Yes, I'm better now. Please, you must go." She watched as he climbed the hill, calling out as he went, and even in her grief she felt amazement that Julian could collect himself so quickly and lock away in some secret place the terrible emotions tearing at him.

Julian insisted on carrying his father's body back to the house himself, and going up the back way, he laid him in his bedroom. Dr. Walters did a quick examination and concluded that Lord Hambledon had indeed had a heart attack and rolled down the hill striking his head on a rock, evidenced by the bloodied stone they had found close to the body. When he had finished, he left Julian sitting alone with his father and searched out Mrs. Merk, as Julian had requested, to inform her of the death.

Julian finally shook himself out of his thoughts and sought Bryonny out in her room where he found her still and shaken, but in control. Gently he suggested that she put on a dress and accompany him downstairs to give the news to Cynthia and Philip. He waited outside while she changed from her breeches and when she emerged he offered her a supportive arm, which she badly needed.

Cynthia and Philip had been engaged in a polite game of backgammon. Neither had mentioned anything about the strange absence of the family over dinner, preferring to accept Mrs. Merk's excuse that they were involved in a pressing business matter. Cynthia's attention had been very distracted as had Philip's, and dinner had largely been conducted in silence. At the sound of people approaching the library, they both looked up in anticipation. Cynthia looked at Bryonny coldly. Philip jumped up from his chair, sending the pieces flying.

"Lady Bryonny! Lord Richmond . . . What has—"

Julian cut in brusquely. "Please sit down, captain, I have something I must tell both of you. My father collapsed and died late this afternoon. Apparently he had not been well, but nevertheless, his death was unexpected." He spoke clearly and concisely, his voice void of emotion. "Therefore, I am sure that you will understand why I am sending you back to London in the morning. You will take my carriage, of course. My apologies to you both. Please excuse us, it's been a trying evening." He took Bryonny by the arm and led her out, not giving Philip or Cynthia a chance to respond to his shocking announcement. They were left alone as before, staring at each other in horror.

"Thank you for your help, Bryonny," said Julian outside her bedroom door. "I know this has been very hard on you and you've held up well. Do you think you can sleep?"

"I doubt it, but I'll try to lie down. And you, Julian?"

"Don't concern yourself with me. I have much to think about, but right now, I'm going to have a word with Dr. Walters. Just get yourself into bed, and this time stay there. You mustn't forget about Dr. Walters' orders, despite everything. Good night." He turned abruptly and left, leaving Bryonny no choice but to do as she'd been told.

Julian retired to his room after he had finished a long conversation with the doctor, in which he learned the details of his father's heart condition. He sat for a long time with his head in his hands until he was shaken from his thoughts by a knock on the door. Slowly rising, he went to open it.

"Julian, I beg your pardon for intruding, but I very much wanted to convey my sympathies. Is there anything I can do?"

Julian's eyes were dark and inscrutable. "Thank you for your concern, Cynthia. I'm afraid there is nothing anyone can do. I think it's best if I'm alone."

"Yes, of course, my lord. I wouldn't want to disturb you." Cynthia spoke carefully.

"Cynthia, I do feel very badly that this should have happened while you were visiting. I hope the shock has not distressed you unduly. You must get your rest now for you have a long journey ahead of you tomorrow. I'll speak with you when I return to London."

"I shall wait to hear from you there, Julian."

"It probably won't be for some time, for there will be much to do here, though there is my work to consider. But all that is beside the point. We should both get to bed; it's very late. Good night."

"Good night, Julian." Cynthia turned quickly with a soft rustle of skirts and left, shutting the door gently behind her.

Julian sighed, pulling off his waistcoat, and decided to go back and sit with his father a while longer. It would be the last opportunity he had.

Bryonny heard Julian enter his father's room. She had lain awake in the dark, unable to sleep. Her throat was dry and constricted. For some reason, she'd been unable to cry since the first shock by the river and there was a hot, hard knot in her chest. She slipped out of bed and pressed a damp cloth to her face, and throwing a heavy shawl over her shoulders, she quietly knocked and entered Lord Hambledon's bedroom through the connecting door. Julian was sitting by the bed and he looked up briefly but said nothing. There was no need: his eyes mirrored his feelings.

Bryonny pulled up a chair next to him and softly slipped her hand into his. His fingers closed around hers and held. So they sat for most of the night until Bryonny finally fell into an exhausted sleep and Julian carried her to her bed and pulled the covers up around her. Then he went back to keep his vigil.

"Marie, I don't like it at all! This has put a thorn in all our plans." It was early morning and Marie was hurriedly packing.

"Not necessarily, madame. You will be marchioness that much sooner, now the old marquess is dead."

"No, that's not what I mean. This visit has been a disaster! Lord Richmond has behaved strangely from the start, and I am more convinced than ever that it has something to do with his young cousin. But now what am I to do?"

"I don't know, madame, for there will be no Season now for Lady Bryonny, and the two of them will be alone up here, together under the same roof for the required year."

"Yes, don't think that had escaped me, Marie. I don't know, I just can't believe that Lord Richmond can be attracted to a raw, gauche girl who hasn't even been out! We all know his reputation, Marie. He has always pursued more mature women."

"Perhaps you were mistaken in his attraction. You said that he came to your room last night, after all."

"Yes, and like a fool I made a show of maidenly modesty. I had an idea that the longer I kept him from what he wanted, the more he would want it. It was the wrong game to play with him, for he went straight down into his cousin's arms."

"Yes, madame, but when you saw them come upstairs is it not possible they had just been talking?"

"Yes, it's possible, I suppose. It just didn't appear that way, Marie! He might as well have been wearing no shirt at all and she was in her nightdress, for heaven's sake!"

"Yes, but she is his naive little cousin, still a girl, madame. They share a house together, after all. Why should she not be in her nightdress at that time of night, knowing she has nothing to fear from her cousin. You say he wants to see you in London. How can you despair?"

"Yes . . . I suppose it's not all bad, Marie. In his grief he will need comforting, will he not? I have a full year to play my cards, for he won't be going out into society. But I cannot afford to take any chances with that girl, Marie."

"No, madame, you cannot, although she doesn't hold a candle to you. But I have an idea, and if it works, you shall be Marchioness of Hambledon in a year's time."

An hour later, Julian's carriage set off carrying Philip, Cynthia, and a thoughtful Mademoiselle Dupris. They had discussed Marie's plan carefully and now all that remained was to present it to the captain and hope that he would agree. Cynthia waited until they were close to London and had been gingerly discussing the tragedy before she spoke.

"Captain Neville, I was wondering what you thought of the relationship between Lady Bryonny and Lord Richmond—I mean Lord Hambledon, now, of course."

"Just how do you mean, Mrs. Ashford?" asked Philip carefully.

"Given that they are distant cousins and relatively unacquainted, did you not feel that they seemed to spend an unorthodox amount of time together?"

"I really hadn't noticed, Mrs. Ashford."

"Come now, captain, let's be honest with each other. I suspect we both have the same purpose in mind and I think we can help each other."

"And just what would that purpose be?"

"Marriage."

"Marriage!" Philip choked, then recovered his composure. "You think that they—"

"I don't mean their marriage to each other, captain. I am absolutely serious about this. I think if we don't intervene, their attraction to each other could well grow and result in their marriage, and I, for one, have no intention of sitting back and letting nature take its course." Cynthia sat forward in the carriage, her eyes fixed determinedly on Philip.

"Mrs. Ashford, I haven't the faintest idea of what you're talking about."

"Please, captain, spare me the protestations. I saw the way you watched her. Don't try to tell me you haven't been sniffing around in the hopes of making a match. But let me make something perfectly clear to you. There is no way that you will ever secure her without my help."

"I see you've worked the situation out very carefully, Mrs. Ashford. So just what is it that you have in mind and why are you so interested in my welfare? And do you really think we should be discussing this in front of your dresser?"

"Mademoiselle Dupris knows everything, never fear. Your welfare does not concern me in the least, captain. However, I am determined to marry Lord Hambledon, and I need Lady Bryonny out of my way. You are in the perfect position to remove her."

"Remove her, Mrs. Ashford?"

"Marry her, captain, and we will both have what we want." Cynthia spoke forcefully.

"In the first place, Mrs. Ashford, I cannot imagine that you think Lord Hambledon would be attracted by a little girl with a mind of her own who runs around in breeches and gallops astride stallions like a boy—"

"Breeches!" gasped Cynthia.

"Yes, breeches. She spends more time down at the stables than she does anywhere else, behaving like a stablehand. Don't tell me that you think Lord Hambledon is interested in her—it's laughable! Anyway, Lady Bryonny has not yet discovered men, believe me."

"So," said Cynthia, her face flushing with anger as comprehension dawned. "I see a little better now. I think I understand what happened the other night. . ."

"What happened the other night?" repeated Philip blankly. "I'm afraid I don't understand you."

"I happened to see Lady Bryonny and her cousin in what might be construed as a compromising situation. I had thought he was making love to her, but it could be simply that they were arguing."

"Arguing about what?"

"It's not of importance," said Cynthia, unwilling to

admit that Bryonny had been responsible for her embarrassment at the stables. "But still, even if that was the case, I take no chances; the situation makes me uneasy. She won't be in love with that stallion forever, captain, I assure you. Little girls have an alarming way of growing up overnight, and something tells me your Lady Bryonny is right on the brink."

"And you think I can help push her over. Tell me, Mrs. Ashford, how do you think I'm going to convince Lady Bryonny to marry me when she's in love with a stallion, for pity's sake? She treats me like an adored brother." Philip sat back and folded his arms across his chest.

"I can encourage the match. Of course, we must come up with some way of making Lady Bryonny fall in love with you; that part is best left up to you, but you must do it soon. She's young and impressionable and seems to be genuinely fond of you. She is obviously not to be going up to London this year, and her chances of meeting anyone else are slim. She trusts you and hasn't another friend in the world as far as I can tell. It shouldn't be too hard. And all the better if you can turn her affections away from Lord Hambledon."

"She already claims that they despise each other, and if they were in fact having a late-night argument, it only proves the point."

"Nonsense. Look at the way they behaved at the dinner table—one would have thought that there had been no one else in the room with the way they were going on. It's been my experience that where there is attraction, angry sparks often accompany it. Such a relationship is only bound to deepen if they are left alone."

"Yes, I think I see what you're getting at, Mrs. Ashford," said Philip slowly. "There's only one thing. Are you aware that Lady Bryonny is heiress to one of the larger fortunes in Great Britain? And even if she did consent to marry me, what makes you think the grand new Marquess of Hambledon would give his permission? The last marquess hardly would have, I can assure you," he said with a frown.

"You have greatly surprised me, captain! No, I didn't know that she was an heiress, and now I understand much better why you want to marry her. That I can respect. But I can see why you also might be concerned. Howeover, there is something perhaps you haven't considered. Lord Hambledon might not want to be saddled with a young innocent girl as ward until such time as he can bring her out and see her married off. If you can find a way to quietly court her during her year of mourning, at the same time as turning her affections from her guardian, then perhaps he will be happy to accept your suit for the sheer sake of convenience. Lord Hambledon does not have a reputation for being overly concerned with the affairs of ingenues, that I can promise you. And she will most likely be relieved to be taken off his hands; Lady Bryonny is no match for Lord Hambledon. He'll have her terrified of him in no time if he behaves in his usual fashion. So all you have to do is convince her that you're in love with her before her mourning is over, and you'll have no competition from any other sources. And in me you will have a powerful ally. I have plans of my own for Lord Hambledon, you must remember, and once he is under my influence, there is little I will not be able to accomplish."

"That I do not doubt, Mrs. Ashford," said Philip with a smile, heartily disliking the woman but seeing that he might indeed need to be in her confidence if he was to achieve his end. And Cynthia Ashford had just possibly found a way to put that end within reach.

"Are we agreed, then?" asked Cynthia, sensing a capitulation.

"We're agreed," said Philip.

Chapter Eight

LORD Hambledon was buried the following day, and the next few days were spent receiving visitors, a task which Bryonny found almost unbearable. Julian was impeccably polite to everyone who came, doing and saying all that was expected of a bereaved son, but when they were left alone, he withdrew into his shell, spending most of his time in his father's study. Night after night he retired into that room and sat for hours behind the closed door, and Bryonny would often hear him climbing the stairs to bed in the cold, gray hours before dawn. She suspected there were nights when he did not go to bed at all, but he never appeared disheveled and was unfailingly cordial to her, although distant, behaving as if she were a complete stranger and guest in his house. She began to miss the Julian of old, despite how infuriating he could be; this man worried her, his impassive facade giving lie to the raging emotions she knew he had to be keeping in check. If he didn't let them out, he would break, she feared, but she had no idea how to reach him. After three weeks of this strange behavior, she could take no more and decided to speak to Cook.

"Aye, child, you're right about the man, but I fear there is nothing you can do to help him. He will come to terms with his father's passing when he's ready, and there's not a body on this earth he's going to show his grief to. He's always been like that, even as a small boy. I think it started when his mother died. He adored

132

her, you know, and was heartbroken when she passed on. There's no way you can prepare a child for losing his mother, but I never saw him cry again and he was only five. It wasn't natural, but there you are. He learned to hide his feelings early, that one." Cook shook her head sadly.

"It just doesn't seem right for him to be locking himself away from the world like this, Cook. I really would prefer him to rage and scream at me; at least that way, I'd know he was back to normal, at least feeling something."

"You take my word for it, the quieter that boy becomes, the more is going on in there. His way is to drown his sorrows in the brandy bottle, is my guess, from the way the cellar's been going down. But as I say, there's no point fretting yourself, child, because he never has listened much to anyone but himself. He's hurting, and he's dealing with his pain the only way that he knows how. One of these days you'll turn around and he'll be right as rain."

"I suppose you're right, Cook, but it still seems to me that no one can hold that kind of thing in and be the better for it." Bryonny paced up and down the kitchen.

"Aye, but don't forget, pet, that a lot more has happened to him than just losing his father. He's taking on a whole new life and responsibilities that maybe he didn't expect just yet. That's not easy for any man, but here is one who has always savored his freedom. Give him some time to get used to the idea."

This was something that Bryonny hadn't taken into consideration, and she went away with a slightly different perspective on Julian Ramsay, and determined to change things between them.

Julian had been leaning back in his chair, his feet propped up on the windowsill, staring across at the serene, glassy lake with half-closed eyes when a light tap came at the door. Startled, he sat up and called, "Yes? What is it?" He expected Simms or Mrs. Merk with some problem, but never Bryonny to enter.

"Julian, forgive me for disturbing you—"

"Bryonny! What on earth! What are you doing here? Are you ill?" Julian jumped to his feet. The rigid self-control he kept clamped on himself when around her was not in place, and his defenses were down.

"No, I'm perfectly well. I couldn't sleep."

"Well, make yourself some hot milk, for God's sake! If you've come for sleep, you've come to the wrong place." The mask slammed back down.

"I know. That's why I'm here. I need to talk to you." Bryonny walked over to him. "Julian, you can't go on doing this to yourself night after night."

"Doing what, my dear girl?" He looked down at her, raising his eyebrow in lazy inquiry. "Just exactly what is it you think I'm doing?"

"Oh, Julian, just for once, let's not play games. Your father's dead, and I know how much that hurts you, but you can't keep on tormenting yourself like this." She pointed at his brandy glass. "That isn't going to bring him back to you."

"Oh, Bryonny, my sweet, you always go for the jugular, don't you?" He tossed down the contents of his glass in one swallow. "Torment, did you say? Ah, yes, torment. And speaking from the tender bloom of youth, I suppose you know all about it?" His eyes were unreadable in the dim light.

"Do I not, Julian? You seem to forget my father and brother were killed not so long ago. Do you think that was easy? And your father had become like my own to me, so I'm not feeling terribly happy myself. Don't you presume to have a corner on misery!"

Julian ran a hand through his dark hair and his eyes dropped from hers. "I'm sorry, Bryonny—forgive me. Ignore what I say; it's best I'm closeted away from the world for a while. You can see I'm not fit for human company. You'd best go back to bed now." He turned from her to stare out the window again.

"I'll go if you wish it, Julian, but know I'm here for you should you need someone." She stood on her tiptoes and leaning over his shoulder, she kissed him gently on the cheek.

Julian spun around. His arms went around her waist and he pulled her to him, his mouth coming down hard on hers. For a moment Bryonny was overwhelmed, her body reacting instinctively to his touch as she softened against him, the blood pounding in her veins as his mouth opened against hers, but she came abruptly to her senses and began to struggle away from his strong grip. And then she found herself staggering backward as he suddenly released her.

"Get the hell out of here, Bryonny. Now!"

Bryonny stared at him, shaking with rage. "How *dare* you! I offer you support and caring and you respond in a typically brazen manner—and then try to turn it around on me! I should have expected no less from you!"

"I told you to leave. Do it, or I swear to God you'll regret staying." He spat the words out from between clenched teeth, his eyes as black as coal.

"Oh, I'm leaving, Julian Ramsay. I'm leaving—I'm getting as far away from you as I possibly can!" She turned on her heel and fled out the door and out of the house, her hands covering her face. She stood on the steps for a long moment, trying to stop the shaking that wracked her, a shaking caused as much by fear as by anger. She had glimpsed a violence just beneath Julian's surface, a violence unmistakably directed at her. He had looked ready to strangle her, and no doubt would have done just that if she hadn't run out. It was clear he despised her, and chillingly clear that she couldn't stay at the Abbey any longer.

Despite the coolness of the night air, she couldn't face going back into the house so, hugging her arms around herself, she wandered down to the lake and sat by the bank. For a long time no coherent thought came to her; she gazed into the water, swallowing against the sick knot of misery in her throat. The water lay still, still and black, to all appearances serene, harmless. But with a shudder, Bryonny remembered when it had closed over her head, sucking her down into its depths. Julian . . . *Had* it been an accident?

A twig snapped, impossibly loud in the hushed night, and Bryonny started, looking in the direction of the sound. Julian stood only yards away from her in the shadow of an elm.

"Bryonny . . ." He started toward her.

"No! Oh—no!" She jumped to her feet, her eyes wide with fright, and she backed away, coming up short against the edge of the steep bank. It was happening all over again, she thought above the terrified pounding of her heart. "Please . . ." Her breath caught on a sob, and frantically she looked around for an escape.

Julian stopped abruptly, looking at her in amazement. "My God . . . You think I'm going to hurt you, don't you?"

"I . . . here, before . . ."

"For the love of God, when are you going to get it through your head that I had nothing to do with that!"

"No? Then who?" But she relaxed her guard just a little.

"How the devil am I supposed to know?" he said in exasperation. "I still think you were hit by a branch—but forget about that. Bryonny, I would never intentionally hurt you, believe me. You have no reason to be frightened."

"No? And just now, in the house, did you not threaten me? You certainly succeeded in frightening me half to death. Was that not your intention?"

Julian ran a hand through his hair. "It's what I came to talk to you about. Look, there's no need to stand there like a frightened rabbit. Come here and sit down. Bryonny, please?" He held his hand out to her.

Bryonny looked at him suspiciously, but she moved toward him and sat, pointedly refusing his offered hand.

"Obstinate," said Julian under his breath, then lowered himself down next to her. "Bryonny . . ."

"I can't see what you could possibly have to say! I've had quite enough of you for one night—in fact I've had enough to last me a lifetime! I think it would be best if I went home to Jamaica."

"Jamaica?" he said somewhat unsteadily. "One kiss is enough to send you fleeing across the entire ocean?"

"*Stop*, Julian. It's bad enough to behave as you did—you can't change it by turning it into a joke."

"Oh, for God's sake, Bryonny, don't you see?"

Bryonny's eyes, clear and skeptical, met his. "No, I'm afraid I don't see at all, Julian." Her voice was cold.

Julian was silent for a long moment. Then he looked at her intently. "Bryonny, listen to me carefully. To begin with, I never should have touched you the other night, especially not in my father's house. You were his charge, and your welfare his responsibility, and I should have respected that. Nevertheless, against all reason it happened. But now everything has changed. Now, you are *my* charge, *my* responsibility, and it's my job to look after you, to see to a good marriage as your father wanted so much for you. I have no right to behave in any other way but guardian toward you, no matter what my inclination, I know that." He took a deep breath and continued.

"Bryonny, we must pretend none of this has happened. We must go back to the beginning and start over, this time as guardian and ward. Can you do that? Can you forget all that has happened between us, the anger, the accusations, especially the—kisses, for which I take full responsibility, owing to my, ah, brazen, nature?" He smiled tightly.

"Oh," said Bryonny softly, "you don't ask much, do you, cousin? You think you can kiss me like that, then throw me out of the room as if it had been my fault, and have it an hour later as if it never happened. You want a clean slate, for me to forget everything."

"Yes, I do. Surely you can see how important it is that we try to change things between us?"

Bryonny looked at him carefully, considering his words and remembering her own resolution. Then she said, "For Uncle Richard's sake I will try—I think I can try, as long as you promise to hold to your words. You can't continue to treat me as a stranger one minute and then—then behave like that the next. If we can just be civil to each other, I'm sure we can work it out. I don't much like it when you lose your temper, but I truly can't bear it when you turn me away as if I don't exist. I thought perhaps it was because you resented having me handed to you as an unwanted responsibility. Do you?"

"No, Bryonny!" Julian smiled and shook his head. "I've had much on my mind; I'm sorry if you've felt ignored. Such a thing didn't even occur to me, I assure you. I know that Father's death has upset you terribly and I haven't been very helpful, but I've been having a hard enough time dealing with my own problems. However, I will do my best to live up to our agreement. I truly am sorry about what just happened, Bryonny. I've been feeling at a loss, and I think just having a warm, living woman in my arms overcame me for a moment—and I wanted you to leave because I didn't trust myself. Do you see?"

Bryonny looked away. "Then you weren't angry with me?"

"No, you little idiot, I was angry with myself. It was unforgivable, and it won't happen again. And there you have my most humble apology. So. Suppose we both go to bed now." He stood and gave her his hand to help her up, and this time she took it.

"Obstinate, but not altogether unforgiving," he said with a chuckle.

"You don't deserve me, Julian Ramsay," said Bryonny, unable to resist smiling.

"I daresay I don't, Bryonny Livingston, but it appears I have little choice in the matter."

"Devil!" she said, pounding his arm.

"I'm afraid I'd have to agree. The devil and the she-devil; a hellish pair indeed. Here, watch the step. I'll just get a candle and light you upstairs."

After that night, Julian made an effort to be more companionable, although he still had times when he withdrew into himself and retreated into the study for long hours. He and Bryonny fell into a carefully guarded neutrality and both were careful to do and say nothing to upset it, but after a week or two, it became almost natural to them, and they slowly settled into a comfortable companionship almost without realizing it.

Julian went to London occasionally on business. But he didn't go out, with the exception of dining with his good friend, Andrew Montague, who also acted as his solicitor. And of course he visited Cynthia Ashford and, as he intended, it didn't take him long to persuade her into bed.

His sorrow gradually wore at him less, although he remained very uncomfortable with the circumstances surrounding his father's death, turning them over and over again in his mind until late in the night. But this he discussed with no one, keeping it a dark secret inside himself.

August came with long, hot days and pleasant nights. Bryonny and Julian fell into the habit of riding together in the early mornings, and they often played chess in the evening, talking quietly and easily with each other. Although they had their share of disagreements, there were no serious altercations and they lived easily together. Bryonny felt that they had become friends, good friends, and was content with her life, and with Julian.

And then one day in mid-August their hard-won peace was shattered. Julian was hard at work in the study when he heard Bryonny's voice coming from the hall.

"Philip, what a surprise! How absolutely wonderful to see you!"

Julian's face darkened and he rose from his desk and went into the hall. "Why, if it isn't Captain Neville. To what do we owe the honor, captain?" he drawled.

"I was passing, my lord, so I hoped you wouldn't mind my impertinence in stopping. I realize you are in mourning, but I was anxious to see how Lady Bryonny was faring."

"She's faring very well, thank you, captain."

"We both are, Philip. I'm so very happy that you came, and we hope we can press you to stay for the night, isn't that right, Julian?" She fixed him with a firm eye.

"Oh, but of course, you will stay, won't you, captain?" Julian said with less than enthusiasm.

"Oh, no, my lord, I couldn't possibly intrude upon you. As I said, I merely wanted to see Lady Bryonny."

"Don't be ridiculous, Philip. We'd love the company. I'll just go tell Cook there will be one more for dinner. Julian, do call for a footman; Philip can have the same room he used before. Won't Mrs. Merk be pleased! She adores you, you know." Bryonny gave him a big smile and Julian looked even more sour.

Bryonny had a wonderful time that evening, but she was well aware that Julian was less than happy with Philip's presence. He treated them both with icy politeness, and although he didn't leave them after dinner as she thought he might, he didn't go upstairs when they retired.

After tossing and turning for a couple of hours, Bryonny finally became resigned to the fact that she was not going to fall asleep and decided to go for a walk. She pulled on a simple dress and crept downstairs, checking first to see that there was no light coming from Julian's study or the library. Relieved, she slipped through the library door and into the garden. There was no moon, and although the night was crystal clear and the sky was clustered with brilliant stars, it was very dark. She wandered through the garden, enjoying the stillness and the quiet, wondering what on earth had come over Julian to make him so unpleasant to Philip. She was well aware of the fact that he disliked him, although she had never understood that either. But that was no excuse for being so rude. Still, perhaps she should have asked him privately first before she had impulsively issued the invitation.

"You really ought to watch where you are going, Bryonny. You're positively lethal in the dark." The deep voice loomed up out of the darkness, causing her to stifle a small scream behind her hand.

"Julian!" she gasped. "Whatever are you doing down there—you scared me half to death! Don't you *ever* announce yourself?"

He lay stretched out on his side in the grass next to the garden wall, dressed only in an open cambric shirt, pantaloons, and boots. He reached out a hand to her. "Come, sit down here with me, Bryonny. You'd be amazed at how beautiful things look from here."

"Julian!" Bryonny landed on the grass.

"There, now isn't that better? Tell me, my sweet; what are you doing taking a stroll in the pitch black, hmm?"

"I might ask you the same question, dear cousin. One does not expect to find a body lying full length in the garden in the middle of the night."

"No, I suppose not. But then, I felt a need for some fresh air after such a stuffy evening."

"*You* have the nerve to call the evening stuffy! If there was anything stifling in the air it was you, you beast!"

Julian looked up at her lazily. "Ah, and did you find me stifling, my love? You would have preferred me to leave you alone with your dear Philip?"

"Oh, Julian, don't be ridiculous, and he's not my 'dear' Philip."

"No? Then what would you call him? After all, you did fawn all over him this evening. What other conclusion am I to draw?"

"You are the most infuriating man that ever walked the earth, Julian Ramsay! I did *not* fawn all over him! You were in the most foul temper, in any case, and hardly worth speaking to. How you can misconstrue an innocent friendship and turn it into a blazing romance is beyond me! In any case, I don't see that it's any of your business."

"Ah, but there you're wrong, Bryonny. It's very much my business. You're forgetting that I'm your guardian and it's my responsibility to see that your virtue stays intact until you marry."

"Rest assured, dear guardian, Philip has never touched me. So far, the only person who has ever threatened my virtue has been you, if you recall!"

"Oh, yes, I recall quite clearly, Bryonny," he said, and the tone of his voice made her cheeks flame. He sat up, leaning toward her, his arm resting lightly on his knee, his eyes glittering through the darkness.

Bryonny glared at him. "Oh, you're totally impossible! No matter what I do or say, you manage to twist it into something else! I wish I could fathom what goes on in that black head of yours."

"Now that is something you really don't want to do, my love. Suffice it to say, I take a very real interest in your affairs. You don't begrudge me that, do you? After all, it is my duty."

"The way you carry out your so-called duty compared to the way your father did, is very different, to say the least."

Julian burst into laughter. "I'm not quite sure how to take that, Bryonny."

"I can't think why you find that so funny," said Bryonny, looking extremely annoyed. "Would you care to explain?"

"No, I wouldn't." Julian grinned and idly picked a tightly furled yellow bud from the rosebush growing against the wall behind his back. "Here, a token for you. Its beauty can't compare with yours, but it's the best I can do on the spur of the moment." He tucked it behind her ear.

"Spare me the gallantries, Julian. Save them for those who would appreciate them."

"My, such sharp words from such an innocent face! So the rose has thorns, does it?"

"That should come as no surprise to you, my dear cousin. And in case you were not aware of it, roses have thorns for self-defense, to keep them from being handled and crushed."

"Have they, now," said Julian with a little laugh. "Fancy that. I shall have to study up on them. But speaking of thorns, it's getting late and young girls need their sleep. You want to be bright-eyed and fresh for the captain tomorrow, don't you?"

"Will you *stop* treating me like an infant, Julian?" said Bryonny, her eyes flashing.

"And how would you have me treat you, my sweet? Like this, perhaps?" He cupped her chin in his hand and leaning forward, kissed her lightly on her mouth. She caught her breath and pushed him away. "Julian! You said you wouldn't! You promised me!"

"Yes, I did, didn't I? But that was a long time ago, and this was simply a cousinly kiss, Bryonny. Surely we've come that far?" He rose to his feet, offering a hand to help her up.

"Oh, Julian, you're such a wretch!" She brushed her dress off, trying to regain her composure. Julian laughed again, a long, deep peal.

"I know. Come, off to bed."

He unexpectedly stopped at the top of the stairs and took her by the shoulders, turning her to face him. Her eyes met his warily and he grinned. "You know, I have grown unexpectedly fond of you, Bryonny. It's too bad, really. I shall miss you when you're gone." Bending down he kissed her cheek. "Good night, my sweet, sleep well." And without giving her a chance to reply, he strode across the hall to his room. Bryonny stared after him, completely confused.

The next afternoon, Bryonny and Philip walked in the hills, Bryonny in a dark green silk gown with tightly buttoned sleeves and a high neck, and a demure bonnet. They had managed to avoid Julian all day, and he them, although he had instructed Lucy not to let Bryonny out of her sight. The sun beat warmly down as they strolled along, chatting easily. Lucy followed at a comfortable distance, but as watchful as Julian had quietly insisted she be.

"I'm very glad you came, Philip. I've missed you." She smiled up into his deep brown eyes with their little creases at the corners.

"I've missed you too, Bryonny. Do you know, it seems to me that you've changed somehow. I can't quite put my finger on it." A light breeze ruffled through his fair hair as he regarded her quizzically.

"Have I? I can't imagine how. Nothing has hap-

pened; Julian and I have been living very quietly. You
are the first guest we've had."

"You know, Bryonny, I get the distinct feeling that
your cousin doesn't care for me." He shot her an
inquiring glance.

"You mustn't let him worry you, Philip. If anyone has changed, it is he. He's quieter, more withdrawn than he used to be, I think. Of course it's
understandable."

"It's not just that, Bryonny; he watches you like a
hawk. He didn't take his eyes off you all night; you'd
think I'd been about to abduct you!"

"Oh, that. He's taking this guardian thing a little
too seriously, if you ask me. I think he's got some
foolish idea that you're going to sweep me off to
Gretna Green in some sort of seedy elopement, and is
playing the suspicious, overprotective father. Actually,
I find it rather amusing."

"How do you feel about your cousin, Bryonny?" He
sat down on a broad, flat stone and offered her his
hand to help her down.

"Feel about him? Oh, I've grown very fond of him,
really." A small smile played at her mouth as she
remembered Julian's last words in the night. "Of course,
he has a terrible temper and can be impossibly arrogant and overbearing, especially when it comes to
what he considers to be his 'male domain.' "

"What do you mean by that?"

"Oh, he won't let me have anything to do with my
own affairs, for example. We're forever arguing about
it. I want to learn how to manage my own money, for
one, but the farthest he's gone is to give me a small
sum to invest on the 'Change."

"Well . . . from what I gather, you have a sizeable
fortune. Perhaps it's only wise."

"It's not that, Philip. Under the terms of my father's
will, I don't receive my inheritance until I'm either twenty-
five or I marry. As I have no intention of marrying, I
want to learn how to control my own estate. I know it's
unconventional, but there you are, and at this rate, I
won't learn a thing until I'm in my midtwenties!"

"I see," said Philip thoughtfully. "I can't say Julian's attitude surprises me very much, from everything I've seen. He's not one to take your feelings into consideration."

"No, that's not true, Philip. Underneath all his bluster he's actually very caring and sensitive. I think that's why Uncle Richard's death hit him so hard."

"I can imagine it did. I overheard part of the argument they had that afternoon."

"What argument?" Bryonny looked at him in puzzlement.

"Oh, then he didn't tell you about it? Not that I'm surprised; I didn't think he would. I've often wondered what it was about to have made him so angry."

"What in heaven's name are you talking about?"

"He stormed out of the study saying something like, 'I warn you, I'll do anything to stop you.' He was in a fury. Then his father went after him, and the next think I heard Lord Hambledon was dead."

"Philip, what are you implying?" asked Bryonny sharply. "Do you mean that you think it wasn't an accident, that Julian was responsible?"

"No, I'm not implying anything. I just thought the whole thing was odd, and then the way he reacted afterward, so cool and calm. I can't wonder that he's felt terrible about his father's death if those were the last words he spoke to him."

"I can't believe it!"

"I'm sorry, Bryonny, I didn't mean to upset you," interrupted Philip. "I know so little of the story. Julian rushed us away the next morning and it's been on my mind since, with his hot temper."

"A display of temper is perfectly normal for Julian, believe me, and usually blows over quickly. I suppose I can see why it alarmed you, though. How awful to have had an argument just before Uncle Richard died. I wonder what it could have been about?"

"I wish I could tell you, but that's all I heard. Bryonny, there's something else I wanted to ask you about that has had me worried." Philip looked at her with concern.

"What could that be?" asked Bryonny, amused.

"I understand that the same day you fell into the lake and the doctor had to be summoned."

Bryonny explained what had happened, underplaying it considerably, and slanting it to sound as if she had slipped. "But you're terribly kind to be concerned, Philip. You've taken such a kind interest in my well-being. In fact, by all rights, it should have been you to drag me out."

"That's just the thing, Bryonny. You've had more accidents in the time I've known you than any one person should in his lifetime, and they've all been near or at the Abbey. I'm not sure this place is healthy for you!"

"You sound positively superstitious, Philip," said Bryonny with a smile. "But believe me, I've been perfectly healthy and safe since then. But it's growing late. We'd better start back." She stood.

"Yes, and I must be on my way, I'm afraid, but I'm sure your cousin will be delighted at my departure. However, despite his attitude, I hope it would be acceptable if I should stop by and see you again?"

"Don't worry about Julian, Philip. His bark is far worse than his bite. I would be delighted, and the sooner, the better."

He smiled at her in easy comraderie, and they strolled back to the house.

Philip took his leave to Julian's vast relief, exactly as the captain had predicted, and for the next two weeks the subject of Philip was carefully avoided between Bryonny and Julian. Bryonny wondered over the reported argument, but finally decided to leave it alone. She didn't want to upset Julian, and it was really none of her business.

Chapter Nine

JULIAN strode into the library where Bryonny was engrossed, surrounded by a pile of books. "Bryonny, we're expecting a guest for dinner."

She looked up in surprise. "A guest? I thought you had sworn off guests, Julian. Isn't this coming rather quickly on the heels of the last?"

"This is a little different. Andrew Montague is coming up from London with some legal business for me."

"Oh . . . So I am finally to meet your mysterious friend Mr. Montague!"

"Yes, you are, and you are to behave yourself, is that understood?"

"But of course, my lord! How could you think otherwise?" She shot him a grin.

"Why is it that I don't believe a word of it, my lady?"

"I can't imagine. Don't worry yourself, Julian, I shan't embarrass you in front of your friend."

"That will be a vast relief. Now why don't you run and change? And Bryonny—remember that Andrew is a gentleman of refined tastes and manners." He delicately touched a nostril and Bryonny smothered a laugh, then rose and swept him a broad curtsy.

"As you wish, my lord." She gathered the books up into her arms and, staggering slightly under the load, made her way upstairs, Julian looking after her as she went with an expression best described as doubtful.

* * *

An hour later, Bryonny was shimmering in a dress of lilac silk with knots of velvet ribbons falling from the high waist. Lucy had dressed her hair with a velvet ribbon of the same color and her auburn curls were arranged becomingly around her face. She restrained herself from dashing down the staircase, instead descending it at a sedate pace.

"Bryonny, you look quite lovely," said Julian, his eyes sweeping over her with warm appreciation.

"Thank you, Julian," replied Bryonny, her face suddenly flushing with heat, and was thankful to be released from his gaze by the sound of the doorknocker.

Julian unceremoniously opened the door himself and he and Andrew greeted each other with a hearty embrace, both talking and laughing at the same time. Bryonny watched them from the bottom of the steps, thinking that they might have been brothers, so apparent was the affection between them. They were both unusually tall, and two pairs of broad shoulders strained against the black cloth of their swallow-tailed evening coats. Dark heads were bent together, but when Andrew looked up, she saw that his eyes were a clear, startling blue. They caught her where she stood, and finely etched eyebrows rose slightly in surprise. She looked down quickly, and Andrew's attention was distracted by Julian's clapping him on the arm.

"Enough of the greetings, my friend. Come, you must meet my ward."

"Yes, indeed," replied Andrew with a smile. "I think I must."

"Lady Bryonny Livingston, may I present the Honorable Andrew Montague. Careful, Bryonny," Julian said with a laugh, noting the expression in Andrew's eyes as he bent over her hand. "He may look like a lamb, but I assure you, he's a wolf in sheep's clothing."

"Then you two have much in common," smiled Bryonny.

"Bravo! Well spoken, my lady! This is a pleasure. You must call me Andrew, or I shall feel that I must be on my best behavior which, despite what Julian says, is impeccable. He only wants company for his own terrible reputation. Julian, you cad, why didn't you tell me you were hiding such a beautiful ward out in the country? Keeping her to yourself, are you?"

"Keeping her away from you, Montague. As Bryonny's guardian, her well-being is my responsibility, and I know full well that it wouldn't last long with you around. Be warned."

"Pure and simple greed is what it is, Hambledon, you can't fool me. So, my lady, shall we ignore his dire warnings and become the greatest of friends?"

"It's Bryonny, and I think that's a splendid idea. I shouldn't pay any attention to Julian, anyway. He's far too used to bullying people about and getting his own way. It will do him good to be ignored for a change."

"Watch out, Andrew. You have no idea what you're letting yourself in for when you offer friendship to Bryonny. Nobody warned me, but as your dearest friend, I think you ought to know that the lovely lady standing before you is in fact a stubborn and rebellious little hellion!"

"Only to those who treat me with no respect or consideration, my dear Julian. Andrew should be quite safe." Bryonny smiled smugly, and Andrew roared with laughter.

'I think you've finally met your match, Julian." Andrew slung his arm around his friend's shoulder and Julian grinned at him.

"I will never meet my match, Andrew, you can be sure of that. Shall we go into the library? I have some fine brandy I think you'll appreciate."

By the end of the evening Bryonny felt as if she'd known Andrew all of her life. He was easy and open and blessed with a good sense of humor, and Julian was more relaxed than she had seen him around other people with the exception of his father.

The next day went quickly, and Julian and Andrew spent much of it closeted away together.

"Damnation, Andrew, I don't see why I have to go rushing off to Spain, prime minister or no. Doesn't the man know I'm supposed to be in mourning?"

"Naturally he does, Julian, but he impressed on me the fact that there was no one else for the job. It's why he asked me to come, counting on my ability to persuade you."

"He knows me too well, but I can't say I can fault his strategy. All right, then, I'll go, of course, but I'm not happy about it. I don't like to leave Bryonny here by herself. The girl's capable of getting into more trouble than you can imagine."

"Speaking of Bryonny, Julian, what are your plans for her?"

Julian looked at him sharply. "My plans?"

"Yes. For her future, I mean. She's a beautiful young thing and I imagine she'll be snapped up as soon as she has a Season. That is what you have in mind, isn't it?" Andrew leaned back and crossed his arms, regarding Julian with a wry smile.

"My plans, my friend, are my own. You and Bryonny both shall know them when the time is right."

"I see. As I thought. And Mrs. Ashford?"

Julian sat up straighter in his chair. "Mrs. Ashford? What the devil does she have to do with it?"

"A good deal, as I see it. You know your mistress is scheming for your title?"

"Nothing of the sort. She knows I have no intention of marrying her. She's an interesting diversion, nothing more; you know I've never been able to resist having the latest rage. But how did you know about it? I thought I'd kept it very quiet." Julian raised his eyebrow inquiringly.

"We are close friends, my dear Julian, and so are our valets."

Julian laughed. "By God, it's true, too. You can't keep a thing from them, can you? But nevertheless, if only you and our valets know, then who is to think twice?"

"Not a soul, my friend, not a soul. But I've never trusted the woman and I think you take it too lightly. In any case, and I don't mean to upset you, don't you think you might consider taking a wife? Not Cynthia, of course, but you need an heir, you know, and rather badly if you don't want everything Ramsay to go to your pigeon-brained third cousin in Scotland."

"I'll worry about my pigeon-brained third cousin and thank you to keep your nose out of it."

"I had only thought that Bryonny might fill the position admirably. After all, she's young, beautiful, and intelligent— "

"Oh, for God's sake!" roared Julian. "Must you be quite so infuriating, Montague?"

"Sorry, no offense intended," said Andrew mildly. "Why don't we get back to a safer subject, like the business in front of us. About your trip south . . ."

There was much laughter and joking over dinner that night, and Bryonny's eyes sparkled with pleasure. She enjoyed Andrew tremendously and reveled in the easy friendship that he shared with Julian and was extending to her.

"You are the most difficult fellow to fathom, Julian," said Andrew in the library after dinner. "This afternoon your mood was as black as sin when you decided you had to go to the Continent, and now you're as jovial as can be. What happened to cheer you up—or shouldn't I ask?"

"The Continent?" Bryonny looked at Julian in puzzlement.

"Oh, I beg your pardon, Julian! I assumed you'd told her."

"No, not yet, but I suppose I should. Bryonny, my sweet, I'm afraid I'm going to have to go for a while. I have some tricky business to perform, and it can't be put off. I only learned today."

"Oh, Julian!" Bryonny's eyes were dark with disappointment. "When will you go?"

"Very shortly, but with luck I shan't be away too long this time. I am sorry, Bryonny."

"I think it's all a ploy to get you away from my company," she said with an attempt at a smile.

"That's it," said Julian. "But would you blame me? Seriously, my sweet, it shouldn't take more than a month. You won't be too lonely, will you?"

"No, of course not. In any case, I'm sure Philip will

stop by once or twice, and that will help to pass the time."

"Surely you don't mean Philip Neville!" said Julian, his face darkening.

"Who else would I mean, Julian, and why are you looking so apople<u>c</u>tic?"

"I don't want him coming near the place, Bryonny, and that's the end of the subject!"

"But Julian, whyever not? I know you haven't developed an overwhelming fondness for him, but he's harmless enough."

"I don't like him, and I don't trust him, and he's not suitable. Don't argue with me, Bryonny, my mind's made up."

"But Julian, that's not in the least bit fair! Your father liked him well enough—"

"Don't bring my father into this, Bryonny. I'm your guardian now, and I'm telling you that you're not to communicate with Neville while I'm away and that's an end to it!"

"Oh, I see," said Bryonny furiously. "It's all well and fine for you to fraternize with whomever you choose, suitable or not, but I'm to be locked away from the one friend I have."

"Just what do you mean by that?"

"Exactly what I said. You have your Mrs. Ashfords as you please . . ."

Julian's mouth drew into a tight white line and his eyes went as hard as steel. He spoke coldly, each word bitten off. "I beg your pardon, ma'am?"

Bryonny, suddenly aware she had just committed the gravest faux pas possible without realizing it, blanched. "I—I'm sorry, Julian. I didn't mean to be rude, but surely you can see—"

"I can see what? What is it, exactly, that I am meant to see?"

"Nothing . . ." she said in a small voice, wondering how she could possibly recoup the situation.

"Nothing. I don't think so. What I do see, Bryonny, is that you have no manners or sensibility whatever. You are an impertinent, spoiled little girl, and the faster I'm rid of you, the happier I'll be. I anxiously await the day that some poor fool takes you off my hands, and it couldn't be too soon. I do hope you realize that I don't find this an enjoyable situation, or has your enormous sense of your own importance precluded that possibility from your mind?" He spoke with deadly calm but his fury was palpable.

Hurt, angry tears sprung to Bryonny's eyes. "It is not I who has an enormous sense of importance, Julian. That honor goes to you, I believe. And believe me, Julian Ramsay, I intend to be away from you as soon as I can, but it will be on my terms, not yours!" She jumped up and ran from the room.

"That was a little harsh, don't you think?" asked Andrew quietly.

"Harsh! Not harsh enough. That girl should be hung, drawn and quartered, and it would be my pleasure to do it personally," spat Julian, giving full vent to his rage. "I've had it up to here with her damned rebelliousness and ingratitude! Poison's too good for her!" He stood up abruptly almost knocking his chair over, then slammed out of the room.

"Hmm," said Andrew to himself, looking after his friend. "This is a fine kettle of fish." He settled back to finish his wine and contemplate the situation.

Andrew left the next day, but not before taking Bryonny off for a few quiet words after noting how unhappy she seemed, and not missing the fact that she and Julian had not exchanged a single word.

"Bryonny, listen to me. You mustn't upset yourself like this. Julian has a filthy temper, I know, but it's like a summer storm; all wind and rain and then the sun comes out again and all is well. Surely you know that?"

"I know what I said was unforgivable, Andrew," said Bryonny looking away, "but I had no idea that Cynthia was, was his . . ."

"His mistress? Bryonny, I don't mean to be indelicate, but believe me, it means nothing to him. Arrangments like this are very common, but you must understand that Julian didn't take kindly to having his ward bring it up, and that I can understand. I suspect he's much more upset with himself than he is with you. Please, don't take it to heart."

"How could you expect me to do otherwise, Andrew? It's not the fact that Cynthia is his mistress that upsets me, although personally I think he's an idiot. I met her, you see, and it was perfectly clear that she was after no less than his title and his pocketbook and won't give up until she gets both! But much worse than that is that he made it very clear I'm a millstone around his neck, and lord only knows I don't wish to be! Well, I'm glad to know what his true feelings are, and believe me, they're reciprocated! Just let him try to marry me off. He'll find soon enough that I won't be bullied! I'll find my own way to escape his yoke, I promise you that! Oh—I beg your pardon, Andrew," she said, suddenly mollified, "I didn't mean to speak of your friend in such a manner, but surely you can see that the situation is untenable for us both?"

Andrew smiled and took Bryonny's hand. "I think there's a great deal about my friend that you don't yet know, Bryonny. He holds his cards close, that one. But we'll speak another time; I must be on my way now. Take care, and try to reconcile your differences if you can find it in your heart."

Bryonny refused dinner that night, instead staying in her room with a tray. Despite what Andrew had said, she knew there was no making peace with Julian when he was in one of his moods, and she didn't particularly want to make peace with him in any case. She had had enough of his insufferable pride, and she had been deeply hurt by the revelation of his true feelings toward her. She crawled into bed with a book, turning page after page without seeing the print.

Julian walked the grounds trying to calm his anger, which had only been aggravated by Bryonny's refusal to appear for dinner. He knew he would have to have a talk with her, but was in no mood for it at all. She was a damned nuisance who caused him no end of trouble, and every time he thought he had the situation under control, she managed to upset it.

From the very beginning Bryonny had created problems. Nothing had gone the way it was supposed and it had made his position extremely difficult. Perhaps going away would be a good thing; it would give him a chance to think things through and decide his next course of action. But Philip Neville bothered him. He could definitely make trouble, and Julian strongly suspected that he had already. Bryonny had to be kept away from him. Time was what he needed, a month or two would see which way the wind blew and then he could act. Feeling extremely agitated, he turned the corner of the east wing and wandered into the orchard.

Bryonny couldn't concentrate on her book. Thoughts of Julian and their argument circled around and around in her head and she cringed internally each time she remembered the impulsive words she had spoken in anger. She jumped out of bed and paced the room and finally went over to the window and peered out into the dark night. The half-moon hung in the tops of the apple trees casting a muted, misty glow through their lush branches. The orchard was wreathed in shadows. Bryonny threw open the window and leaning out, she drank in a deep breath of the rich, moist night air. She felt thoroughly miserable and although she had certainly been partly at fault, there was no excuse for the way Julian was treating her. He had reason to be angry with her, but his behavior went far beyond that, and she was not going to be treated like a naughty child. She'd had enough of that from Julian. He probably expected her to wash his feet with her tears of apology!

"If you think for one minute that I'm going to back down and crawl to you on my hands and knees, you're sadly mistaken, Julian Ramsay," she spat into the dark. "You're cold and cruel, and how I was ever deceived into thinking otherwise is beyond me! You are beneath my contempt, and the sooner you leave, the happier I'll be. I would marry a toad sooner than spend another year under your roof—I despise you!" She pulled the window closed and flung herself back into bed, but felt no better for venting her anger, for the truth of the matter was that she did not despise Julian at all.

But the man who had slipped into the cover of the shadows when she had appeared at the window took her at her words and they cut deeply. Wounded pride brought soft but bitter words to his lips. "Fine, Bryonny, you shall have it the way you want it! You have solved my difficulty for me; when I return I shall see to it that you are off my hands permanently, and there will be an end to this hell. And you damned well deserve what's coming to you!"

The next two days passed without any lessening of the hostility between them. Julian spent most of his time away, and when he was at the Abbey, Bryonny avoided him as much as possible. The angry tension began to take its toll on Bryonny, and a cold, heavy misery numbed her spirits. The servants were all aware of the situation and hushed words were exchanged between them. No one knew the cause of the trouble; Bryonny did not even confide in Lucy, and when Mrs. Merk tried to find out the reason for Bryonny's indisposition she was curtly shut off. The staff tiptoed around Julian for fear that the slightest thing would set him off. Things were definitely not as they should be.

"Mrs. Merk, I would like you to summon Lady Bryonny to my study, please."

"Yes, my lord."

"You may tell her that I will see her immediately. I will brook no delay!"

"Yes, my lord," whispered Mrs. Merk, and quickly scurried away. Whatever had become of the nice Master Julian of old?

"He said what?" cried an outraged Bryonny as Mrs. Merk delivered her message. "Thank you, Mrs. Merk, you may leave me now; you needn't escort me in chains, unless that was also part of your instructions. I shall be there shortly." Her eyes snapped with their old spirit and her cheeks were flushed with anger. She sat down and consciously tried to control herself. There was no point losing her temper now. Taking a deep breath, she went downstairs.

"Sit down, Bryonny, I must speak with you." Julian's voice was cool, his face remote. "I am leaving for Spain tomorrow, and I would like to give you your instructions. You will stay here, naturally, under the supervision of Mrs. Merk. You are not to see Captain Neville under any circumstances. And you *will* behave yourself in my absence. I hope I've made myself understood. Do you have any questions?"

"Goodness, no, Julian. You've planned it all out with great attention to detail, and I'm very appreciative, indeed. There's just one small thing. I intend to do precisely as I please, so *you* might as well be warned. I do hope you enjoy your trip to the Continent, and don't waste your time worrying yourself about me. Safe journey, Julian." Bryonny didn't give him a chance to answer. She walked quickly out of the room, softly closing the door behind her.

Julian stared at the door with narrowed eyes. Then he leaped out of his chair and, spinning around, he smashed his fist against the wall.

Bryonny once again took her dinner in her room that night, pleading a headache. When she rose the next morning Julian was gone, and she went immediately down to the stables and took Bedlam out for a long ride. She found a small glade in Three Mile Wood and dismounted, leaving Bedlam to graze while she lay down on the soft grass, gazing up through the tangle of boughs to the sky beyond, her hands behind her head.

The wood was perfectly still, emanating a sense of deep peace. Bryonny drew in a long, aching breath and released it. She felt horribly empty, as if there were a gnawing hollow at the center of her being. She couldn't believe that she and Julian had come to such a point of enmity. They had been good friends for such a long time now, or so she'd thought, and yet lurking just below the surface had been this canker waiting to be exposed. Well, if he intended to wash his hands of her as quickly as possible with no regard to her happiness, then she would take matters into her own hands. She would not allow him to force her into marriage—she'd have to find another way out.

Bedlam drifted over to her and nuzzled her shoulder, blowing softly through his nostrils. She pushed his head away with a little laugh, then suddenly and inexplicably she burst into tears, covering her face with her hands and crying as if her heart were breaking. But after a minute she cut herself off, and angrily wiped her tears, defying her misery.

"Stop it, you fool. What's done is done, and there's no point in giving that callous swine the satisfaction of seeing that he's hurt you. And by God, he doesn't deserve your love in any case!" And then she paled as her words echoed back to her from the woods, the meaning finally and inexorably becoming clear to her. Remounting, she turned Bedlam's head for home and pushed him into a gallop, but there was no escaping the fact that defiance was not going to erase the feelings in her heart.

"Captain Neville," said Cynthia, pressing home her advantage, "now is the perfect opportunity, don't you see it? With Lord Hambledon out of the country for at least a month, you have a free hand!"

Philip turned from the window where he had been gazing out over St. James's Square, apparently deep in thought. "I do see it, naturally, Mrs. Ashford. But it simply isn't as easy as you seem to think. I have to earn Bryonny's trust. I can't just show up on the doorstep and ask for her hand in marriage. These things take time, and I have been working on it. And furthermore, I happen to think that Bryonny's feelings are more than half engaged from what I saw on my recent visit, which proves out your earlier contention. Not that I think for one minute that he returns the sentiment. And believe me, Lord Hambledon was not the least bit pleased to see me."

Cynthia shifted delicately on the sofa, not at all

happy with Philip's pronouncement despite the fact that it confirmed her own thoughts. "I'm quite certain you will find the right way to persuade Lady Bryonny to marry you. I happen to know that Lord Hambledon and his ward have had a bad falling out, so she won't be entertaining any fond thoughts of him at the moment, which is all to the good."

Philip frowned. "A falling out? Concerning what, may I ask?"

"I have no idea; he wouldn't discuss it except to say that he was washing his hands of her for once and for all. Naturally, he was speaking from pique as there's absolutely nothing he can do about the situation—"

"Don't be too certain of that, Mrs. Ashford," interrupted Philip curtly, repressing his own sudden worry. "Thank you so much for the enlightening interview. I think I will pay a visit to Bryonny after all. Good day, ma'am."

Chapter Ten

"**P**HILIP!" Bryonny came running up to him as he was dismounting his horse. "Oh, dear, you really shouldn't be here, you know. Julian's away and I've been forbidden your company." She shot him a mischievous grin and shifted the basket of flowers she'd just picked from the cutting garden.

"I know," he said, bending down and kissing her cheek.

"You know?" she asked with surprise, as much at the kiss as his foreknowledge. "I don't see how, but then what are you doing here?"

"I'll explain all of that. I know this is unexpected, but I must talk with you and it couldn't wait." He tied his horse to the posting ring outside the front steps.

Her smile faded. "What could possibly be so important that it couldn't wait?"

"Why don't we go inside? I haven't much time, or I would be more observant of the formalities."

"Oh, Philip," she said, taking his arm and leading him up the steps. "You know perfectly well that there's no need for formality with me. I wouldn't know what to do with it in any case!"

Mrs. Merk was passing through the hall as they entered, and she stopped abruptly, looking at Philip with blank astonishment. "Captain Neville!"

"Good afternoon, Mrs. Merk," he said, amused by her dismayed expression.

"My lady, you know what Lord Hambledon's orders were . . ."

"I do, Mrs. Merk, but the captain has only stopped briefly. It wouldn't be very polite to show him the door, would it? Where's the harm?"

"I don't like it, my lady," she said, looking at Philip with worry. "I'm meant to be in charge, you know."

"I do know, but I shan't say a word about it if you won't. Why don't you bring us tea, Mrs. Merk," she said, firmly dismissing the woman, but Mrs. Merk refused to be dismissed.

"A word with you, my lady?"

"Oh, all right," said Bryonny impatiently. "Philip, please wait for me in the library? I'll be in directly."

Mrs. Merk waited until he was out of earshot, and then said, "You know his lordship expressly forbid him, poppet, and I reckon I know his reasons even if you don't." She shook her head vehemently and deep lines stood out between her eyebrows. "The captain's ambitions should be lying in other directions, and he doesn't belong sniffing around here. I know what I'm speaking of, my girl, and gentlemen's thoughts lead in one direction and one direction only!"

Bryonny burst into laughter. "Mrs. Merk, you're very sweet to be concerned, but I assure you there's no need for it. Captain Neville is a friend, nothing more. And if you're worried that Lord Hambledon will have your head, don't be. It will be our secret. Now why don't you get that tea?" And still laughing, she went to join Philip.

"What was that all about?" asked Philip curiously.

"Oh, nothing at all. Just Mrs. Merk being her meddling self. She's afraid she's going to be in terrible trouble if Julian finds out you were here."

"I see. Why don't you tell me why I've suddenly been forbidden to see you?"

"I can't really tell you why, any more than to say that for some ridiculous reason Julian's taken a severe disliking to you."

"And what do you think he's going to say if word gets back to him that I came?"

"He won't be pleased in the least, of course, but it doesn't make any difference. I don't think I could sink any lower in his estimation."

"Bryonny, why? What's happened?"

"We had a terrible argument; it's not important now, but at the time I think Julian was prepared to kill me."

"Don't joke about it, Bryonny. I don't trust that man and his temper."

"Don't be ridiculous, Philip. He would never do me any physical harm, although he made it very clear that he wants me out of his life. I suppose he'll try to marry me off as soon as decently possible." She sighed miserably.

"No. No, I don't believe that's it at all. You must get away from Julian as soon as possible, Bryonny. I've been thinking a great deal about the situation and it doesn't seem right."

"What situation? What are you getting at, Philip?"

"I don't want to alarm you, but I sincerely believe that you might be in danger. It's what I came to talk to you about."

Bryonny threw her head back and laughed. "Really? What sort of danger? Is it my virtue that you're concerned about? I assure you, you needn't be."

"I'm serious, Bryonny. It's your life that concerns me."

"Come now, Philip. It's not as bad as all that. It was only an argument."

"Listen to me. I haven't wanted to speak before this, but I feel I must now. Has it ever occurred to you that your accidents might have been intentional attempts on your life? From what you told me, Julian is your only relative. Wouldn't he inherit if you died?"

"Yes, he would, but that's irrelevant. You're seeing danger where there isn't any, Philip. Julian wouldn't do such a thing. He has a fortune of his own, for heaven's sake."

"Perhaps not large enough. What do you really know of his situation?"

"Well, nothing, really. But there have always been more than adequate sums."

"And first your godfather handled the Livingston affairs, and now Julian."

"Oh, for heaven's sake, Philip, if you're implying that either one of them skimmed a single penny from—"

"Perhaps not his father, but Julian? Has he ever let you see the books?"

"You know that's an ongoing argument, Philip. It doesn't mean that he's in any way dishonest."

"Just take my point for a moment. If that were the case, it would explain why he's so adamantly against your having anything to do with your finances. And I don't think he has any intention of seeing you married, if I'm correct."

"What *do* you mean?"

"I mean that anyone so intent on getting your money that he's willing to kill for it, is unlikely to hand it away on a silver platter to another man, and certainly he isn't going to take the risk of having the books examined."

"Absolute nonsense. And what did you mean by willing to kill?" asked Bryonny, by now thoroughly annoyed.

"I don't think Lord Hambledon's death was an accident, Bryonny. I believe that Julian and his father were arguing about money that day and that Lord Hambledon probably refused to give Julian whatever he'd requested. I think that Julian lost his temper and killed his father in an incontrollable rage."

Bryonny stood up abruptly. "You go too far, Philip!"

"I haven't even begun! Bryonny, I don't mean to upset you, but your entire family was killed. Perhaps that wasn't an accident either. Perhaps you were meant to die with them, and since then, two more attempts have been made on your life; once with that gunshot in the woods, and then when you were thrown into the lake! No," he said at Bryonny's look of surprise, "I didn't believe your story about having slipped."

"But Julian wasn't even there when the gun went off in the woods, he was out of the country!"

"Can you be absolutely certain?"

"I really don't want to hear any more about this, Philip. It's completely absurd and in any case, I could turn around and say the same thing to you. You were there all three times, *and* when Uncle Richard died. It would make about as much sense if I accused you!"

"But Bryonny, I have no motive; and even if I did, I wouldn't be stupid enough to stay around and always be discovered on the scene! Look, I've become very fond of you, and I don't want to see you hurt. It's the only reason that I would ever speak of this to you."

"Wait, Philip, there's a large hole in your melodrama. You forget that I've been living with Julian for the last few months and I've been perfectly safe."

"Perhaps for the moment. I doubt Julian thinks he could get away with another murder so soon after his father's. He'd be incredibly stupid to try something right away and invite suspicion."

"Oh, this is ridiculous! And speaking of inviting suspicion, Philip, just what suddenly compelled you to come up here and tell me all of this? How did you know Julian was away?"

"Cynthia Ashford told me."

"Cynthia? I wasn't aware that the two of you were friends!"

"We're not. You might say that we are co-conspirators."

"Now I'm quite convinced you're out of your mind. I suppose you know that Cynthia is Julian's mistress?"

"Good lord, Bryonny! Yes, I'm aware of the fact, but it surprises me a good deal that you know that!"

"Why, because well-bred young women aren't supposed to know about such arrangements? Well, I'm sorry if I shock you, but I'm not a fool, you know."

"No, of course you're not. Well, that does make it easier to tell you this next thing. You see, Cynthia realizes how precarious her situation with Julian is. She's not content being his mistress; she wants to be his wife."

"I came to that conclusion the first time I laid eyes on her. So?"

"So, she's jealous of you, and very worried that you might steal Julian away from her. After all, she's well aware of his reputation, and she cannot like the idea of having a beauty like you right under his nose. Therefore it's in her best interest to get you out of the way as soon as possible."

"Me! She thinks I'm going to steal Julian away from *her?* Oh, that's very good, Philip. Tell me, where have you come up with all this? Your imagination really is running riot today."

"It's quite true, Bryonny. I was a bit nonplussed when she approached me and laid it all out. You see, she's under the misguided impression that I'm after you for your fortune. I think Cynthia can only see life in terms of pounds and shillings, but most importantly, titles, and the higher, the better. She informed me that she would help me in my pursuit of your hand so that you would be safely married and out of her way, and Julian would be all hers. It's twisted, I know, but I took her up on her little scheme so that I could keep an eye on her—and you."

"I don't believe it! Of course, it does sound exactly like something Cynthia would dream up. But why you of all people?"

Philip shot her a sidelong look. "I find that a singular remark," he said quietly.

"Oh, Philip, don't take offense. I only meant that there must be other men she could have gone to, whom she knows much better than you. Surely she's aware that Julian would never approve of you!"

"I don't think she is aware of that, but she does know that you and I are friends. That's a good beginning, coupled with what she assumes to be my greed. She and that peculiar companion of hers got it into their heads that I should conduct a smear campaign on Julian to put you off him. Ironically, that seems to be the very thing I'm doing, but believe me, it's not on Cynthia's behalf! She's a desperate woman, Bryonny, and I believe there's more going on than meets the eye."

"How very interesting that you should think so," said Bryonny thoughtfully. "I wonder how far she's prepared to go . . . And Julian, fool that he is, certainly doesn't see it. But never mind that. It does make sense that she should attribute her own nasty motives to you."

"It never occurred to her to do otherwise. But then, marrying you is quite an appealing idea, so who am I to complain?"

"Then you are after my fortune, Philip?" asked Bryonny with a grin.

"But naturally, my dear Bryonny. The only difference between myself and others is that at least I'm honest about it."

"An admirable quality in any man."

"Only to a certain point, beyond which it would be foolish to stray. But as you know, there's no love lost between myself and Julian, and as for Cynthia—well, suffice it to say that to thwart them both would give me nothing but pleasure."

"I see. Well, I must say, it's nice to have a champion. I don't believe a word of your fantasy about Julian, but I'm very glad that you told me about Cynthia. It's better to be forewarned."

"But don't you see, that's exactly what I'm trying to do. Bryonny, I'm very serious about all of this. But there is a solution, you see, and I've come to present you with it."

"And what is that? I can't run away, Philip, even if I did believe you."

"No, but you can marry me, Bryonny. I've thought it all out very carefully. It's the only way to keep you safe. If you marry me, then you and your inheritance are safe from Julian. He would have no reason to kill you. I would be your husband, and your money would be safe, do you see? But I think we should marry before he returns. God only knows what he'll try next!"

"Philip, it's very kind of you to offer, but I can't accept. In the first place, I don't love you, at least not in that way. You're like a brother to me, so this is ridiculous!"

"I do know that, Bryonny, and I don't expect you to see me any other way. The point is, I don't want to see you hurt or dead! We could elope. I obtained a special license this morning. And I swear, you would keep control over your money. I know how strongly you feel about that—and one other thing. It will be a marriage of convenience, I promise."

"I can't, Philip. It wouldn't be right. And I don't believe your theory, so there would be no point to it."

Philip sighed in exasperation. "I wish I could talk some sense into you, Bryonny, before it's too late! It is only because I want to protect you that I'm in such a state of agitation. Your emotions are so involved that you cannot see clearly."

"Just what do you mean by that, Philip?" Spots of anger burned in Bryonny's cheeks.

"I think I know a little of what you feel for Hambledon, Bryonny. It may not be obvious to others, but I know you too well. He's been known to take in other young women before this with his good looks and charm, but never were the stakes so high. And personally, I think the man's quite mad—look at his irrational behavior. You yourself have told me about his rages—if he's capable of killing his father, then why not you? He'll stop at nothing to get what he wants! And you're so blinded by your feelings for him—"

"Philip, you're being impertinent!" Bryonny stopped for a moment, controlling her own emotion. For days now, although it seemed like years, she had been painfully aware of the feelings she held toward Julian. That she was in love with him, and had been for months, was painfully clear to her, but it only made her more unhappy to realize that it was not the secret she had thought it. But there seemed no point in denying the fact, not to Philip, who read her so well.

She spoke with a quiet voice. "I would thank you to collect yourself. My feelings toward Julian are nobody's concern but my own, and I assure you, I expect him to feel no other way toward me than is appropriate for a guardian toward his ward. I think it's high time you put away your fantasies and not bring up the subject again. I will not marry you, and I beg you to stop making a fool of yourself."

Philip fingered his brow in frustration, then sat down and took Bryonny's hand, looking at her earnestly. "Then at least will you consider what I've said? Surely you can see there must be some truth in it?"

"No, I'm afraid I can't. But I can forgive you despite how foolish I think your accusations are. I can see how you've put everything together, and there are a few coincidences, I have to give you that, but you simply don't know Julian as I do."

"Oh, for the love of God!" said Philip in complete exasperation. "You're in love with someone who doesn't exist! The man's either ruthless, mad, or both!"

"Philip! Stop this immediately! I have great affection for you, but that does not give you the right to intrude in something which most emphatically does not concern you."

"My dear Bryonny, I'm most sorry if I've upset you unduly. But as you wish, I will refrain from mentioning it again, if you'll promise me just one thing."

"What is that?" she asked warily.

"Should you ever be in trouble, or see any evidence that what I've said might be true, you'll come to me? My offer of marriage is sincere."

Bryonny smiled. "You are incorrigible, but you do have my promise."

Just then, Mrs. Merk entered with a tea tray. She had heard only the last few words spoken between them, but she needed to hear no more. She put the tray down with a bang. "Your tea, my lady," she said coolly and quickly went outside again.

Bryonny smiled at Philip. "I think that was Mrs. Merk's way of letting us know that she thoroughly disapproves of our tête à tête."

"Indeed? How very unfortunate for her," replied Philip lightly.

But neither realized how very thoroughly Mrs. Merk disapproved.

The next three weeks went by in an agony of slowness for Bryonny. She dreaded Julian's return as much as she anticipated it, and as the days dragged by, her dread grew. How was she to survive under the same roof knowing that she was in love with him? When she had been unaware of her feelings it had been an easy matter; there was no way that she could have inadvertently revealed herself, but now? Surely Julian would see it and only mock her. Her life seemed suddenly to have gone quite mad. First had come Philip and his insane suspicions, not to mention his extraordinary proposal, then there was the fact of Cynthia and her bizarre scheming, but finally, finally and in the end, there was Julian—but she wouldn't think about him; she couldn't.

Lucy quietly came in with water. She had sensed Bryonny's melancholy since the coldness had developed between his lordship and her mistress. Although she privately had her own thoughts on the matter, she had refrained up until now from making any comment. But the time had come to shake some sense into her mistress, no matter what it brought down on her head. And tonight she would see to it that Lady Bryonny was as beautiful as she knew how to make her.

"Are you ready to dress for dinner, my lady?" she asked pointedly.

Bryonny looked at her with surprise. "I can't see why you would get such an extraordinary idea into your head, Lucy. Since when have I dressed for dinner?"

"It's time you started, my lady, begging your pardon. You've been moping around long enough the way I see it, and there's no point in letting yourself go.

I have it in my mind that tonight you're going to look
as pretty as can be, if to please nobody but myself. It's
been a sad job being a lady's maid and nothing to
show for it."

Bryonny smiled. "Oh, dear. That never crossed my
mind! Very well, then, Lucy; if it will make you happy,
dress away."

Lucy grinned broadly. "I think the deep blue satin,
my lady. You haven't worn it for the longest time, not
since before old Lord Hambledon passed on, God
bless his soul." She went to the armoire and rustled
inside, well pleased that her ploy had worked.

Bryonny submitted to Lucy's administrations with
resignation, but soon was caught up in Lucy's infec-
tious spirit.

"Oh, you shall look like a fairy princess tonight, my
lady, just you wait and see! Now, let me see. I think
the string of pearls his lordship gave you for your
eighteenth birthday. Yes, that's exactly right!"

Bryonny stood up with a rustle and went to examine
herself in the mirror. The dress fell from the low
neckline in a long sweep to the floor gathered only by
the high bodice. Lucy was right; the pearls set the
dress off perfectly, the milky beads resting coolly against
her skin. She remembered well enough when Julian
had presented them to her, his long fingers fastening
the clasp around her neck.

"These are for you, Bryonny," he'd said gently as
she'd protested. "They were my mother's and I know
she would have wanted you to have them, and we
both know my father would have felt the same."

Bryonny's fingers touched the pearls briefly, then she
dropped her hand, pushing the memory away along
with the accompanying pain. "Thank you, Lucy. You've
wrought a miracle, indeed. Now what?"

"Why, now you go downstairs to dinner, my lady,
what else?"

"Simms won't believe his eyes," said Bryonny with
a little laugh.

"He's not the only one, my lady," said Lucy
smugly.

* * *

Bryonny started down the stairs feeling very silly but glad to have indulged Lucy's whim. And then she halted abruptly, her heart stopping in her chest.

Julian was standing at the bottom of the staircase and he looked up as she appeared. His eyes caught hers and held, and she felt as if they burned right through her. The pulse bounded painfully at the side of her throat and she thought her legs would give way, but somehow she forced herself on through her shock.

"Julian, I . . ." She could think of nothing to say. All she seemed to be aware of was the wild beating of her heart. And Julian, Julian here in front of her, his presence so solid, so real.

He took her hand in his and kissed her fingers lightly. "Bryonny."

She swallowed hard. "Welcome home, Julian."

He smiled at her, that wide, attractive smile and it turned her bones to water. "Thank you. It's good to be home. You look very beautiful, my sweet."

"Thank you. I—I had no idea you were back . . ."

"Oh, I see." He frowned. "Do you dress like this every night?"

"No! It was Lucy. I thought she was playing at some game, but she must have known. I mean—it was very wicked of her not to tell me." Bryonny blushed furiously with confusion.

"And had you known would you have done the same?"

"Why, yes! Oh, Julian, I'm sorry; I don't seem to have my wits about me. You took me by surprise."

"A pleasant one, I hope."

"Yes, naturally . . ." She felt like a complete fool.

"I'm very gratified to hear it. Have you decided to forgive me?" He spoke softly, but his words went through her with a shock.

"Oh, Julian, there's nothing to forgive; it was as much my fault and I, too, am sorry."

"Then we'll say no more. I have something for you."

He retrieved a little box from his pocket and placed it in her hands. "Come, open it. It's nothing but a small way of apologizing for the harsh words I spoke. I didn't mean them, you know."

She was taken aback but she couldn't seem to react. She finally raise the lid; inside lay a spray of roses worked in diamonds and pearls. Her breath caught in her throat and her eyes flew to his. "Julian—I can't possibly accept . . ."

"Can you accept my apology, Bryonny?"

"Yes, yes, of course, but . . ."

"Then you can accept this." He took the box from her fingers and removed the broach. "Do you remember that night in the garden?" he said as he pinned it to her dress. "I spoke the truth then, or what I knew of it. Roses become you, my sweet. There." He stepped back and looked at her carefully.

"Thank you, Julian," she said simply.

"Shall we go in for dinner?" He offered her his arm and led her into the dining room.

Julian made a point of keeping the conversation light, but there was a palpable tension in the room. The glowing candles and Julian's deep voice talking softly across the table made it difficult for Bryonny to concentrate on the meal. Her appetite seemed to have fled as she watched his face in the flickering light, its strong planes accentuated by the shadows, his intelligent gray eyes meeting hers and sending a shiver down her spine, his graceful hand pushing back a stray lock of hair that had fallen over his forehead. The wine sent a pleasant warmth through her body and she leaned her chin forward on her hand as she watched him.

"Bryonny?"

"Mmm?"

"You haven't heard a blessed word I've said, and you've hardly touched your food! What's happened to the girl with the appetite of a horse?"

Bryonny smiled and stretched. "I don't know."

"That's all you have to say for yourself? Something is very wrong if you're not eating, and you've barely said a word all dinner."

"Haven't I? I beg your pardon. I suppose I've become disused to company."

"It must have been very dull for you here by yourself. But perhaps you will like my suggestion. I've been thinking; I've been meaning to pay a long overdue visit to Shelbourne Hall to be sure it's running smoothly, and I thought that you might like to come along. It's time that you begin to take a part in your own affairs and we can go over the running of the estate together."

"Do you mean it, Julian? Oh, I'd like that! But what made you change your mind?"

"I've had quite a bit of time to reconsider. You were right—it's what my father would have wanted, and I know that you're more than capable of dealing with your finances with a little guidance. Why don't we leave tomorrow? It will make a pleasant change for you."

"That would make me very happy, Julian. Thank you." She smiled at him softly.

"Good. We'll take Mrs. Merk and Lucy with us. We should get to bed now. We'll leave in the morning, and you should be well rested. It's a long journey."

"You're really not angry with me?" she asked, hesitating.

"Of course not. You're stubborn and disobedient, but it's become apparent to me that it's no good trying to control you since you're determined to do things your own way, so I might as well surrender gracefully." Julian smiled ruefully.

"I never thought to hear you speak the words, my lord. They come as a tremendous relief."

"Don't be too overconfident, my sweet. As they say, you may have won the battle, but you haven't won the war."

"We shall see." Bryonny rose, and with a quick backward smile at him, she went upstairs.

Julian sat for a while longer, lost in thought. He was vastly relieved that Bryonny appeared to have forgiven him and better yet, that she'd agreed to go to Shelbourne. It was private and remote and if everything went well, he would have the conclusion he planned with no one around to interfere. Smiling to himself, he went into his study and unlocked a small drawer. Removing its contents he slipped it into his pocket and went upstairs to bed.

Chapter Eleven

SHELBOURNE Hall came into view, standing proudly on its distant hill near the cliffs, the golden sunshine of late afternoon pouring down its walls and mellowing the dark stone. The air was warm and stirring with a pleasant breeze which carried with it the faint tang of salt.

"Welcome home, Bryonny." Julian helped her down from the carriage. From the distance came the sharp cries of gulls who winged and hovered over the ocean.

Bryonny turned to him in uncertainty. He took her hand in his and gave it a squeeze. "I know," he said simply. They went inside.

"Lady Bryonny, 'tis good to see you, indeed, and fine to have a Livingston inside these walls again." The old bailiff, Mr. Alwyyd, was in the great hall to greet them. "Lord Hambledon, we're grateful to you for bringing the lass to visit. It's been overly quiet here since the tragedy. My sympathies, Lady Bryonny. The rooms are being turned out upstairs and I've had a bit of food and drink laid out for you. It won't be much tonight, but it should tide you over until morning. My apologies, my lord, my lady, but we weren't quite prepared, you see."

"Not at all, Alwyyd," said Julian. "I'm sorry we didn't have an opportunity to give you earlier notice of our arrival. I hope it hasn't created a problem."

"No, indeed, my lord. This way." He led them into

the sitting room where the holland covers had been hastily removed.

Bryonny was content to let Julian converse with the bailiff. She clearly remembered the last time she had sat in this room, when it had been filled with merry laughter. So much had happened.

"Bryonny, would you like to take a walk before we change for dinner?"

"Oh, I would, Julian. I know just where I want to go." She thanked Mr. Alwyyd for his efforts and led Julian outside, heading unerringly to the south. They passed through a meadow and further on. A herd of fat sheep, looking for all the world like balls of cotton tossed onto a backdrop of green felt, grazed contentedly on a distant slope. The soft wind blew about them and the air was filled with a sense of contentment. Bryonny drank it in; this was what she had needed. They walked in quiet companionship, neither needing to speak.

The wind picked up over the cliffs, and Bryonny stood near the edge, looking far down into the ocean below where the waves crashed against the sheer rock. The gulls circled and plunged steeply on the air currents in search of fish, their constant crying carried off on the wind. Julian sat off to one side on a cushion of springy thrift, his arms resting on his knees as he gazed off into the distance. Finally, as the light began to fall steeply in its western descent, casting long, deep shadows, he rose and approached her. "It's time, my sweet. Dusk is approaching."

"Yes—but isn't it magnificent, Julian? Standing here makes me feel so small in the scheme of things, as if my problems could hardly matter."

"Are you going to start waxing poetic on me, Bryonny?" he said with a little smile. "I should have known it was bound to happen with the way you've been looking so faraway since my return." She gave a little shiver, and he put his arm around her and pulled her close to warm her, and together they stood looking over the ocean.

Bryonny relaxed against the warmth of his body,

leaning her head against his chest. In that moment she felt as if time had ceased to exist, had wrapped her in complete peace and then simply stopped.

"Do you believe in fate, Julian? You, personally?"

"Hmm . . ." He glanced down at her, then looked away.

Bryonny studied the fine line of his profile as he gazed out over the churning ocean, his face expressionless. For a moment she thought he'd forgotten her, but then he spoke.

"I personally think, my sweet, that one makes one's own fate. There is probably a thread that guides us, but we decide how to weave it. Everything comes down to choices, right or wrong. A slightly skewed form of free will, if you like."

Bryonny considered this carefully, her mind set very much on one thing. "But suppose one makes the wrong choice—or makes no choice at all, just mindlessly drifts along without taking a stand for oneself or for one's beliefs? It seems that once set on such a course there is no turning back . . ."

"There is always a way back, Bryonny, if one has the will to find it."

"And the courage . . ."

"But then that is also a choice," he said with a smile.

"How can that be a choice? There are many who don't have will or courage to begin with!"

"They aren't qualities that one is necessarily born with like shining virtues, Bryonny. A courageous person is someone who is capable of acting in spite of his fear, just as a person with will is someone who can force himself to go on despite his despair."

"I suppose . . ." For some reason her father flashed into her mind. "But then that comes back to fate. We take what life deals out and go on as best we can."

"True, from one point of view. But suppose we look at it in ethical terms. Assume for the sake of argument that a man is confronted with a situation—perhaps to which fate has led him—in which his moral sense is challenged. He knows what is ethically 'right,' but you see, he need not make that choice, despite what his conscience might tell him. He's just as capable of setting off on the path to his own destruction perfectly well aware of what he's doing, but perhaps able to rationalize his actions. Murder is an excellent example."

"Murder?" said Bryonny with a start. "I assume you mean premeditated murder?"

"Exactly. Cold-hearted, calculated murder. It's not so difficult to understand, Bryonny, or so uncommon. This might come as quite a shock to you, my innocent, but we all know people capable of such a thing. But come, dear philosopher, we really must head back. And you're quite misled if you think I have any of the answers. I'm just as capable as the next person of choosing a destructive path, and quite consciously at that. Of course, I never claimed to have a conscience."

"I don't believe you're capable of evil, Julian. Stupidity, perhaps, or acting in your own self-interest, but never deliberate evil."

"And how am I meant to take that, I wonder? I'm hard-pressed to decide whether I've just been insulted! But you're quite right, I am more than capable of acting in my own self-interest, so be warned. And speaking of that, my stomach is beginning to growl, so if you don't mind?" He took her hand and turned her back toward the house.

Bryonny pulled away from him with a grin. "Oh, no—I'm not having anything to do with a self-confessed man of no conscience. You sound far too dangerous!" She tore away across the cliffs, and Julian watched her for a moment as she ran, her dress whipping around her small form. Then he took off after her, catching up to her in no time as she reached the meadow. She exploded with laughter as she tried to get away, but he grabbed her around the waist with a cry of victory and they fell to the ground in a tangle, Julian pinning her underneath him.

"Julian, stop it! Let me go!" she laughed breathlessly, but she quickly sobered at the expression in his eyes and went very still. And then just as suddenly as he had grabbed her, he released her and stood.

"You shouldn't offer up such an invitation to a desperate man, Bryonny, especially, as you say, one without a conscience." He gave her his hand to help her up, then walked away from her. A moment later he called, "Here, look at this. Do you know what this is?" He picked a handful of a tiny white flower whose climbing tendrils wound their way over an old stone wall.

"It's white bryony."

"That's right. It bears your name. A flower with a beautiful blossom but whose berries are quite deadly. You, my sweet, are the flower, and I the berry." He pointed to the bright red clusters.

"Indeed? Quite a pair we make." She looked away from his laughing eyes.

Julian tucked a sprig behind her ear. "But then you can't have the berry without the blossom."

"I'm most impressed with your knowledge of botany, Julian. I never would have guessed that your interest ran to flowers."

"Oh, you never know when such things will come in handy. But I consider myself quite an expert in flowers—certain varieties, that is."

"Such modesty, Julian, is so typical of you. Tell me, did you pick the flowers for me, or to show off your incredible store of knowledge?"

"Neither. I picked them for myself so that I might have a reminder of our curiously intermingled destinies. But let's not have any more talk about fate before dinner. It makes a man lose his appetite, no matter how hungry he may be." He shot her a strange look, then abruptly left her, striding across the meadow and disappearing over the knoll.

Dinner was a very quiet affair. They ate in the enormous old dining hall, the table set in front of a massive fireplace that four people could easily have sat in. Silver candelabras glowed on the snowy cloth set with fine crystal and china. Courses were laid and removed; Alwyyd had done a remarkable job in the little time he'd had, and somehow a green pea soup was produced followed by a compote of pigeon, a haunch of lamb with mint sauce, fresh carrots, beans, and new potatoes, and a trifle to finish. But despite this tempting display, neither Julian nor Bryonny did much more than toy with the food in front of them. Bryonny looked up at the end of the meal and found Julian watching her intently, his eyes very dark but as usual, inscrutable. Her cheeks went hot and she felt as if she could not get enough air. Julian's close presence was suffocating her, and she could bear it no longer.

"Please excuse me," she whispered as she stood, not meeting his eye. "I think I'll go outside as it's such a beautiful evening."

Julian politely stood but said nothing, his eyes following after her as she left, the faintest of lines drawn between his brows.

The moon swam golden in the misty sky, throwing columns of soft light down among the trees wreathed in deep shadows. The grass was heavy with dew but Bryonny walked heedless of her wet slippers, unable to think. She was only aware of her burning senses and a sharp, overwhelming misery that gnawed at her heart. It had never occurred to her that love could be so painful, so physically overwhelming. It was almost more than she could bear at times to be in Julian's presence, yet she felt empty without him.

She had no idea how long she had been walking but finally she turned back toward the gardens. A tangle of roses climbed up an arbor, throwing off a heady perfume into the night. Bryonny was sharply reminded of the night in the Abbey garden when Julian had so casually detached a rose bud and tucked it behind her ear. She reached out a hand to pick a bloom from the vine, but as she pulled at its stem, a thorn pricked her finger. Her eyes swam with hot tears which had nothing to do with the drop of blood welling up and she sank down on the stone bench beneath the canopy of blossoms and leaned her head back against the strong, winding roots. Julian had talked of choices, but what choice had she? She couldn't possibly go to him and confess her feelings; he would think her a fool. But she couldn't go on like this, either. The tears spilled over and angrily she wiped them away.

And then her heart contracted painfully as a tall figure detached itself from the long black shadows.

"Bryonny?" Julian came toward her and reaching out his hand, he cupped her face gently. "Why the tears?"

"Julian—not now," she pleaded, jumping up and walking away from him, feeling completely defenseless.

He came up behind her and turned her to face him. "Can you not talk to me, tell me what is troubling you?"

"Oh, Julian, it's not that I cannot talk to you. It is what I would say that would turn you away from me and that I couldn't bear." Her words hung in the silence between them.

"Is it this, my love?" He gently pulled her closer and his arms went around her, fitting her body to his as he lowered his mouth onto hers.

"Oh, please, don't!" Bryonny twisted away from him in distress. "You—you don't understand!"

"I don't understand that I love you, that I want you and need you as much as you do me? You're wrong, Bryonny—I understand all too well and it's just about killing me. Let's have done with the games." His control was stripped away and his face was naked with his need.

Bryonny stared at him in disbelief. "You love me?" she asked shakily.

"My sweet fool, could you not tell? I've loved you for a very long time, loath as I was to admit it to myself. There's something that galls about having had one's heart and soul stolen by a snip of a girl who spouted on about independence and treated me with monumental disdain. But as I haven't had a decent night's sleep in months, I thought I'd better come clean before I went completely mad."

"I—I never guessed." Bryonny was stunned.

"And I didn't mean for you to. But as I said, I've had time to think while I was away, and the only thing I seemed to be able to think of was you. I knew I couldn't come home and live with the charade of being only your guardian. You're very much more than that to me, Bryonny." And he drew her into his arms again and this time Bryonny responded to his kiss with all the love and longing she'd been suppressing for so long.

Now it was Julian who pulled away, looking intently down at her in the moonlight. His voice was thick and strained as he spoke. "Bryonny, my dear love, will you marry me?"

Her eyes searched his face for a long moment. "Julian," she said softly, "do you know what you're asking?"

"Oh, yes, I know exactly what I'm asking."

There was no need to consider. She looked full into his eyes. "Then yes, Julian." Her voice was soft but clear. "Yes, if you want me, I'll marry you."

"Thank God! If you had said no, I would have behaved in an extremely dishonorable fashion!" And so saying, he scooped her up off her feet and carried her into the house, up the stairs and into her bedroom. He kicked the door closed and set her on her feet.

"Now, Bryonny—you and I have some unfinished business." He looked at her for a long moment and then reached around behind her and began to unfasten her dress.

She stood quite still as he slipped it down over her shoulders to her waist, his fingers tracing its path over her skin. It fell in a heap to the floor and he drew her to him in a long kiss, his lips burning hers with their heat. The hardness in his groin pressed against her sending waves of violent arousal through her and her legs felt as if they would no longer hold her. Then he slipped her shift down and it followed the same course as her dress. Julian drew in a long, shuddering breath and once again picked her up and gently lay her on the bed. His own clothes were thrown to the floor in no short time and Bryonny could see for herself the full evidence of his masculinity. She felt no embarrassment, rather an all-consuming desire, and reached out for him.

He came into her arms, his length stretched out against her, and he raised himself up and looked at her hard, examining her face for her reaction. Her eyes met his fully and what they held was unmistakable. He bent his dark head and pressed his fiery lips to hers, then to the soft hollow of her throat where her pulse wildly leaped as he slid his hand down to cup her breast. She shivered as his thumb found her nipple, stroking it in circles as his other arm encircled her hips. She drew him even closer as his mouth burned a trail down her neck to her swollen breast where he took the taut, upthrust nipple into his mouth, capturing the peak between his teeth, flicking it with his tongue. A sharp wave of pleasure stabbed through her and she moaned softly as his hand drew ever lower circles along her silken skin, across her flat abdomen, down the curve of her hip to her buttocks and up her thigh until it paused at the juncture. She was limp with desire, and a tide of intense sensation overcame her as his hand slipped between and caressed the silky folds, his fingers gently exploring. Her breath came in short gasps and liquid heat poured through her as her hips arched to meet his hand. Never had she felt such pure, piercing excitement and yet she ached for something more.

"Ah, God, Bryonny, my love." Julian's jaw was clenched with the effort of retaining control. Unable to wait any longer, he raised up, positioning himself between her parted legs and gently thrust, breaking the barrier that separated them and momentarily halting at Bryonny's sharp cry before driving deep into her.

Bryonny had stiffened at the brief, unexpected stab of pain, but as he began to slowly move within her, she was caught up in his rhythm and as he increased the pace of his strokes she began to spiral toward a desperate, achingly sweet unknown, meeting thrust for thrust as they became faster and more frenzied. The muscles of his back rippled under her fingers and their breath came in quick gasps. Her hips rose and stayed, pulling him into her very soul and she froze and then shuddered again and again, with small sharp cries. She thought she would die from the pleasure and then he surged up, grasping her buttocks, groaning in wave after wave of release, and bringing Bryonny with him as she crested once again in unbelievable ecstasy.

It was long minutes before their breathing quieted and Julian collapsed onto his side. "My God, Bryonny!" He reached down to draw her into a gentle kiss. "If I'd known that was waiting for me, I would never have stayed myself so long!"

"Oh, Julian—I had no idea! Nobody ever told me it was that wonderful—in fact, I'd gathered the opposite from the whispers I heard, although watching the horses, I always thought that both the stallion *and* the mare seemed quite happy."

Julian laughed. "I don't know about stallions, but that was a unique experience for me, my love." He kissed her neck. "But I'll tell you what. If you give me a few minutes, we'll see if it was just beginner's luck or a more permanent state of affairs."

Bryonny smiled dreamily, stroking the hair that curled at the back of his neck, and Julian pulled her close and kissed her nose, whispering, "Vixen," with laughing eyes. But as Bryonny rolled over and regarded him lazily, her hair falling around him, her silky breasts pressing against his chest, the laughter died away to be replaced by something more volatile. He pulled her down to him, capturing her mouth with his own, playing with her lips, gently biting, running his tongue along the sensitive inner skin. As he explored the sweet, wet heat of her mouth he could feel her trembling arousal.

This time their lovemaking was more leisurely as Julian tasted and explored every inch of Bryonny's body, his hands stroking, teasing, lingering until Bryonny begged for him to take her. He did, this time with smooth, powerful strokes and once again their blood raced as they spiraled upward in fiery arousal. Julian slipped his hands under Bryonny's hips, and lifting her, he turned in one movement until she was sitting astride him.

Her eyes widened for a moment and then she threw

her head back and laughed with sheer uninhibited pleasure. Her eyes closed as she moved on him, finding her own rhythm, and when she opened them again, it was to find Julian watching her. For once his eyes were most definitely not inscrutable, and what she saw there made her breath catch.

"Bryonny, my love," he whispered raggedly. "Bryonny. . . ."

She leaned down until she was pressed full against his chest, and kissed him. "I love you," she murmured against his lips. He groaned, and his arms, bands of steel around her back, flexed and rolled her over. He lifted her legs and thrust deep, deeper than she would ever have thought possible, and her muscles tensed under him, and again as she shuddered and cried out his name, convulsing against his searing manhood until he exploded with an animal cry of agonizing pleasure.

They collapsed into each other's arms, both too exhausted to move, but finally Julian, concerned for the burden his weight was on her, managed to raise himself up on his elbows. He could not bear to pull away from her and so he rolled to his side, raising her knee over his lean hip and pulling her full length against him. She opened her eyes and smiled in contentment. "For an unprincipled rake you do have a way about you, Julian Ramsay," she whispered.

"Delighted you think so," he murmured sleepily, his breathing deepening. Bryonny smiled to herself and then she, too, slept.

Streaks of vermilion and pink began to lighten the sky. Bryonny opened her eyes to find Julian leaning on his elbow gazing down at her. She reached up and stroked his face, and he bent down to kiss her. "Good morning, ma'am."

"Oh, it is that! I've never felt so wonderful!"

"Hmm . . . No maidenly modesty, I see. You seem to have been made for love, Bryonny—I suspect we're going to have a great many children."

"What a nice idea. I've heard this is how one goes about it, so let's start right now."

"This minute?" Julian laughed, flashing his strong white teeth. "You lusty wench! If I didn't know better, I'd swear you'd been at this for years! I can see you're going to keep me a busy man, and I can't say I object." He lowered his head and kissed her lightly, then deepened his kiss as he felt her responding beneath him. He stroked her neck, her breasts, trailing his fingers over her abdomen. Then his fingers dropped between her thighs, stroking in little circles until she gasped. They lingered there, continuing their slow circling until she opened under him and quickly Julian entered her in a smooth, strong thrust. Their eyes remained open and locked and Julian dropped kisses on her hair, her forehead, the corner of her mouth as he rocked above her and brought them both to a shaking climax.

Then he fell onto his back with a groan and Bryonny snuggled up against his side.

He brushed the hair out of her face with his long fingers, stroking her cheek. "Bryonny, my love," he said. "Never, ever have I experienced what I have with you. I suppose it's because I've never been in love before—and then you came along and shook me to my very foundation. Now, suddenly, I find myself pining for marriage and children. Ridiculous." He dropped a kiss on her mouth. "That reminds me."

He rose from the bed, completely unconcerned with his unclothed state. His long, lean body was beautifully proportioned and sleekly muscled. Bryonny ran her eyes over it as he strode across the room, and she smiled with pleasure at the sight. Retrieving his coat, he withdrew a small box from the pocket.

"I brought this in the hope that you would agree to marry me."

Bryonny sat up and opened the little box. Inside was a square-cut emerald ring flanked by two diamonds. "Oh, Julian, it's beautiful! It's absolutely beautiful!" He took it from her and slipped it on her finger, kissing the palm of her hand.

"I don't think its fire quite matches yours, my love," he said with a grin.

"But Julian—do you mean you *planned* to ask me to marry you?"

Julian burst into laughter. "Oh, did you think I only asked you in the heat of the moment?"

"I didn't know—it was so unexpected. I still can't quite believe that it happened at all!"

"Believe me, my love, it happened. You should know by now that I plan everything very carefully, no matter how unexpected it might seem. I just wanted to wait until the time was right, and truthfully, I could wait no longer. Do you have any idea how long I've wanted you?"

"No—that is, I knew you had something on your mind that night so long ago in the library, but I thought it was your habit to take what you found."

"It is most certainly not my habit to go about seducing virgins, Bryonny. I really should have waited until our wedding night, but I'm afraid I wouldn't have survived that long. I don't know what you've done to me, but I feel as if my loins have been on fire for a good time."

"I am mortally sorry, my lord. You must let me know if you should ever be afflicted with the condition again."

"I can guarantee it, my love."

"Oh, good," laughed Bryonny. "I think I could grow rather addicted to the sport! And I certainly wouldn't have traded the last few hours for the sake of propriety!" She reached up to kiss him.

"Oh, no, despite your disregard for propriety—and as your guardian I must say I'm shocked, Bryonny Livingston—I must be out of here before the servants are up and about. Whatever would Mrs. Merk say if she came in with your water and found me lounging stark naked in your bed?"

"Master Julian!" said Bryonny, pulling a disapproving face that looked remarkably like Mrs. Merk's. "This is most unfitting, and I warn you, if you're not out of that bed this minute, there shall be dire consequences!"

Julian applauded. "Exactly, my sweet. So you see,

to avoid dire consequences I shall be off to my room, rumple my bed until it looks as if I had nightmares the whole night, indent the pillow, throw my clothes on the floor, and look the picture of innocence. Mrs. Merk will never be the wiser. Brilliant, isn't it?"

"Absolutely inspired, my love. Oh, Julian, I've never been happier. Do you know, my only sorrow is that your father is not alive. I think our marriage would have made him very happy, don't you? If it hadn't been for that miserable accident he would at least have lived long enough to see us wed. It's such a shame."

"Let us not talk of that, Bryonny. There are some things better left alone."

"But why, Julian? I loved him. I don't want to forget him."

"He loved you, too, perhaps too much for his own good."

"Whatever do you mean? We were very fond of each other, but it certainly did him no harm." Bryonny looked at him in puzzlement.

"You did him no harm, it's true. But that doesn't change the fact that his death was no accident, Bryonny. No, leave it. I should have said nothing."

"But Julian! You can't say such a thing and then just change the subject without explaining!"

"Hush now; look, the sun is up. 'O, now be gone; more light and light it grows.' Words to the wise."

" 'Then, window, let day in, and let life out,' " said Bryonny with a smile, watching him pull on his trousers.

He looked up sharply and his eyes were dark and troubled.

"Julian? What is it?"

"Nothing, Bryonny." He paused as if he were going to say something else, but then thought better of it. "And as that poor Romeo finished, 'One kiss and I'll descend.' " He crossed over and did just that, in something of a regretful fashion, then gathered the rest of his clothes and slipped quietly out.

Bryonny looked after him for a moment, a smile on her lips, then gave a little shiver of pure happiness, and shook her head in sheer amazement. Julian had asked her to marry him. It was incredible, really. And her Uncle Richard *would* have been happy, she knew that with absolute certainty. Her brow creased as she pondered Julian's strange words, but then dismissed them from her mind, knowing he would explain only when he was ready.

A half hour later, Julian tapped at Bryonny's door, and she opened it to him, still wearing her robe.

"Good morning, ma'am. You must have had a restless night. It's not like you to be still abed at this hour."

"I couldn't sleep for thinking of the man I'm to marry, my lord. I'm so pleased that you gave your blessing to the union."

"What else could I do? You forced my hand. He's a scoundrel to be sure, but how could I deny you your heart's desire? Just remember, I warned you. I only hope you won't live to regret it."

"Never!" said Bryonny warmly.

"Hmm," said Julian, leaning toward her.

Bryonny caught a movement in the hallway close behind them. "Careful," she whispered. "Mrs. Merk is on the prowl."

Julian retreated a step. "I wanted to tell you that I'm going down for my breakfast and then I'm off to Alwyyd's house to have a look at the books. Why don't you join me there as soon as you've eaten. Take your time, there's no rush. We have quite a few preliminaries to go over."

"That sounds fine, thank you, Julian. I appreciate your attention to detail."

Julian's smile widened at her words. "My pleasure, my dear. Indeed, I find attending to your details most interesting." He turned and said with feigned surprise, "Mrs. Merk!"

"Good morning, my lord," she said with a scowl. "Your breakfast is awaiting you, my lord. My lady, your hot water. I'll see that your breakfast is laid out directly."

"Thank you, Mrs. Merk," said Julian politely, echoed

by Bryonny, who threw a highly amused look at Julian, and then followed into her bedroom after the woman, wondering if she had divined things already. Surreptitiously, she slipped the ring off her finger and put it in the bedside drawer. Mrs. Merk would hear when the time was right.

Lucy arrived to help Bryonny into her clothes and then, when Bryonny had gone downstairs, began to make the bed. Her eyes widened when she pulled the covers back, and she sat down in rapturous surprise. Her dreams had come true. His lordship had bedded her mistress; love had triumphed as she knew it would. Quickly, Lucy bundled the sheets up and made the bed with fresh linens. These sheets she would wash herself, for she did not think that Mrs. Merk—or anyone else for that matter—should be enlightened as to these goings on.

Mrs. Merk had put out porridge for Bryonny, which usually she ate with great enthusiasm, but this morning she found she couldn't eat a thing. Lovesick, she thought with an internal laugh. Her attention was distracted by the barn cat who had busied himself rubbing against the side of her chair, purring loudly.

"Why, Thomas! How on earth did you get in here? Up to your usual tricks, are you?" She gave the enormous white tom cat a good scratch behind his ears, and he closed his eyes in ecstasy while his purr escalated to the level of a roar. Bryonny grinned. She had developed a fondness for Thomas, who enjoyed flaunting the conventions as much as she did, and had absolutely no regard for his proper station in life. He opened his eyes and looked up at the table expectantly.

"Here you are, then, you great silly thing," said Bryonny, putting her bowl of porridge on the floor. "Although you certainly don't look as if you need it. If anything, you're fatter since the last time we met. But I can appreciate that a steady diet of mouse might pale after a time, and you can save me a scold from the dragon in the kitchen."

Thomas leaped into the bowl head-first and gave Bryonny not another thought, and she laughed and leaned back in her chair. It was then that she noticed a note that Julian had propped on her cup, and with a little rush of pleasure she unfolded it.

My dearest love,
   Thank you for your gift of last night. I shall carry its memory through the rest of my life. Do your remember our discussion on the cliffs yesterday, concerning destiny? I do believe that we were fated from the very beginning, our threads tied irrevocably together. But as you've seen, fate or no, in the end everything comes down to choice, and so I concede myself the point. I told you yesterday that I am a man of no conscience, but that's not entirely true. I think I have found my conscience in you. Whether I can live with it is another question, but it appears it must be my burden to bear from here on in. You have given me great happiness, Bryonny. I can only hope in this moment that I have made you happy as well. I do love you, you know.
   Now eat up your porridge like a good girl and join me at the bailiff's house.

                                                        J.

Bryonny refolded the note and tucked it into her pocket with a wide smile. Julian. How was it she hadn't guessed at his feelings before? She had often thought him to be fond of her, yes, but the only real emotion he had ever exhibited toward her had been anger. Until last night. And if there was one thing he knew how to do, she thought with a little chuckle, it was to surprise her. She sipped her tea, lost in her thoughts, and a good half-hour had gone by when a strange noise distracted her and she looked down.

Thomas had fallen to his side and lay there twitching, blood and saliva oozing from the corner of his mouth. In alarm, Bryonny dropped to her knees, wondering whether he was choking, but he was breathing, very rapid shallow pants. The cat's legs shot out stiffly in one final convulsion, and then, with a long sigh, his body went quite still.

Bryonny's hand went to her mouth as she stared at the animal. Then slowly she bent down and picked him up, but he lay limp in her hands, his chest unmoving. Thomas was dead.

She sat there for a long tome, but looked up as Mrs. Merk came into the room with another pot of tea.

"My lady, I beg your pardon as his lordship said you weren't to be disturbed, but I thought you—*what* are you doing with that dirty old animal!"

Bryonny spoke very softly. "Tell me, Mrs. Merk, were the porridge and the milk you laid out fresh?"

"Fresh, my lady?" said Mrs. Merk in confusion, her eyes fixed on the cat as she put the teapot down with a rattle.

"Yes. I—I'm afraid the cat collapsed after eating from my bowl."

Two spots of color appeared in Mrs. Merk's cheeks. "No—how terrible! But yes, my lady! Everything was fresh this morning. I would never serve you old porridge, or soured milk for that matter! As it happens, Master Julian made that porridge for you himself."

"J—Julian! *He* made the porridge? Are you quite sure?" Bryonny's blood washed cold with shock.

"Why yes, my lady, and very odd, I thought it. I've never known him to do such a thing, but he said it was the only thing he knew how to make, and that you needed your strength and he was going to see to it personally. He wouldn't even let me taste it; he said I'd make a sour face just for the pleasure of it. Well! Not that I wouldn't be surprised if Master Julian's cooking would poison anyone, but I should think the poor cat had sickened of something."

"Yes, I expect you're right," said Bryonny, feeling as if she had just had the wind knocked out of her.

"You ought not have been feeding your breakfast to the cat, my lady. If it was inedible, I would have made you some more. Shall I bring you another bowl? I'll make it fresh myself if you like."

"No, thank you, I—I'm not hungry. Tell me, how long ago did his lordship leave?"

"Well, let's see now. He had a quick bite of breakfast, then made your porridge. He left shortly before you came down, a few minutes I would say. In fact, he seemed to be in a bit of a hurry."

"I see. Thank you, Mrs. Merk. Please, will you see that the cat is buried . . ." Bryonny rose and handed the woman the little body. No hint of the turmoil she was feeling showed on her face. She picked up her cloak and went out into the cool morning air. The bright sunshine dazzled her eyes, but she was unaware of the fine morning.

She turned toward the north path that led to Mr. Alwyyd's cottage, but after a few steps she faltered and stopped. She could not make herself go on, no matter how hard she tried to rationalize her fear. Pulling her cloak around her, she headed toward the cliffs, her body held stiffly as if she were very cold, her face drained of color. Her mind was reeling, entertaining thoughts that were an impossibility, but she could not push them away.

Reaching the pathway that gave onto the rock, she took herself to the edge of the cliff and there she stood, looking down over the turbulent ocean which crashed relentlessly against the sheer gray face, sending up great lashes of spray and foam, pounding, again and again, the incessant noise matching the pounding in her head. She pressed her shaking hands against her temples as if to ward off the words that screamed at her . . . too many attempts on your life . . . Master Julian made the porridge . . . white bryony, the berries a deadly poison . . .

"No! No—it can't be true! Not Julian!" Her anguished words were picked up by the wind and carried away, blending in with the screaming of the gulls. Bryonny dropped to the ground, her fingers digging into the rock as she fought against the violent sobs that threatened to choke her.

'Eat up your porridge like a good girl . . .' Dear God. Not just one isolated incident which could be pushed away, but a series of events, and in each one, Julian. The evidence was too strong to deny. It *had* to be Julian. There was no one else.

Finally she forced herself to straighten up, her body still shaken by great shuddering gasps, and shakily she got to her feet. She had been blinded to the truth by her feelings, had allowed Julian to manipulate her. He wanted her dead, for whatever reason, and her life was still in danger. There would be time for tears later, but for now she had to get away. Her decision made, there was no time to lose. She headed back to the house, but her footsteps slowed as she reached the rise of the hill, then stopped. She stood there for a long moment, a small, solitary figure silhouetted against the vast sky, feeling in that moment as if all happiness, all life, were draining out of her, to be forever left behind. She forced herself on.

Chapter Twelve

PHILIP opened the door in shirt and trousers. "Bryonny! What on earth? My God—what's happened?" He pulled her inside and gestured Lucy in behind her.

"I'll explain it all to you, Philip. Do you think I could have something to eat and drink, and Lucy, too? We've been traveling since early morning." Bryonny was exhausted, dark circles ringing her eyes.

"Of course; I'll just call my man. Come, sit down. Lucy, why don't you go back to the kitchen and rest yourself?"

"I'm sorry to arrive at such a late hour, Philip, but I didn't know what else to do!"

"I'm glad you came to me, Bryonny. Why don't you tell me what's brought you to London like this?" He sat her down and looked at her calmly, waiting until she was ready to speak.

"Oh, Philip, you were right about everything. I've been such a fool." She leaned her forehead on the heel of her hand, feeling utterly numb.

Philip frowned. "Why don't you start at the beginning? Something's obviously happened to badly upset you. Is it Julian?"

Bryonny raised her eyes to his. "It seems completely impossible, Philip, but I've been over and over it, and no matter now painful it is, I just can't see any other explanation! There are so many things, now that I look back on it—things he did and said that perplexed me—but now I can see . . . And then this morning! I'm so frightened, and I didn't think I had any choice but to run away!"

"What happened this morning, Bryonny?" prompted Philip quietly.

"We were down at Shelbourne. Julian made porridge for me. Mrs. Merk said he'd never done such a thing. Then he—he left to see the bailiff. I had no appetite, so I gave my porridge to the cat. It died, right there in front of me when it had been perfectly healthy only half an hour before!"

Philip slowly stood. "And you believe Julian poisoned the stuff?"

"Yesterday he picked some white bryony—he knew the berries were poisonous, he told me so. And before that, he talked about some people being easily capable of—of premeditated murder, for personal gain. He said it was easy to understand, and that he was perfectly capable of—oh, never mind. We were just having a philosophic discussion and I thought nothing of it then, it was just Julian being—well, you know. He's always saying things like that. He wrote me a note this morning, and it was the same thing, about living with the burden of his conscience . . ." Tears welled up in her eyes and angrily she brushed them away.

"May I see it?"

"No—I'd rather . . . It wasn't important, other than that. And after last night, I can't believe he'd do such a thing but I can't think of any other explanation!"

"What happened last night?"

She drew a jagged breath, then forced herself to continue. "He . . . he asked me to marry him."

"What!" Philip made a visible effort to control himself. "And did you turn him down? Is that why he attempted to poison you?"

"No. I accepted." Bryonny looked away.

"I—see. Yes, of course you would. Suppose, then, you explain to me why he would bother to ask you to marry him one night and the next morning try to kill you. Where's the gain?"

Bryonny blushed furiously. "We spent the night together."

"So . . . I might have guessed. No, don't look so mortified, Bryonny. It only makes sense. You know Julian's reputation as well as I, I daresay, and it should have come as no surprise. If he thought he had to propose in order to bed you, why not? Why not take what he so obviously desired if he planned on killing you the next morning anyway?"

"But—but it wasn't like that!" Bryonny burst out. "Nobody could pretend to . . ."

"My dear girl, I don't mean to be indelicate, but what do you know of such matters? It's an easy thing to make a woman, most especially an inexperienced one, believe she is passionately loved. And Julian is an old hand at it."

Bryonny bit her lip and said nothing.

"You've obviously given some credence to my story or you wouldn't be here," said Philip gently, sitting next to her and taking her hands. "But would it help to go through it one more time?"

"I've done nothing but go through it, Philip! Everything can be seen in two lights: the carriage accident, the first time I met Julian . . ."

"What happened then?"

"He nearly ran me over with his phaeton."

Philip looked at her in surprise. "I didn't know about that."

"I never thought it worth mentioning. It was my fault as well."

"This is not the time to be defending Julian, Bryonny. Don't forget the gunshot in the woods—in light of everything else, it seems hardly a coincidence."

"Yes, I know—I only just remembered overhearing Mrs. Merk's saying something about mistaking Julian's carriage outside the gates that day and it was only two days later that Julian actually arrived. It's possible—it's just possible. Then the next time I saw him, I had the accident in the lake. But then there was the time we had together at the Abbey until now, and everything was wonderful—oh, there were a few terrible arguments, of course, and once when I was truly frightened, but it came to nothing."

Philip shook his head. "It's too much to be coincidence, Bryonny, and I know that you see it, as little as you may want to. So . . . Perhaps he, too, saw that you were becoming attached to him and decided to wash his hands of you. Why not remove you to Shelbourne, conveniently remote, where he personally made you porridge—an unprecedented act—after obtaining some poisonous berries. Can there by any question left in your mind, Bryonny?"

"No, but somehow I still can't believe in my heart that Julian . . ."

"The words of a woman deeply in love. I'm afraid history is littered with them, Bryonny. Can you forget Lord Hambledon's sudden death following a violent argument with his son, the son who supposedly loved him?"

"No," she whispered. "That's something else. Julian said this morning that it hadn't been an accident."

"*Did* he? You surprise me! I wouldn't have thought he'd admit to such a thing!"

"He didn't, exactly. He only said that, and would say no more. Oh, Philip . . ." Her voice broke.

"It's all right now, Bryonny. You did the right thing in coming here, and I'm very gratified that you did, indeed."

"I almost didn't; I didn't want to burden you with my problems. But there was no one else—Julian's friend Andrew would never have believed my story and probably would have turned me back to Julian. And then there was the promise I made you . . ." The words trailed off.

"You poor thing, what a terrible time you've had." Philip's expression hardened. "Damn the swine, I can see how easy it was for him to seduce you with his charm. He'll clearly stop at nothing to get hold of your money. He's a cold-blooded murderer, Bryonny, and I'm going to see to it that he never gets near you again!"

"But how, Philip?" Bryonny looked hopeless.

"You're going to marry me. I still have the license and we'll be married first thing tomorrow morning. I think it's the only way. Julian's bound to follow you. I can't imagine he'd just sit back and wait once he realized that his little murder attempt failed and you've caught on to his game. Now he has more reason than ever to kill you!"

"Philip, I know you're right, but you don't understand. I *can't* marry you. You know I don't love you— I've given myself to another man—it wouldn't be fair to you. You deserve somebody much better, and you deserve happiness. I can't give it to you!"

"But you can, Bryonny. It's more than I ever expected. As for marriage, I told you the other day that I certainly don't expect you to open your bed to me. It couldn't matter less that you're not a virgin. The only thing that's important to me is that you're kept away from Julian. And once we're married, he's lost any chance to get his hands on your fortune. He has to hand it over to me by law."

"Yes, I suppose you're right." Bryonny leaned back in the chair and closed her eyes, holding back the tears that burned at them. It no longer mattered, nothing really mattered, and if Philip wanted to be noble and fancied himself in love with her, then so be it.

"Yes, then Philip, I'll marry you. I think you're mad to sacrifice yourself like this, especially after I've been so stupid. But I can't see that I have any other choice, and I appreciate your offer. I suppose we should consider it a marriage of convenience, like so many others. I assure you, I will not stand in your way. You must feel quite free to go about your own business."

"Good girl. It won't be so bad, I promise. I'll sell out my commission; I've been meaning to anyway, and this gives me the perfect reason. But for tonight, I think it's best if you and Lucy stay at an inn. We don't want Julian catching up with you before we're married. He's bound to come here in the end, you know. Whom else would you run to? Ah, good, here's some supper for you. Eat up—you look as if you haven't eaten in days!"

"I suppose I haven't, really, Philip, thank you. You're

a good, dear friend. I'm so terribly sorry to have dragged you into this."

"I'm not, Bryonny. I am a very gratified man, believe me."

"Oh, Philip. I appreciate your devotion, I really do. And I'll do my best not to make you unhappy."

When Bryonny had managed to eat a little of her supper, she requested a private interview with Lucy. "Lucy, I'm going to marry Captain Neville tomorrow morning. You are quite free to go, but will you stay on with me?"

Lucy was stunned. "But my lady! You can't do that—it's Lord Hambledon that you love, I know that. Why would you want to marry Captain Neville?"

"I can't explain, Lucy. Something very bad happened between Lord Hambledon and myself. Captain Neville is being very kind and helping me out of a scrape. Besides I'm very fond of him."

"Oh, but my lady! You don't have to worry about last night. I know his lordship's going to come after you and ask you to marry him, and your virtue will be restored! So you see, you don't have to marry the captain after all!"

It was Bryonny's turn to be shocked. "How did you know about last night, Lucy!"

Lucy colored. "The sheets, my lady."

"Oh," said Bryonny, blushing herself. "I see. I hadn't thought of that."

"It's all right, my lady. I think it was a wonderful thing. You've been pining for each other for the longest time."

"Lucy, you're incorrigible, and I hate to shatter your hopes, but I'm afraid you have it all in a jumble. I don't want to see Lord Hambledon ever again. Will you stay with me? I think I'm going to need a friend. I know I'm taking you away from your family, and your friends at the Abbey. Would you mind that so terribly?"

"No, and of course I shall stay with you, my lady, but I think you're doing the wrong thing. I won't say any more about it, but I just wanted to say my piece, begging your pardon, my lady."

"Of course, Lucy. I appreciate your devotion."

Three days later, Lucy opened the door to a furious knocking and blanched when she saw Julian standing there, fury blazing in his eyes.

"Well, Lucy, where is she?"

Lucy turned and ran. A minute later, Philip appeared. "What the hell do you think you're doing here, Hambledon?"

"I came to speak with my ward, Neville," he said in icy tones.

"Then it's a pity that it's a wasted trip. She doesn't want to see you now or ever, Hambledon, and there's absolutely nothing you can do about it. You have no more authority over her now that she's married me."

"Married . . . She *married* you! That's impossible! Where's the proof?"

"You doubt it, Hambledon?" said Philip, drawing the paper from his wallet and handing it over. "A copy, of course, but perfectly legal as you can see. Please, keep it. Consider it a sentimental reminder."

Julian, reeling with shock, scrutinized the paper, then looked up with narrowed eyes. "I suppose you think you're very clever, Neville. I smell a rat, and we both know where the foul odor is coming from. I have no proof yet, but when I do, be warned."

"Idle threats, Hambledon. There is nothing you can do. I would appreciate it if you would have Bryonny's affairs immediately transferred to my man of business." He retrieved a card from his pocket and casually offered it to Julian. "His address."

"I don't believe Bryonny entered this marriage of her own free will, Neville. I don't know what you did or said to coerce her, but I will find out."

"Oh, I think you're just put out that she ran from your bed into mine, Hambledon. Oh, yes, she told me everything. Just remember that it's my bed she's warming now and give up gracefully."

Julian's face had gone white with rage. It took every ounce of self-control not to level Philip then and there.

"You bastard, Neville—you conniving, murderous bastard!"

Philip took a step toward him, his eyes glittering. "I should call you out for that . . ."

"I wish you'd be that foolish, Neville. It would be my pleasure to kill you and I'd welcome the excuse. I know exactly what you're up to and I won't believe for a minute that you didn't entrap Bryonny until I hear that she married you gladly from her own lips."

"It's quite true, Julian." They both turned to see Bryonny standing at the top of the stairs. She was very pale but calm, and descended the steps to stand next to Philip. "I married Philip of my own free will. He did nothing to coerce me. It's what I wanted. My choice, Julian."

"Bryonny . . ." His hand went out toward her and then dropped to his side as she took a step back. "Bryonny, I don't understand . . ." Julian's face registered his shock. "*Why?* After everything—"

She cut him off abruptly, trying to still the trembling that racked her body. "I don't care to explain any further, Julian. I believe you know exactly why. Philip is my husband now, and our relationship, legal and otherwise, is at an end. I think it's best if you leave now, and don't return."

Julian hesitated for a long moment, his eyes raking Bryonny's face, and she looked away, unable to bear the scrutiny.

"I see," he finally said, his voice as cold as steel. "As you will have it, ma'am." He turned on his heel and walked to the door. He turned back for one moment. "I'll be watching you, Neville." His eyes were black as coal. The door shut quietly behind him.

Julian went straight to Andrew's office where he found him in the middle of a chaotic mound of papers.

Andrew looked up distractedly. "Julian! What are you—good God, man, what's wrong!"

"It's Bryonny. She's gone and married Neville." He sank into a chair.

"No! That captain you told me about? It's not possible!"

"I'm afraid so. God, Andrew, what a disaster." Julian put his head in his hands.

"What happened! How could you have let her do such a thing!"

"I had nothing to do with it, believe me! I asked the girl to marry me at Shelbourne and she accepted. Things couldn't have been better between us. The next thing I knew she was gone—no note, no explanation. I've been chasing her all over the blasted country. She wasn't at the Abbey, and then it occurred to me that perhaps she'd gone to London to see Neville for some idiotic reason. And now I hear that she and Neville were married three days ago. *Married,* for God's sake! She says it's what she wants, but she won't explain, she won't even talk to me!"

"Julian, I'm sorry. This makes no sense!"

"I know—I *know!* Of course, it makes perfect sense from Neville's point of view. I've suspected for a long time that the bastard was after Bryonny's money. I even suspect that he was responsible for my father's death."

"What!" exclaimed Andrew. "What are you saying?"

"Neville was having an interview with him the day Father died, and I interrupted." Julian filled Andrew in on the little he had heard. "I know it sounds far-fetched, but I think Father must have had something on him and Neville killed him to keep him quiet."

Andrew looked at his friend somewhat skeptically but said nothing.

"I can't explain it to you any better than that, but with all the other things . . ."

"What other things, exactly?"

"Somebody took a potshot at Bryonny a few months ago. It was put down to a poacher. Then the day my father died she took a little dip in the lake and nearly drowned. She claims someone pushed her. Neville was there both times, *and* when her father's carriage went off the road, come to think of it—but it doesn't make sense. It would get him nowhere to kill Bryonny if he was after the money, which obviously he was. And Bryonny doesn't love him, I'm sure of it, yet she married him. *Why?* What could he have told her and why will she not see me? She owes me at very least an explanation!"

"I don't know, Julian. Bryonny seemed to me to be too smart to be taken in. I'm as baffled as you are. Perhaps he has some hold over her?"

"No. No . . . Bryonny herself—what she said in the entrance hall . . ." Julian's voice trailed off.

"I'll keep my ear to the ground and see what I can find out. I'll do anything I can to help, you know that. Why don't I start with some research on Neville?"

"You can try, but I might as well warn you, I looked into Neville's background before this. There was nothing I could find on him. Orphaned young, brought up by a respectable family, good schools, and straight into the army. That's it. *Damn* this whole blasted thing! It's the very thing I was trying to avoid, aside from falling in love with Bryonny myself, which I also hadn't counted on. The maddening thing is that I don't see any solution to the situation. The marriage is legal." He flung the certificate on the desk. "The only way out is for Bryonny to come to me and ask to have the thing annulled. Typical! I might have known she'd manage to create some kind of catastrophe. I should have trusted my original instincts; the girl's never done anything but turn my life upside down. I'm probably well rid of her!"

"Don't worry, Julian. Somehow we'll get it sorted out."

Julian merely shook his head, then turned away.

Upon hearing the news, Mrs. Merk packed up her trunk, said her good-byes to the shocked staff, who could not quite absorb what had happened, and ordered a carriage to take her to London and straight to Captain Neville's door to offer herself as housekeeper. She felt more than responsible for the dreadful situation and was not about to shirk her duty. She would see to it that the post was hers. In her reticule she carefully slipped the bottle of laudanum that Dr. Walters had left with the old marquess during his illness. That should take care of everything. Without a backward look, she passed permanently over the Ramsay threshold after twenty-five years of service.

January rolled around and the snow began to fall, lying thick and crisp upon the ground. Bryonny had been tired and listless since her marriage, a condition she had put down to her unhappiness, but severe enough to keep her mostly confined to her bed, sleeping the days away as if in a drugged stupor. And now she finally knew the cause and had been trying to think of a way to tell Philip.

But before she found the courage to summon him to her bedroom, Philip knocked on her door late one afternoon. "Bryonny? May I come in?"

"Of course, Philip. The door is open." She pushed herself up in bed.

"How are you feeling? Better, I hope, although from looking at you I doubt it. You're as pale as ever. Bryonny, I do wish you'd let me send for the doctor—it's only stubbornness on your part that you won't let yourself be bled. Mrs. Merk's possets aren't doing you any good—for all I know they may be harming you; God only knows what's in them. Lizard's tails, I shouldn't be surprised; that woman is as close to a witch as I've ever come across, and I'm convinced she cast a spell over me to make me mad enough to take her on as housekeeper." Philip sat down on the edge of the bed and took her hand.

"It's nothing to do with Mrs. Merk, Philip, and she's only trying to be helpful. It would break her heart if I sent her possets away, and I'm sure they're harmless. But there's no need for a doctor in any case. Philip, there is something I must speak to you about." Bryonny looked at him anxiously.

"It will have to wait for a moment. I've come to tell you something very important. I don't want to upset you, especially when you're not well, but you must know."

"What, Philip? What is it?"

"It's Julian. He's meddled with your inheritance again and this time, there's nothing I can do."

She breathed again and looked away. "Oh. What has he done now?"

"He's found a clause in your father's will that states if he disapproves of your marriage, he can tie everything up until you're twenty-five. The worst part is, and this is what has me so worried, the worst part is that if you die, all still goes to your next of kin—him! We're back in the same position. There's no reason that he shouldn't try to kill you again!"

Bryonny covered her face with shaking hands. "I can't believe it," she whispered. "The nightmare begins again. Oh, Philip, there must be something we can do!"

"The only exception to the clause is if you produce an heir. Then it's all turned over immediately, and he's out of it. But that's a hopeless situation for us."

"No, Philip," said Bryonny quickly, looking excited. "No, it isn't at all!"

"What do you mean? Are you suggesting that we— you want to . . ." Philip looked completely taken aback.

"No, I'm not suggesting that at all. Philip, listen. It's what I wanted to talk to you about. I've been trying to find a way to tell you this, but now it's the perfect solution!"

"Well, what is it, Bryonny?" said Philip impatiently, looking puzzled.

"I *am* going to have a child!"

"What . . . ?" he asked in confusion. "But how?"

"It's Julian's child, don't you see, Philip? It's due in April but we'll tell everyone May and Julian will never be the wiser. What can he do?"

"My God, Bryonny," whispered Philip. "I don't believe it."

"Oh, Philip, I'm so sorry. I hope you don't mind too much—"

"Mind! Bryonny, I'm elated! This is perfect, I never dreamed of such a thing. Don't you see? It's the ultimate revenge. Julian's own child stealing the fortune he lusts for right out from under his very nose. It's too good to be true!"

"Yes," said Bryonny slowly, "I can see that, but neither he nor the child can ever know the truth, Philip. You must promise me that."

"It's enough that you and I know, Bryonny. Is this what you wanted to talk to me about, the reason you've been so ill?"

"Yes. I haven't known for very long myself; it was sheer stupidity on my part."

"Never mind all that. We must see that you get healthy and fit. I have an idea. Why don't we go to Shelbourne? The country air will do you good and you've always loved it there."

"Yes, but now it holds such terrible memories for me, Philip."

"Nonsense. It will be the place your child will be born. What could be happier than that?"

"I don't know, Philip. I'm just not sure I want to go back."

"I understand your feelings, but you must think of the child. I want you as far away from Julian as possible in case he gets any ideas in his head before it's born."

"I hadn't thought of that!" gasped Bryonny. "Oh, but Julian wouldn't—he couldn't—"

"I couldn't what, Bryonny?" The bedroom door had flown open and Julian stood framed in it. He had pushed past Mrs. Merk, with one quick look of surprise to see her there, but had immediately dismissed her and taken the stairs two at a time.

"What the hell do you think you're doing!" Philip leapt up from the bed and started toward him.

"I couldn't what, Bryonny? What amazing stories has Neville been weaving for you now?"

Bryonny had gone completely white, but she spoke evenly and quietly. "Leave him alone, Philip." She turned to face Julian, her small fists clenched in her lap, the knuckles bloodless. "He has been weaving me no stories but the truth, Julian. He's just told me of your latest attempt to keep my inheritance from me."

"Bryonny, I've come to explain about that. I must talk to you, but privately. Please, it's important." His eyes bore into hers.

"Anything you have to say to me you can say in front of my husband, Julian."

"Bryonny, be reasonable!"

"I insist." She stared down at her hands.

"All right, then. I can see I have no choice in the matter." He shot Philip a look of contempt, then took a deep breath. "Bryonny, I haven't tried to meddle with your inheritance, but did what I have because I want to see you protected, I swear it! I don't know what drove you from Shelbourne that day, but I love you, you must believe that! I can't begin to imagine what Philip has said to take you in, but it's not true, any of it."

"That's enough!" shouted Philip. "I will not have you filling my wife's head with any more of your filthy seductions and lies and upsetting her. You might as well know, Hambledon, that all of your plotting has failed. Bryonny was just telling me the good news when you interrupted. We're expecting a child in May."

Julian froze, the color draining from his face. He looked at Bryonny for confirmation. "Is it true?" His voice was no more than a whisper.

"Yes, Julian, it's true." She cringed inwardly at the lie and the devastated expression on his face.

"I see. Are you happy, Bryonny?" He spoke the words painfully.

"Yes, I'm very happy. I love my husband and I'm looking forward to having our child."

"Then there's nothing more to say. I wish you well, Bryonny." He looked at her one last time and left the room.

"My God, Julian," said Andrew. "Do you suppose it's true? Couldn't it be a ruse to keep you from invoking the clause we found?"

"She looked as sick as a dog, and anyway, I can't imagine Bryonny would lie about a thing like that. Damn!" Julian ran a hand through his hair. "I hadn't counted on this. What the devil is going on! I can't believe Bryonny would sleep with that monster!"

"He is her husband after all, Julian. It's within his rights, you know. Of course, we still don't know why she married him in the first place."

"You know, for one incredible moment I thought it might be mine, but it's impossible, with the dates. Had it been April, it would have been another matter."

"Dear God!" Andrew looked shocked. "Are you telling me that you and Bryonny . . ."

"Yes. Yes, and don't look so scandalized. It was certainly of her own free will, believe me, and I had proposed, you know. I thought at first that was why she'd run away—sudden remorse and all that nonsense— although it seemed completely out of character. But it doesn't matter anymore, Andrew," he said bitterly. "She's having his child. Isn't that proof enough that I mean nothing to her? Damn her, anyway! She swore she loved me, then ran off with Neville. You should have seen the two of them cozied up on the bed together. Why should I care any longer? She lied to me. It's finished."

Andrew was wise enough to keep silent.

That night Julian went to St. James's Square. The butler showed him in immediately.

"Lord Hambledon!" Marie hurried forward, her eyes glowing with delight. "Let me take your hat and cloak. I shall fetch madame immediately."

"Thank you, Mademoiselle Dupris." He paced the salon abstractly, his face void of emotion, his heart as cold as stone.

Cynthia received the news that Julian was downstairs with tremendous relief. Despite the fact that Bryonny had married Philip exactly according to plan, she had been devastated by the fact that she had not heard a word from Julian since then. She hadn't been able to fathom what had gone wrong and had spent the last four months in a terrible state of anxiety, but there was absolutely nothing she could do about it. And now, now Julian was back and she determined that this time he would not get away. She took great care in her dress, thinking hard the entire time, and by the time she went downstairs, she had decided exactly what she would do.

"Julian! What a wonderful surprise! I thought you'd forgotten all about me." Cynthia knew she looked dazzling, powdered and lightly perfumed. He stepped up to kiss her hand.

"I'm sorry I've been so remiss in my attentions, my dear. I've been extremely distracted; I hope you haven't taken offense. I'm in town for a short while. Would you like to go to the theater, the opera perhaps?"

"Oh, I would like that, Julian! You have been upsetting, staying away for so long, but I forgive you. I've missed you."

She welcomed him back to her bed, quite sure that he would not leave it again.

Mrs. Merk sat in her room in a state of shock. The one thing she had tried so hard to prevent had happened. She could scarcely believe it! But she had heard it shouted from Philip's own lips after Master Julian had practically run her down and stormed into Lady Bryonny's room. She wished she had heard more. How could she have missed the signs? The laudanum had been working so well . . . Too well, perhaps, for it had disguised the symptoms of pregnancy to her. When could it have happened? She was sure she had kept Bryonny too well drugged for that sort of thing to go on. No, it must have occurred in the few days before she had arrived. There was no other explanation. But then the baby should have been due a month earlier. She couldn't work it out.

"Lucy! Lucy, come here, please. I must talk to you."

Lucy came running down the hallway. "Yes, mum. I've just been out on errands for the mistress."

"Never mind that. How long have you known about the child, Lucy?"

"Oh, did Lady Bryonny tell you then?" said Lucy in surprise.

"Not exactly. Answer my question."

"Not even a week, mum. She asked me to keep it a secret until she told the captain."

"Yes, well she's told him now, and Lord Hambledon, too."

"Lord Hambledon was here, mum?" Lucy's eyes opened wide.

"He was, and kicking up quite a fuss. What I want to know, Lucy, and thought you might be able to tell me, is whether the master and mistress have been, well—together. I don't meant to be indelicate," she added at Lucy's crimson blush, "but with the mistress being so ill, I wondered. I was surprised to hear of the child."

"Oh, yes, mum. They have, you know. Not often-like, but once or twice." Lucy blushed again at her lie, but as she'd promised her mistress, the secret of her child's true father was safe with her.

"I see. Thank you, Lucy, that will be all." Mrs. Merk went back into her room and closed the door behind her. So. It was true then. Dear Lord, what was she going to do now?

Mrs. Merk sighed heavily, and shook her head. "Oh, Philip. You've gotten yourself into a terrible predicament and I don't know what I'm going to do."

Chapter Thirteen

PHILIP took Bryonny down to Shelbourne the next day, traveling in simple stages. She said very little during the journey, her mind far away on earlier days when she had traveled this route. It had been autumn then, rich with color. Now it was bleak, bleak and bare. Winter had stripped the countryside, leaving it in the unrelenting grip of frost and snow. The carriage slipped on the icy road, throwing the occupants from side to side. Drifts of snow had piled up in the ditches and the trees passed as skeletons against the pale sky. Bryonny sat under a blanket, her cheek pressed against the cold glass.

Julian's visit had upset her badly, far more than she was willing to admit. It had been agony seeing him standing there, knowing what he had tried to do, was still trying to do, while she carried his child within her—and yet remembering how much she had loved him, how well she'd thought she'd known all of his expressions, and how he had deceived her even in that. How could returning to Shelbourne be any worse than that experience?

After what seemed to be an interminable journey the carriage pulled up in front of the house. The cool gray stone stood out starkly against the white snow. Philip helped her into the house and up to bed; she was weak and tired and filled with an aching emptiness.

"Sleep now, Bryonny. I'll send Mrs. Merk up with some tea." Philip had been nothing but kindness, seeing to her every need.

"Thank you, Philip. Thank you for everything." Bryonny closed her eyes.

Time went by slowly, Bryonny thinking that pregnancy had to be the worst punishment possible. She'd never felt so ill and tired and she couldn't help but wonder if it didn't have something to do with the deception with which her child had been conceived. And yet she couldn't help but love the life that grew within her, much as she couldn't help loving Julian despite everything that had happened.

The short, dark days of winter gradually began to lengthen as the frost left the air. March arrived, wet and blustery as Bryonny became heavy with her child. She would walk slowly out to the meadow and watch the first hedgehogs stirring, rooting around in the leaves for food. Snowdrops adorned the ground and the first tiny shoots of daffodils began pushing up through the sun-warmed soil only to be covered again by an overnight snowfall.

"Have you had your walk yet today, Bryonny?"

"Yes, Philip," she said with a tolerant smile, "and I've had my morning rest and my afternoon rest. You're worse than a mother hen!"

"Only because I care for you, Bryonny, and the child. You have no idea how much it means to me, and I want you both to be healthy. Has he moved much today?"

"Oh, yes. He—or she—has had his exercise, too, never fear, and now we're resting. We're both behaving ourselves, Philip." Bryonny smiled fondly at him. "You know, I don't know who creates more of a fuss—you, or Mrs. Merk."

"Oh, Lord," groaned Philip, "don't mention that woman's name to me. I swear she's becoming queerer all the time. It was against my better judgment to take her on in the first place, but she seemed so heartbroken at the prospect of losing you that I couldn't find it in my heart to refuse her! It was a major tactical error, I must say. Today she created the most terrible fuss in the kitchen, demanding that Lucy give her your lunch to carry up. I was most impressed with Lucy. She actually stood up to the woman. She's very protective of you, you know. Mrs. Merk was in a state. She stood there sputtering as Lucy made off with your tray."

"I don't know what I'd do without her. I think you're right—Mrs. Merk is becoming more peculiar, but I imagine it's because of my pregnancy. She's jealous of Lucy, and resentful of me because I won't let her hover. Poor woman. You know, she lost a child of her own, and I'm sure that has something to do with it."

"No, I didn't know that. An infant?"

"No, a little boy of five, I think. He and his father died from some fever, as I remember."

"That's how old I was when my mother died." He sighed, remembering. "Her name was Mary. I only have snatches of memory of her, like fragments of a dream. My foster parents used to tell me stories about her, and how courageous she was. I've never stopped missing her."

"What about your real father, Philip? You never talk about him."

His face darkened and he looked away. "He deserted my mother before I was born."

"Philip, that's terrible!"

"Not as terrible as what he did six years later. He was responsible for my mother's death—her murder, I should say."

"Philip! Whatever do you mean?" said Bryonny with horror.

"I don't know how it happened, exactly, but I know it to be true. All I can say is that there was an inheritance involved. Motive enough. My mother gave me up to my foster parents in order to protect me from him. And then he killed her. I suppose he would have killed me, too, if he'd known where to find me."

"Oh, Philip, no wonder you're bitter! How dreadful to go through your life knowing such a thing!"

"I didn't know anything about it until my foster mother died. She had a letter hidden away that explained everything."

"But what of your father? What happened to him?"

"He's dead," said Philip curtly. "I don't really want to discuss it any further."

"Oh, of course not . . . I'm sorry, Philip. But what an incredible story! You've had the most difficult life, and look at you now. You haven't been affected by all that tragedy. But you're right—we shouldn't think about the past. We have much happier things to look forward to. Just think, Philip only a few short weeks and we'll have the babe to fill our lives."

"Yes. A few short weeks. No time at all." Philip rose and went to the window, looking out over the cliffs.

"What on earth is it, Cynthia, that could be so urgent you summoned me up to London immediately?" Julian was exceedingly cross. If there was one thing he abhorred in women, it was emotional scenes. He scowled, looking at Cynthia who was tearfully dabbing at her eyes. The relationship had palled a long time ago, had never had anything in it, really, except as a matter of convenience. He should never have gone back to it.

"Julian, I know it must have put you out, and you were good to come so quickly. I didn't know what else to do!"

"Cynthia, do calm down and tell me what this is all about. Whatever it is, I'm sure we can fix it." He looked at her impatiently.

"Oh, Julian . . ." She wrung her handkerchief. "I've just discovered that I'm with child! There hasn't been anybody else but you, you must believe me! And now, and now I just don't know what to do . . ." She started crying afresh.

"Dear God," said Julian. His heart sank. He couldn't believe anything so awful had happened. But then, his life had been so miserable that this couldn't possibly make it much worse. He took a deep breath.

"There's only one thing for it, Cynthia. We'll have to be married." God help him, he thought.

"Married! Oh, Julian, you would hate me if you felt I'd forced you into marriage!"

"Don't be ridiculous." He spoke tonelessly, looking over her head. "It's the only solution. To have the child out of wedlock would ruin you, and I won't have a bastard child running around—what do you take me for? Why don't you make any arrangements you want for a quiet wedding. You couldn't be more than a few weeks along, so we have a little time. We might as well make it look as respectable as possible, don't you agree? Shall we say in a month, or even a fortnight if you prefer. Will that give you enough time to organize it?"

"Oh, yes," breathed Cynthia gratefully. "Julian, thank you! You've saved me—I'll make you very happy, I promise! You know how much I love you." She went to him and offered her cheek. Julian kissed it, thinking that this was possibly the worst mistake of his life.

"I've gone and done it now, Andrew," he said glumly, walking into Andrew's office.

"Julian! You're an unexpected sight, but a glad one. Sit down. Now what have you done?"

"Mrs. Ashford is in the family way, and I'm the proud father, so she tells me."

"Julian, no!" Andrew looked as if he didn't know whether to laugh or be mournful for his friend.

"I can't see what you might find amusing in the situation, Andrew. I've had to offer to marry her and quite honestly, I find the prospect appalling."

"You poor man. I do sympathize. But you know, with the way you've always shared yourself around, so to speak, it was bound to happen sooner or later. Maybe she'll produce a son and you'll have an heir at long last."

"But I don't want a son, Andrew. Once I did, but no more." His eyes were black with misery.

"I know, my friend. Any news?"

"Nothing. Nothing at all, and Bryonny's child is due in two months. That doesn't leave much time. Well, there's no point hanging around London. I think I'll go home to brood over this latest disaster in the catastrophe my life has become."

"My condolences, Julian. And have a safe journey; we don't want anything untoward happening to the bridegroom before the nuptials."

"Oh, stuff it, Montague. I'd swear you were taking a perverse pleasure in my misfortune."

"Not at all. However, you've needed something to give you a prod to bring you out of your black humor. I'm sure marriage to Cynthia will at least make life interesting again."

"Thank you for all your support, my friend. By the way, will you be my best man? It will be a very small ceremony—I hope."

"I'd be honored. Just let me know the date and I'll be there to get you stinking drunk and try to make it as painless as possible."

Julian returned to Hambledon Abbey and George took one look at his face and knew there was more trouble, if that was possible. The master had been impossibly moody and curt the last few months. Christmas had been more like a dirge than a celebration and his mood had affected everyone.

"Did things not go well in London then, my lord? You're looking more ill-tempered than when you left."

"Things went very badly in London, George. And I'm going to be looking a good deal more ill-tempered yet before this is all over. But you'll hear about it soon enough. I'm in no mood to talk."

"Yes, m' lord."

Julian shot him an irritated look and then strode off to the house. "Where's that new housekeeper, Cook, what's her name?"

"Do you mean Mrs. Humphrey, my lord?"

"Yes, that's the one. I need to talk to her."

"She'll be shocked to her very core, no doubt. It will probably be the first time you've spoken to her since she came eight months ago—aside from grunts, that is."

"That's quite enough of your acid tongue, Cook."

"Yes, my lord, whatever you say." Cook smiled complacently.

"You can tell her that I'm to be married. I'll be bringing home my new wife in a month's time. See that she has a chamber appropriately prepared, and the nursery wing will have to be made ready, of course. No point in marrying if you don't fill the nursery, isn't that what you've always told me, Cook?" He fixed her with a quelling eye.

"Why, Master Julian! That's the most wonderful news! And the way you've been acting of late, who would think you were a man with marriage on your mind?"

"I've been a man with marriage very much on my mind, Cook. Now enough of your chatter. I have work to do."

He closed himself off in his study and began to sort through a pile of papers, and with irritation he realized that he had forgotten to ask Andrew about a legal matter concerning trade agreements. He went to the bookshelf, wondering where in his father's law books he should begin to look. He pulled down a volume at random and began leafing through it, growing more impatient by the minute, his mind not fully on the task. A loose piece of paper fluttered out from between the pages and he glanced at it absently, then more sharply as the words took hold. It was a letter, dated twenty-five years before. He sat down slowly, reading intently the whole time, an incredulous expression coming over his face. "What in sweet hell. . ."

My darling Philip,

I write this letter the evening before I must give

you up forever. I do this only to ensure your own safety. Should you ever read this letter it will mean that I am dead, killed at the hand of the Earl of Carlyle. He did not want anyone ever to know who your father was and has threatened me, but I don't think he will stop there. He has found me after all this time, and I think he fears I will blackmail him. I wouldn't but I am afraid for my life, and for yours. Your father promised to marry me, but deserted us before you were born, Philip, and because you are his firstborn and come of noble blood and a great fortune, I fear that one day the Livingstons might come after you, afraid that you might try to claim your rightful inheritance. If that should happen, use this letter to protect yourself. It will only be given to you by your foster parents if you should need it. Remember that I love you, shall always love you, and what I do now, I must, for you.

Your mother,

Mary Neville

Julian sat for a moment in silence as the import of the letter slowly sank in. "My God—I don't believe it! So *that's* what Neville's been up to! It all makes sense now—and there's the motive, the dirty bastard! Bryonny, you poor girl," he said slowly, as further meaning sank in. He thought quickly. He knew Bryonny was at Shelbourne, for being her trustee, he'd been told to direct her monthly allowance there. He would have to go to Shelbourne and without further delay. Neville had to be stopped.

Quickly, he scribbled a note to Andrew, telling him to meet him at Shelbourne with all haste. He franked it with his signature. "Simms, give this to George. Have one of the boys post it. Then tell George to get the carriage ready and a good, fast team. I'll want Dougal, too. We're off to Shelbourne Hall and there's no time to waste."

"Yes, my lord," said Simms with a neutral expression, and took himself off with great dignity, burning to know what was happening now.

"Cook," Julian said, going directly to the kitchen, "I want you to make up a big basket of food; we'll need wine and brandy, too. Enough for two days and three hungry people."

"Yes, my lord, but where are you—"

"There's no time for explanations, Cook, just get on with it and quickly. I'll be back shortly." He strode off.

Cook stood looking after him in utter amazement. This had been a day of days. And was there ever a man so changeable?

Within half an hour, all was ready. Julian had thrown some clothes into a bag, taken the basket of food and drink from Cook with a curt thanks, and gone quickly off to the stables.

"Right, let's get started. George, we're going through without stopping except for changing horses. We'll keep to the turnpike, and we're going directly south-east toward Winchester. You and I will share the driving, with Dougal as a back-up. Are we ready?"

"Yes, my lord," said George, swinging up into the box.

George drove the first shift, leaving Julian to sleep. He lay with his head back against the seat, his mind thoroughly occupied with going over and over the letter and its implications. He hadn't had time to think it through clearly. His own father must have known the truth, for he'd had the letter. That would be what they'd been arguing about, and of course Philip had killed him to keep him quiet. But what about everything else? And what in God's name was he going to do about it?

The carriage rattled on as night drew in.

The day had been wet and windy, the wind blowing in off the cliffs, and Bryonny had tired of staying indoors. She longed to stretch her legs and so she slipped on some sturdy boots, although with difficulty for the mound of her stomach made it difficult to bend over, and wrapped herself in a thick cloak, creeping down the steps and out the door before anyone could find her and object. The fresh air smelled delicious, tangy with the rain and damp earth and she decided to head out toward the cliffs. The waves were bound to be up and she loved to watch them seethe and crash against the rock face. She walked slowly and cumbrously, the baby only a month away now and a heavy burden. A pair of kestrals circled overhead, sweeping on the updrafts and then diving in long arcs. Bryonny stopped to watch them spinning and twisting in the gray light.

"Now, Captain Neville, I shouldn't go bothering the mistress with all that attention. She needs her rest, you know, and gentlemen don't understand about these things. I'll just take the tea tray up myself." She tried to pull it from his hands.

"Mrs. Merk!" bellowed Philip, finally losing all patience. "I have had more than I can take of your nonsense! You are driving both Lady Bryonny and me around the bend! I think it's best if you pack your things and take yourself off. Why don't you go back to Hambledon Abbey and plague your precious Julian Ramsay? *He* deserves you!"

Her hands trembled and went to her throat. "You can't mean what you say, sir! Please, I beg you to reconsider . . ." Mrs. Merk's face crumpled. "I shall try to do better, I assure you I will!"

"The sooner you are out of here, the happier I will be. I'll give you a month's wages in lieu of notice. Have one of the boys drive you to the village. You can take the next coach out, and it couldn't leave soon enough for my liking! Good-bye, Mrs. Merk!" Philip took the tray from the shattered woman and went upstairs. He decided to say nothing to Bryonny about Mrs. Merk's dismissal until she had gone. He didn't want Bryonny's soft heart calling her back.

But he found that Bryonny was not in her room. He wandered downstairs, calling her, but she didn't answer. He went back to her room again. And then he caught a movement out the corner of his eyes and went to the window to look out. There he saw Mrs. Merk running across the meadow, and further in the distance, he could just make out the flapping of Bryonny's cloak in the wind.

"What is that crazy old woman up to now?" he muttered. And then with a sudden stab of worry, he ran down the stairs, grabbed his coat and a pistol for good measure, and tore off after them.

Chapter Fourteen

MRS. Merk was out of breath, her hand held to her side where it had cramped. She stopped to collect herself for a moment, panting heavily. She was in a panic—there was no time to lose. If she was to be forced to leave, then it was her responsibility to see that this child was never born. Bryonny must be killed, and now, and it would be a simple thing to dispose of her. She ought to have thought of this before when she had seen the the laudanum had not been working well enough, despite the large doses she had been using. How convenient that the girl had decided to take herself off to the cliffs. A simple push and it would all be over. Poor Lady Bryonny, who had been so susceptible to dizzy spells and was foolish enough to go walking on the cliffs by herself during a wind squall. Such a tragedy, they would say. She hurried on.

Bryonny stood looking over the lashing ocean, loose strands of hair whipping around her face. Her child kicked inside her and she laid her hand on her swollen belly. A noise behind her, just barely audible over the wail of the wind, caused her to start and turn.

"Mrs. Merk! What on earth are you doing out here?" asked Bryonny.

"I have come to take care of you, my dear," said Mrs. Merk, stepping toward Bryonny. "I have come to take care of you and the child."

"Mrs. Merk, I'm sure you're very kind, but I assure

you I am quite well. And to be honest, I would prefer to be alone."

Mrs. Merk's hands reached out and grabbed her, pulling her toward the cliff's edge. "No! What are you doing?" She struggled to free herself but was clumsy with the child and weak with the residue of the recent dose of laudanum.

"Let go of her. Now, Mrs. Merk!"

She gasped and turned, Bryonny held tightly to her. Philip was standing just feet away, a pistol pointed straight at her.

"No, no, you mustn't, Philip—you don't understand! I'm doing this for you!"

"Philip, please! Stop her!" cried Bryonny desperately.

"Let go of her, Mrs. Merk. I warn you; I'll shoot."

"If you shoot me, Philip, then we both go over! Listen to me! Bryonny and her child must die. The marriage and the babe are a sin against God! You cannot allow this to go on!"

Philip regarded her warily. "What are you talking about, woman?"

"She's your sister, Philip! John Livingston was your father!"

Bryonny's eyes widened in shock.

"How do you know that! Tell me!" Philip, completely astonished, was thrown off guard.

"So you did know! I had wondered. Did you find the letter, Philip? Is that how you learned your father's identity?"

"How do you know about the letter? Was it you who took it from Lord Hambledon's study?"

"No. But I had to kill Lord Hambledon to protect you, to keep you safe. I overheard him threatening you."

"My God . . ." whispered Philip. "You? *You* killed him! Why? Why would you do such a thing?"

"Because I couldn't see you exposed."

Philip ran a hand over his face. "You couldn't see me exposed."

"Don't you see? *I* am your mother, Philip. I wrote that letter. I didn't want to you to know the truth, but

I have done everything I could to help you get your inheritance."

"No! My mother was Mary Neville—she was a lady, not a servant!" The gun dropped to his side.

"That's what I wanted you to believe, but I should have known from the day you appeared at the Abbey with your sister in your arms that the truth would have to come out. Perhaps I should have told you sooner, but I couldn't bring myself to; I believed that if I kept silent I could still be near to you. I didn't expect anything more than that."

"I don't believe a word of it! You've made this up!" Philip's voice was icy. "It was you who took the letter and you're using the information in it against me. What do you want? Is it money?"

"Oh, Philip. Listen to me, and perhaps you'll understand. I was ladies' maid at Shelbourne the summer that John Livingston came home. We—we became lovers and then I discovered I was with child. John's father was a terrible man, and when he learned of my condition he sent John away to Jamaica. Then he threatened to throw me out onto the streets. So I left, but even that didn't help. He found me years later and said he was going to take you away from me. I feared for you, so I gave you up to the family who had taken me in while I was pregnant, then changed my name and disappeared. I—I went to Lord Hambledon's household, never dreaming that he and John were cousins until many years later when David, your half-brother, came to England. Do you believe me now?"

Philip had grown progressively more pale as Mrs. Merk's story mercilessly unfolded. "But then my father *didn't* kill you! My God—you, my mother! And all this time I thought you were dead, I mourned you—I even accused my father of your murder! No wonder he thought I was mad!"

"You went to your father?" It was Mrs. Merk's turn to look horrified.

"Yes—with the letter."

"Dear God . . . It all begins to make sense!"

Philip shook his head as if to clear it. "I don't

understand . . . I found the letter after my foster mother died. I assumed—when I learned that my father had come to England I went to him and told him who I was. He didn't believe me. He claimed his son was dead, dead at birth along with my mother. I told him I knew what he'd done to you, and I wanted acknowl-edgment and my rightful inheritance in exchange for my silence. He threw me out. He scorned me just as he had scorned you. I truly believed that he had mur-dered you—Mary Neville had disappeared without a trace—and so there was only one thing left for me to do. I followed him when he left Shelbourne and saw my opportunity then to avenge your death, to kill all the Livingstons and claim my inheritance. Rightfully *I* should have been Viscount Wycombe! I sabotaged the carriage, then followed it at a distance. When nothing happened, I waited until there was a steep embank-ment, then fired a shot to make the horses bolt. Ev-erything went according to plan—except that Bryonny wasn't killed with the others."

"Oh, Philip! But then *why* did you come to Hamble-don Abbey?"

"I was just finishing Bryonny off when Lord Hamble-don's coachmen interfered. I had to explain my pres-ence somehow, and I needed an alibi. I accepted their offer of help. Little did I know that Lord Hambledon would actually be related to the Livingstons!"

"And—and was it you with the gun that day in the woods?"

"Naturally. Unfortunately, my pistol kicked to the right. I didn't have another chance after that with the blasted chaperones dogging my every footstep. And then opportunity finally presented itself, but when I threw Bryonny into the lake after I thought she'd found the letter, that damned Julian pulled her out—on his father's orders, of course. I knew she'd think it had been him, with their mutual dislike of each other, so I'd be in the clear. As I was."

"Julian is innocent, Julian is innocent!" The words beat like a litany in Bryonny's head over the dreadful realization of what Philip had done.

"But Philip, you might have been caught!" cried Mrs. Merk in distress.

"Oh, on reflection, it all worked out much better than I hoped. After all, once I'd lost my letter, I no longer had any proof of my birthright. And then Cynthia presented her plan to throw Bryonny straight into my arms. It was unfortunate that Bryonny's original opinion of her cousin changed so drastically, for it made my task much harder. But everything worked out beautifully, I must say, and I had no need to press a claim or take any more risks."

"But your *sister*, Philip! How could you have married her!"

"Quite easily. I have to admit, I grew fond of Bryonny, and even fonder when she decided to present me with a child who would finally put what I wanted directly in my hands. Poor misguided Julian."

"My God!" cried Bryonny, finally managing to speak through her disgust. "You killed my family and you took from me the man you knew I loved! You've grown *fond* of me?" She stared at him with hatred. "You perverted monster! To think I trusted you! I suppose it was you with the poison, too!"

"Don't be a fool, Bryonny. Your precious Julian was after exactly the same thing I was. You were taken in by both of us. I admit that I was responsible for all your other accidents, but not the poison. That was Julian's hand."

"No, Philip." Mrs. Merk shifted her grip on Bryonny. "I was trying to prevent Bryonny from marrying you. I had warned her against it repeatedly, but the girl just wouldn't listen! I overheard your proposal, and I later heard Master Julian give his permission—although why he did and then kicked up such a fuss—"

"Mrs. Merk, please listen—" Bryonny twisted in her arms.

"—but that's neither here nor there. So I poisoned Bryonny's porridge. I did my best to keep you from committing a sin, don't you see? But then—then I discovered I'd been too late. I waited, hoping that perhaps the child would be miscarried, but it was not

to be. So you must see that I no longer have a choice!
And now Philip, now I find that you knew all along!
It's disgusting!" Her eyes grew wide with madness.
"This child is an abomination and it must die along
with its mother!" She shrieked the last words into the
wind and jerked Bryonny around, forcing her to the
precipice.

"No, Mrs. Merk! No, you're wrong—" Bryonny's
words were cut off as she cried out from a piercing
stab of pain and doubled over.

Julian found the house empty with the exception of
Lucy, who was extremely gratified to see him, and had
to bite her tongue to keep from asking why he had
come. She dearly hoped he had discovered the truth
about the baby and was going to take her mistress
back to where she belonged. But she managed to hold
her peace. "Why no, my lord, I didn't know that Lady
Bryonny had left her bed!" she said when he questioned her. "She was there the last time I looked, only
an hour ago it was. She hasn't been well, you see."

"George, check the stables! See if there's a carriage
gone. Where could they be?"

"I don't know, my lord," ventured Lucy. "But on
Lady Bryonny's good days, she often goes on walks,
out over the meadow or to sit on the cliffs. She says
she likes to think there. I usually go with her to keep
an eye on her, or help her if she becomes tired.
Perhaps the captain accompanied her. He doesn't like
it when she goes out on her own."

"Of course, the cliffs! I don't like it; I have a bad
feeling about all this. Listen now; I'm going out there.
You, Dougal and George stay here. Keep an eye out
for Mr. Montague. And if Captain Neville should return before I'm back, tell him that I have a business
matter to discuss with him."

"Yes, my lord," said Lucy obediently, but beginning to feel alarmed.

Julian checked his pistol and then quickly strode off
in the direction of the cliffs. He reached the bluff, and
his heart jerked to a stop at the sight before him. Mrs.

Merk had Bryonny in her grip on the very edge of the cliff. It was obvious what her intention was. He sprang forward.

"Stop—for God's sake, stop!"

Bryonny was dimly aware of Julian's voice cutting through the howling wind. Philip spun around, raising his pistol, but was flung aside by Julian who lunged toward Bryonny, heedless of the gun. Philip fired, and Julian felt a white hot flash through his shoulder as he reached out to grab her.

Mrs. Merk stepped back in alarm, but there was nothing beneath her foot. For a fraction of a second she swayed, her face registering nothing but blank astonishment, and then she fell backward into space with a scream, one arm still around Bryonny.

For a heart-wrenching moment, Bryonny was pulled along, a cry of terror rising in her throat, and then an iron grip locked around her arm and drew her back with a violent wrench and she found herself lying on mercifully hard ground.

"Bryonny—oh, God, Bryonny, my love . . ." Julian's arm went around her and she looked up through a swimming haze into his white face, somehow unable to believe he was real.

"Get away from my wife, Hambledon." Philip stood over them, his pistol at Julian's back.

"Please! Please do as he says, Julian," pleaded Bryonny in a choked voice. "He'll kill you!" She gasped as another stab of pain flashed through her.

"One more word about *anything,* Bryonny, and I'll kill him here and now! You know it would be my pleasure." He shot her a menacing look and she fell quiet, fully aware that he meant what he said.

Julian slowly stood, holding his right arm close to his body, blood seeping through his shirt. "I believe this issue is between you and me, Neville. Let Bryonny go."

"Go? Go where, may I ask? Let me remind you again that Bryonny is my wife, Hambledon."

Julian's eyes narrowed but he spoke cautiously. "And never should have been, as you well know. The marriage was illegal."

Philip regarded him curiously. "Just how have you come to that conclusion, Hambledon? Is this another one of your ruses?"

"No ruse. I believe it's a question of—parentage."

Philip let out a long breath. "So . . . I see you've discovered my little secret. I always did think you were a little too curious for your own good."

"And now that I know the truth? What do you plan to do?"

"I'll kill you, of course. You've meddled once too often."

"That answer comes as no surprise from you, Neville. It seems you find committing murder very easy."

Philip smiled coldly. "Only when necessary to gain my ends. The carriage mishap was my first experience, and I considered myself fully within my rights."

Julian looked at him with disgust. "I thought as much, once I started putting the pieces together. And then you killed my father to keep him silent."

"Oh, no, cousin. I didn't kill your father. As it happens, my dear mother, whom I just discovered brought *you* up, rather than her own son, did me the favor of killing him—I see you're surprised, Hambledon. Ah, the delicious irony of it. And all along, I thought it had been you; the poisoning, too. After all, why shouldn't one man's motives be the same as the next? No, my mother served me better than I could ever have imagined. And now she's gone, thank God, taking her nasty secrets with her, or I would have had to kill her, too."

"My God . . ." Julian stared at him, appalled. "And Bryonny? What of her?"

"As for Bryonny, I still need her—and the infant. She'll cooperate for the sake of the child if she knows what's good for her."

"It won't work, Neville; I'm not the only one who knows about your scheming," bluffed Julian, desperately wondering where Andrew was.

"Oh, come now, Hambledon. We all know how close-chested you are. I can't imagine you'd tell anyone about your beloved Bryonny's terrible disgrace."

"Bryonny is innocent in all this!"

"Of course she is, but that doesn't dismiss the fact that she's shortly going to give birth to my child. Naturally she must survive long enough to do that, but then I'll have no further need of her. So if you want her to live past the birth, you'll do as I tell you. You'll sign a confession to your father's murder, and the attempts on Bryonny's life, citing her inheritance as your motive. If she even considers exposing me, I'll have it as my security. Her life and the child's will be worthless if she attempts such a thing.

"As for you, you're finished in any case. But if you love Bryonny as much as you pretend, you'll write the confession. You can even die an honorable death. With your own pistol, of course. Such a neat alibi, don't you think?" He retrieved Julian's gun from his pocket and held it up. "It was so thoughtful of you to let it drop as you made your heroic rescue. I'm eternally in your debt for that." He laughed. "What do you say, *cousin*?"

Julian watched him warily. The man was obviously quite mad, and capable of anything. He stalled as he looked for his chance. "I'll do what I must to protect Bryonny and the child."

"Well spoken. I do admire men of honor. And it's so kind of you to be concerned about the welfare of my offspring." He threw back his head and laughed. "Shall we remove to the house for pen and paper?"

Julian's eyes narrowed and his body tensed. "As you wish."

Bryonny could bear no more. "No, Julian! You mustn't listen to him!"

"Silence, woman!" Philip's eyes were wild and glazed. "I warned you—"

A crack sounded out, loud and sharp in the roar of wind and ocean. Bryonny saw Julian fall to the ground, face down. She fainted.

She was aware of a tremendous wash of pain flooding through her, wracking her body until she cried out from the agony. A damp cloth passed over her forehead and a faraway voice said, "Hush, my lady; there, now."

"Lucy?" she murmured, the wave receding.

"Yes, my lady, it's Lucy. You're safe now, safe, and your babe is on the way."

"Lucy. Oh, Lucy, Julian!" It came out on a sob.

"I'm here, my love." A large, warm hand took hers gently.

Bryonny's eyes flew open, the pain forgotten. Julian was bending over her, his gray eyes looking into hers with gentle concern.

"Julian! Oh, Julian, I thought he'd killed you! I thought . . ."

"No such luck, my love." His eyes smiled at her.

"But then what happened?" She gasped as another wave of pain hit her, catching her in its crest and throwing her back into its churning darkness.

"Soon now, my lord," whispered Lucy.

"Sweet Christ, where in the name of heaven is the doctor!" Julian's brow was soaked in sweat.

"I don't know, my lord. Perhaps he couldn't be reached, but not to worry," said Lucy reassuringly. "I helped my mother out often enough when her time came. Are you sure you don't want to leave until it's over, my lord? This is not a place for men."

"Never, Lucy. While Lady Bryonny needs me, I'll be here by her side." Julian spoke with determination, but every cry of Bryonny's tore at him, far more than the searing pain in his shoulder ever could.

Another hour passed as Bryonny struggled against the contractions rending her in two. She was oblivious to everything but Julian's hand gripping hers, his voice comforting her, his hand stroking her damp forehead, and Lucy's tender, reassuring presence as her baby fought to make its way into the world. And then she felt a deep primordial force surge up in her, and gathering all of her strength, she bore down with it, straining against her burden. Again and again she pushed, concentrated deep within herself.

"Julian—oh, Julian!" she cried in anguish.

"Yes, that's it, my sweet love; it's nearly over." His eyes sought Lucy's for reassurance. This was more than he could bear.

"Now, my lady! One more time." And as Bryonny strained, the head appeared, and Lucy's hands were there to catch it as the baby's shoulders and then body slipped effortlessly from Bryonny.

His head was covered with soft, dark down and he cried lustily in an infant's short, jerking wails, and Lucy covered him in a blanket and handed him to his exhausted mother. "Oh, my lady," Lucy exclaimed, "he looks just like his father!" She gasped and covered her mouth. Julian looked painfully away.

Bryonny's eyes filled with tears as she received her son, still attached to her by his cord. "Yes, he does." She smiled at Lucy. "Oh, he's so beautiful!" she whispered, gazing at him with wonder. He was small, a month early, but he was healthy. His tiny fists were clenched and his dark eyes open, blinking at her as if in amazement at finding himself in such an unexpected situation. Bryonny laughed with unbelievable happiness.

"You'd think we'd interrupted him in the middle of a meal, he looks so indignant!" She smiled up at Julian.

But he couldn't meet her eyes. He had fought along with Bryonny to help her give birth to this child, and the miracle he had just witnessed had overwhelmed him; but as he watched Bryonny gaze down at her newborn son with undisguised adoration he was piercingly reminded of the baby's origins. How would she feel when she realized?

He stood and turned away.

"Julian?" It was then that she remembered.

"He's beautiful, my love." Julian turned back and she could see the anguish in his eyes.

"Julian, we must talk," said Bryonny softly, but he looked away from her.

"No. No, I can't. Please, excuse me." Abruptly, he left the room.

Lucy met Bryonny's eyes. "Later, my lady. Right now there are things we still need to do."

"Julian! Is it all over?" Andrew jumped to his feet.

"Yes." His voice was heavy with misery. "A boy."

"I see. How is Bryonny?"

"She's exhausted but she's perfectly well."

"And how is she about the child?"

"I don't think she understands yet. She seems overjoyed. I don't really know how much she took in of what Philip said out there. Dear God, I don't know how I'm going to tell her."

"You'll find a way, Julian. And Bryonny's a strong woman; she'll get through this, with your help."

"I hope so. I dread the pain this is going to cause her, Andrew." He winced as his shoulder grabbed him.

"Here. Drink this. We'd better get the doctor to look at that. Where is the dratted man anyway? I can't believe you just helped to birth a babe! Somehow I never would have imagined it was your style."

"Nor would I. It was—most interesting, Andrew. You'll have to try it yourself someday." The shadow of a smile crossed his face. He leaned his head back against the chair and closed his eyes, his face gray and drawn.

Eventually the doctor arrived, having been detained in another village, and much to Julian's relief, he pronounced that the bullet had gone cleanly through the shoulder, and his lordship needed only proper rest and care before he was as good as new. He looked briefly in on Bryonny, who was sleeping soundly, and did not disturb her, content with the state of her infant's health and her own. He then dressed Julian's shoulder professionally and took his leave, privately holding the opinion that matters at Shelbourne were not at all as they should be, but too wise after forty years of doctoring to intrude.

Chapter Fifteen

BRYONNY was sitting up in bed, her child in her arms, when she sensed a gaze on her and looked up to see Julian framed in the door, a large white bandage visible under his open white shirt. She smiled in relief.

"Julian! I've been so worried about you! Lucy told me you'd been shot! Are you in pain?"

"No, just sore. But never mind that." His voice was husky. He approached her bed and sat down next to her. "Bryonny . . ."

"Julian, *please* will you tell me what happened? Lucy won't say a thing! I've been going out of my mind!"

"Philip is dead, Bryonny."

She bit her lip. "I thought as much. How?"

"Andrew."

"Oh, Julian. Thank God. I was so afraid for you!"

"I know, my love. But you needn't have been. As you see, I'm here in more or less one piece."

"But I saw you fall . . ."

"I thought it would be advisable to get out of the way of Andrew's bullet. I saw him take aim just before you screamed."

"But how did you and Andrew know to come? I was so dreadful to you, Julian! Philip said the most terrible things about you, and God help me, I believed him. Will you ever be able to forgive me?" Her eyes sparkled with tears.

"There's nothing to forgive, Bryonny. If anyone

should be asking forgiveness, it is I. I certainly gave you enough cause to doubt me. In any case, I should have realized what was going on and stopped him. You know I never trusted him; I always suspected that he was after your inheritance. And then when I discovered that he was . . ." His voice broke and he looked down. "Bryonny, I don't know how to tell you this . . ."

"That Philip was my half-brother?" she said softly.

He stared at her. "You *knew*?"

"I only learned about it out on the cliffs, before you came. Philip didn't know that Mrs. Merk was his mother until then, and I heard the story. But I still don't understand how you knew."

"There was a letter. I found it in a law book in the study. I came as soon as I could."

"So that was the letter Mrs. Merk was referring to!" She told him what she'd heard. "And you see, that's why Mrs. Merk was going to kill me; she had it in her mind that the babe was a sin."

Julian avoided Bryonny's eyes and his gaze fell down to the infant. He finally looked up. "Bryonny, about the child. I don't know how you feel. If it's too painful for you to care for him, I'll take him, bring him up. I feel so responsible for what happened to you. And he need never know the circumstances of his birth. He shouldn't have to suffer for what happened."

As the meaning of Julian's words sank in, Bryonny realized that he still hadn't guessed at the truth. A gentle smile played on her lips and she looked down at the baby in her arms, who so much resembled his father. She couldn't believe Julian hadn't seen it and put the pieces together. The child was small but lusty, most certainly not two months early. The humor of the situation suddenly struck her.

"I should certainly think you would bring him up," she said, bursting into gales of laughter.

Julian looked at Bryonny in complete bewilderment. "Bryonny, I'm deadly serious!"

"But of course you are! I've always known you were an honorable man, Julian." Her lips trembled with suppressed laughter and her eyes danced. "It only follows that you'd take responsibility for your son. But do you think I might be allowed to visit him every now and then?"

Julian stared at her. "My—what did you say? For God's sake, Bryonny, are you telling me this is my child?" His voice was barely a whisper.

"Yes, my love, that's exactly what I'm telling you. How could you believe I could ever be with anyone else after what we shared? I never stopped loving you, Julian, even in my darkest moments of doubting you, no matter how hard I tried. The knowledge that I was carrying your child sustained me. It was all I had left of you."

"Oh, Bryonny. My son . . ." He shook his head. "I can scarcely take it in! And after all these months of thinking it was Philip's child! Why didn't you tell me?"

"I couldn't, Julian. Not believing what I did. I'm so sorry." She met his eyes evenly.

"When you ran away from me and married Philip, I thought it was because I'd scared you away after that night, implausible as it seemed." He smiled gently. "I couldn't believe that you really loved him, Bryonny, not after that. But when you told me you were with child, I thought that perhaps you cared for him after all. Nothing made any sense to me. But now I think I understand, although there are still some pieces missing. You—you never shared a bed with him?"

Bryonny smiled. "Never, Julian. I couldn't have married him if it had been so. Philip offered me a marriage of convenience; now we know why he was so gracious. In fact, he was delighted with my pregnancy; it solved all his problems. He hated you, you know—he truly believed you were after the Livingston fortune, and he was going to use your own child to spite you."

"The whole damned thing is unbelievable! My child all along . . ." Julian looked down at the baby tenderly. The infant's eyes were closed, his little rosebud mouth pursed in contentment, his fists resting alongside his cheeks. "He's very beautiful, my love." His large hand gently covered the baby's tiny head.

"I'm so glad you appreciate my efforts, Julian." She smiled up at him.

He laughed shakily, recovering his composure. "I'm just remembering some of my own efforts that went into producing him—just here, as I recall."

"So it was, my lord," she said softly.

Julian cocked his eyebrow and grinned. "It's so satisfying to see the result of my labors." He slowly bent down and lowered his mouth onto hers in a soft kiss. Then he sighed and said huskily, "I've waited eight months, I suppose I can wait a little while longer. Infants really are the most dreadful nuisance."

"Julian, you are incorrigible!"

"Yes, I am. But how can you possibly blame me for my impatience after you left me with such warm memories?" He smiled. "Bryonny, my sweet, I don't usually make a habit of repeating myself, but will you marry me?"

"I think I could consider it, Julian. After all, you really owe it to me to make me a respectable woman." Her smile widened.

Julian looked at her for a long moment, and then he reached down and cupped her face in his hands. "Bryonny Livingston, you are the most impossible, intractable woman a man could ever have the misfortune to have heaped on him, but you certainly do make life interesting." He kissed her again, his warm lips lingering on hers. "And I love you."

"I know. I think you've loved me from the moment you nearly ran me over with your phaeton."

"I don't know if I'd go that far, although I remember the moment well. No, I think I can definitely say that love was not an emotion I was feeling at the time."

"No? Well, nor I for you. I don't suppose, either, as you were verbally abusing me, that you expected I'd be presenting you with a son." She offered him his child with dancing eyes.

"Believe me, the thought didn't cross my mind," said Julian with a smile, taking the little bundle easily.

"In fact, if it had, it would have been a most unnatural one, considering the circumstances, my little stableboy."

"When then, exactly," said Bryonny, smothering her laughter, "did the thought cross your mind?"

"Most exactly that second night when you appeared in the library looking like a water nymph, and I thought I'd been struck senseless. Of course it wasn't a son I was thinking about, rather the events leading up to one. I was extremely amused when you sweetly asked me if you'd invaded my privacy. You had no idea how much!"

The laughter bubbled over. "Julian, you cad!"

"So you've told me often, my love. But look where it's gotten me."

Bryonny sighed happily, leaning back against the pillows as she watched Julian cradle the baby.

"Andrew!" Julian strode into the library.

"My, my, for someone who was looking as if the world had come to an end just an hour ago, you certainly have recovered yourself. Can I assume things went well?" Andrew regarded his friend quizzically.

"That is not exactly the word I'd use. Andrew, Bryonny and I are to be married. And the child—he's mine, Andrew! I have a son!"

Andrew was silent for a long moment as he absorbed this information. "You certainly are prolific, aren't you?"

Julian looked at him distractedly. "What? Look, Andrew, would you do me a favor? Get a minister over here as soon as you can. You'll stand as my best man, won't you?"

"I already am your best man, my friend."

"Dear, sweet Christ! Cynthia!"

"Remember her? The mother of your other child." Andrew regarded Julian wryly.

"Oh, God, Andrew, now what am I going to do?"

"Well, if you will sow your wild oats all over England, you have to expect a few small harvests. Of course, bigamy is always a possibility—I'll never tell. But try to keep it down to two, will you?"

"Andrew," roared Julian. "This is no laughing matter!"

"Oh, but it is, Julian." Andrew grinned. "I think the only one who won't be amused is Cynthia." He decided regretfully to let Julian off the hook. "Especially," he continued, "when you tell her that you know she is incapable of having children."

"What are you talking about, man?" asked Julian in confusion.

"I did a little research."

"What are you getting at? What sort of research could you have been doing?"

"I know it's unethical, but I've had a bad feeling about Cynthia from the start and I decided not to let ethics get in the way. After all, she certainly didn't. You know as well as I that doctors can be bought. Cynthia is barren, my friend, and the only thing she hoped to bear was your title. I remembered that there'd been talk when she'd been married to Ashford; he was desperate for a son to carry his name, and as we know, she didn't produce one. It wasn't a difficult matter to find out what doctor she frequented. He was most cooperative when I dangled a hefty sum in front of his nose. By the way, I just happen to have a bill for services rendered. Now, about that minister."

Julian grabbed Andrew around the shoulders with his good arm, not knowing whether to strangle him or to embrace him. "Andrew, you heartless fiend, I don't know how I'll ever thank you."

"Oh, I have a few suggestions."

"Save it for later. Just get out of here and find me a minister—and don't forget the license."

"Unlikely I'd forget the legal details. That's another twenty-five pounds I'll add to your account."

"Just go," said Julian, laughing.

The minister arrived the next afternoon, after Julian and Andrew had spent a long and difficult morning with the authorities, giving them a story close enough to the truth, with the omission of Philip's true relationship to Bryonny. Satisfied, the police had declared the matter closed. Andrew led the minister upstairs to Bryonny's bedroom, and he had the presence of mind to not blink an eye when he took in the scene in front of him. Julian was stretched out on Bryonny's bed, his arm around her and their heads were bent together over their newborn. Julian uncoiled himself when the minister came in and walked over to greet him.

"Reverend Purcell, the Marquess of Hambledon," introduced Andrew. "And Lady Bryonny Livingston."

The little man bowed. "Are we quite ready?"

"No!" Bryonny said, quickly. "Andrew, could you call Lucy and George and Dougal? I'd like them to be here."

Julian smiled. "They deserve to be, after all they've done for us." Andrew obliged.

Lucy ran in, flushed, a little bouquet of flowers in her hand which she gave to Bryonny. "There, my lady. Now you look like a proper bride."

Julian's and Bryonny's eyes met and they burst into laughter.

George and Dougal came next, Dougal looking terribly pleased and embarrassed at the same time. He kept his eyes down and scuffed his feet, not sure what to do with such unprecendented familiarity, and Lucy went to stand at his side reassuringly. But George went straight over to Bryonny's bed and peered down at the baby. "My congratulations, m'lady," said George, his face creased by an enormous grin.

"Thank you, George." She held him up for George's inspection. "You'll soon be teaching him to ride just as you did his father."

George beamed even wider. "He's a fine looking lad. A fine looking lad, indeed, and if you don't mind my saying, it's high time the two of you were married. But then neither of you has ever done things like ordinary folk, so far as I've ever seen, and this ain't no different." Julian choked and Bryonny grinned in delight.

Reverend Purcell closed his eyes momentarily. Then he composed himself and cleared his throat. "May we begin?"

Julian sat down on the bed again and took Bryonny's hand. "Marry us, Reverend."

They said their vows, Julian grinning all the while, but his smile faded when the minister said, "The ring, please."

"Oh, dear Lord! I forgot about a ring!"

"Naturally," said Andrew, withdrawing a plain gold band from his pocket and handing it to him. Julian shot him a look of gratitude and slipped it on Bryonny's finger.

"I now pronounce you man and wife." The Reverend Purcell heaved a sigh of relief that it was over.

"Thank you, Reverend Purcell. I was wondering if you might do one more thing for us," said Julian comfortably. "As you're here, do you think you might christen our son?"

The Reverend Purcell coughed into his handkerchief. "Certainly, my lord."

"Andrew, would you do us the honor of being god father?"

"I would be proud." His eyes were filled with suppressed laughter. He could clearly see the poor minister's offended sensibilities; he had been careful not to explain the situation in too much detail to the man before he had arrived, saying only that he needed a marriage performed quickly due to unusual circumstances.

"His name, please?"

"Andrew Richard John Ramsay."

Andrew's eyes met Julian's. An unspoken message passed between them, the words unnecessary.

His son duly christened, Julian turned to the minister.

"I thank you, Reverend Purcell, for your services. You may go now." Julian summarily dismissed the little man, who scurried out as quickly as he civilly could.

Andrew followed him downstairs and had a quick word with him. The Reverend Purcell's face paled. "You want me to do what!"

"Just a quick burial. Everything is ready, and it should only take a minute." Andrew and Julian had decided that Philip should have a Christian burial, despite his sins. Mrs. Merk's body had been unrecoverable, washed away in the ocean.

"And just who is it I'm burying, may I ask?"

Andrew couldn't resist. "Lady Bryonny's late husband."

The minister fainted.

Julian and Bryonny decided to stay at Shelbourne for the next six weeks, until the baby was old enough to undertake the long journey back to Hambledon Abbey. He sent a letter home, requesting that a trunk be packed for him and sent to Southampton. Andrew returned to London, bearing a letter for Cynthia. It was his first order of business.

"Mr. Montague! What a pleasant surprise! I suppose you come because you have heard the news of my engagement to Lord Hambledon. I haven't heard from him in a week, and we are to be married in a fortnight. I hope you come with news of him?"

"That is exactly why I come, Mrs. Ashford."

"Oh, what a relief! Tell me!"

"I have a letter here for you which he asked me to deliver."

"A letter? Oh, well, give it to me then." She opened it impatiently.

My dear Cynthia,

I write to tell you that I must call off our engagement. It's awkward, I know, but the fact is that I find I already have a wife and child. I hope that this will not cause you too much inconvenience, but I am certain you will think up some little tale to tell your friends. I regret if this causes you any undue discomfort.

Your servant, etc.,

Hambledon

Cynthia slowly sank into a chair, staring disbelievingly at the letter.

"What does this mean? I don't understand!"

"I'm sure Lord Hambledon made himself very clear, Mrs. Ashford." Andrew regarded her coolly.

"But a wife! A child? It's not possible! He can't do this to me! What about my own child? I don't believe him—I shall sue him for breach of promise!"

"I don't think that would be very wise. I assure you, it's quite true, and aside from that, I'm sure you wouldn't want the word of your little deception spread around London, now would you? And Lord Hambledon isn't very pleased with you at the moment. After all, it's not a very pretty thing to trap a man into marriage with such sort of mistruth, more especially when you know you could never give him an heir. We have a legal name for that sort of thing."

"No!" Cynthia cried. Her lips were bloodless. "No, I will do what he wants. I—I will say that I cried off myself."

"A wise decision, Mrs. Ashford. And in your own self-interest, although that doesn't really surprise me."

"Please. Please, Mr. Montague. I don't know how you discovered me, but I admit to it, so you needn't hammer your point home." Her voice was a dry whisper. "I can only ask you to keep it to yourself, and I swear, I will say nothing against Lord Hambledon. But please, I don't understand. Who is this wife and child?"

"Lady Bryonny is the Marchioness of Hambledon and their son, Andrew, the new Earl of Richmond."

"But this is impossible! What of Captain Neville!"

"Dead in an unfortunate accident. I'm afraid I can tell you no more, but the child is most assuredly Lord Hambledon's. His heir, Mrs. Ashford."

"I see. Yes, I see." She looked up at him, her eyes blank. "I think I would like to be alone now, Mr. Montague, if you please."

"Of course. Good day, Mrs. Ashford." Andrew left her staring out the window. He encountered Marie standing in the hallway, her face a mask of bitter hatred. He could assume she had heard everything.

"I think you had better go in to Mrs. Ashford, Mademoiselle Dupris. She'll be needing some help to get herself out of an embarrassing situation."

He turned sharply on his heel and let himself out.

Bryonny and Julian spent long hours talking about everything that had occurred, from the unfortunate affair between Mary Neville and John Livingston to the final scene played out on the cliffs so many years later. Lucy had found the laudanum among Mrs. Merk's belongings, and so the mystery of Bryonny's exhaustion and dizzy spells was solved. It was only the good luck that Lucy had superstitiously taken to throwing out most of Mrs. Merk's possets that had kept the unborn child from being harmed by the drug. Julian was outraged and it took Bryonny all of one morning to calm him down, but finally had him laughing when she pointed out that poor Mrs. Merk must have originally intended to keep her asleep for the duration of the marriage rather than let her son take his wife to bed. Julian described Mrs. Merk's face when he'd left the house the day he—and she—had learned of Bryonny's pregnancy, and swore that, if it were possible, she'd looked more upset than he had. Bryonny simply said that it served her right for being so nosy. It amazed her that the woman had never caught on about them. Ironically enough, if she had, Bryonny would never have been forced into marriage with Philip.

Bryonny and Julian had long since worked out the misunderstandings that had sent her running from him, and he could bear no grudge, for it was easy to see where his often boorish behavior could have led Bryonny to the conclusions she had drawn, with Philip carefully planting the seeds. Julian could only be incredibly grateful for the timing of the discovery; he had come so close to losing Bryonny forever. She had laughed until she cried when he told her the reason for his argument with his father the day he'd died. He took her teasing in good grace, feeling rather sheepish; he could now see that his outrage had come from pure jealousy which he never would have acknowledged at the time, although when he thought back over it, his father had clearly seen through him. The realization helped to heal the deep wound of their last argument.

He was so grateful to have Bryonny back with him safe and sound that he was reluctant to let her out of his sight. It was as if he needed to make up for all the time they had lost. He didn't sleep with her at night, fearful of disturbing her, but even more fearful that he would not be able to control his strong impulses. Each time that he held her in his arms it became harder for him to pull away.

Bryonny was well aware of his dilemma and found it extremely amusing. She, too, was impatiently looking forward to the day that they could be together again.

"Tomorrow, my love." They were sitting peacefully on the sofa in her room, Julian's legs stretched out in front of him, Bryonny's head resting on his chest as he stroked her hair. They'd had their supper and Bryonny had fed Andrew, sending him off to the nursery with Lucy to be put to bed. The night was still and filled with contentment, the fire sparkling and crackling, reflecting a soft golden glow into the room.

"Yes, tomorrow. I can hardly believe that I'm finally going home, Julian." Bryonny spoke softly.

"There was a time that I never believed you would be coming home, my love. I can't tell you what torture I went through."

"And I. I thought I'd never see Bedlam again."

"You little she-devil!" Julian tugged at a lock of hair. "I thought I'd replaced stallions in your affections."

"I merely replaced one stallion with another," she said with a grin.

"Oh, I see! And am I to be honored by that last remark, ma'am?"

"In truth, I can't remember, my lord. It's been so long since I've had acquaintanceship with either."

"And which have you missed the more?" he asked with a little smile.

She reached up and took his face between her hands in answer.

His heart hammered in his chest and his breath grew ragged as he read her expression. He gathered her into his arms and fitted his mouth to hers, capturing it in a long kiss, and she responded to him, opening her mouth under his, slipping her arms around his neck and pressing her warm body close against him, kindling a fire in his loins.

He gently pulled away, rubbing his forehead with his fingers.

"Julian?" asked Bryonny softly.

"Bryonny, my love, I think it would be better if I retired now."

"Retire, Julian? But it's early yet," said Bryonny as innocently as she could manage, stroking his thigh as she spoke, fully aware of his discomfiture.

"We have a long day tomorrow. It's important that you be well rested." His voice was hoarse.

"In that case I think I must take your husbandly words of advice and go to bed immediately," she said with a smile, unbuttoning the bodice of her gown. Her breasts glowed like white satin in the firelight as she released the ribbon of her chemise.

"Bryonny, for God's sake!" cried Julian in despair. "I'm a man, not a blasted saint!"

"Really?" said Bryonny, her smile widening. "Sainthood never occurred to me, but your manhood begins to come into question."

He looked at her for a long moment. "Is that a challenge, my lady?"

"I would think you'd recognize my challenges by now, Julian."

"And it's been a point of honor that I've never turned one down." He caught her up in his arms, carrying her to the bed and laying her down. Bryonny's fingers reached for his shirt and slowly began to undo its buttons, her hands stroking his chest as she drew it off. Julian's shoulder had healed but the scar was still raw and raised. She pressed her soft lips to it, and then to his neck, her hands going around his back to caress his corded muscles.

Julian, whose control was at its very limit, managed to remove the rest of her clothes without doing too much damage, and paused only to impatiently discard his trousers. Then he lowered his head to her throat, kissing it until she arched her neck back, and he followed the curve down to her full, round breast, tonguing it gently. Bryonny moaned softly with pleasure and his hand found its way over her softly curved abdomen and down, down to her center only to find with surprise that she was very ready for him.

He looked into her eyes, ablaze with passion. "Are you sure, my love?" he asked on a whisper. "I don't want to harm you . . ."

"Sainthood doesn't become you, Julian," she murmured, pulling him toward her. "I'd far rather have the man."

Julian did not delay in fulfilling her request. He opened her to him and sheathed himself in her with a groan of relief. His blood pounded unmercifully as he moved his hips in an ancient rhythm, faster and faster, moving toward an inevitable conclusion as the tide of piercing sensation swept him so high that he felt he could bear no more.

"Bryonny!" he cried as he crested and exploded within her, and then she cried out too, as she pulsed against him, raising her hips to pull him even deeper, the waves of fulfillment crashing through her very being.

And then they were still, their hearts gradually slowing, and finally Julian raised himself and looked down at her, brushing back the wet strands of hair from her flushed face. She opened her eyes and smiled at him.

"Was it worth the wait, my lord?"

"Oh, I don't know. One woman's the same as the next. Is it not so with stallions?" He spoke with a straight face, and then burst into laughter as Bryonny reached behind her and threw a pillow at him.

"You are a callous rake and a notorious womanizer, and not to be trusted, Julian Ramsay!" Her eyes danced.

"It's true, my love, although from now on, I plan to do my womanizing in one place. If the lady is willing to pick up the challenge, of course."

"I'd say that the lady was very willing." Bryonny sat up in bed, letting the sheet fall slowly to her waist.

"Then I'd say she had met her match." He reached for her, his heart beginning to pound once again.

"Honors even," said Bryonny softly, melting into his arms.

Julian packed the last of his clothes away in his trunk and shut the lid. "Bryonny . . ." he said carefully. He turned to look at her where she was brushing her hair at the dressing table.

"What is it, my love?" She glanced up curiously at the serious tone in his voice.

"There's one thing we haven't discussed about going home." He came to stand beside her and gently laid his hand on her shoulder. The sun streamed brightly in through the window and highlighted the burnished strands of her hair.

"Julian?" asked Bryonny, suddenly worried. She put down her brush and turned to face him. "What has you looking so solemn?"

"You do realize that there will be a certain amount of—scandal when people realize that Andrew's conception somewhat preceded our marriage?"

"Oh, is *that* all," laughed Bryonny, relieved it was nothing worse. "To tell you the truth, my lord, it will be interesting to be a scandal, I assure you. And scandal is only what people expect of *you*, Julian; how sad it would be to disappoint them!"

"Bryonny, you little vixen! I can't imagine what well-brought-up woman would bring up his dubious past to her husband!"

"But I wasn't well brought-up, Julian, as you constantly remind me. And you see, I have just managed to scandalize you, so the role suits me very well!" Her eyes danced with mirth.

Julian smiled and dropped a kiss on top of her head. "I would expect no less from you, my love. But seriously, there is bound to be talk, and I don't want you hurt."

"Talk blows over, Julian, and only serves to entertain those with nothing better to do. I really couldn't care less. I have you and Andrew, and believe me, it suffices. But," she added wickedly, "if there is talk, I can imagine from which corner it will come most viciously."

"And what corner might that be?" he said with a little smile.

"You're not to fly into a rage, Julian, but Cynthia is sure to be displeased by the news that her prize has been snatched from beneath her nose. If anyone spreads malicious gossip, it will be she." Bryonny picked up her brush again.

Julian turned and walked over to the window. "You need not trouble yourself on that score, Bryonny. Cynthia will be the last person to make trouble, of that I can assure you. As it happens, I have an interesting piece of blackmail on her and she knows I wouldn't hesitate to use it."

Bryonny looked at him speculatively, but decided to say nothing. "Julian, there's no one other than Andrew who knows the truth about Philip. How on earth are we going to explain—"

"We explain nothing. I don't intend for the world to know the truth. Andrew will simply let it drop that it was a love match between us, and let the world assume that you married Philip to protect your virtue, because you thought I, the notorious rake, would not marry you. It's what Lucy seems to have thought, after all," he said, grinning.

"Well, then, what about Philip's death?"

"Now that is a little trickier. I think . . . I think I discovered that the child was mine, and came to claim you both. There was a duel, and I, naturally, being the better shot—"

"Julian! That's more scandalous than the truth!"

"I know, but I do so like to be a blackguard. And

don't think that's not exactly what I'd have done if I'd known."

Bryonny smiled happily.

"But seriously, I do believe that Philip was killed by highwaymen, and in your grief you summoned me to your side and the truth came out."

"How *boring*! I wouldn't be such a milksop!"

"I'm afraid you're going to have to be in this version, my love. As I said, I intend to say nothing, but Andrew will plant the seeds of the story in the right ear, and that's all that's necessary. It will be interesting to see how it spreads."

"Which ear did you have in mind?"

"His valet's. He's unfailingly discreet, but Andrew will instruct him to pass the news to all his friends, and naturally word will drift upstairs into the appropriate drawing rooms. If Andrew does his job correctly, you'll come out looking like a tragic heroine. I'm already tarnished, and so nobody will be the least bit surprised about my role in the piece. And I do believe that Cynthia will be the first to proclaim that you and I have been in love since we met."

"You really must have the goods on her!"

"Such a vulgar expression, but yes, I do. Ah, Bryonny, about that—there's one last thing you should know. I'm afraid that Cynthia and I were to be married shortly." He watched her for her reaction, laughter lurking in his eyes.

"You what! Julian Ramsay, you cad, how could you! And why didn't you tell me before this?" Bryonny's eyes flashed in outrage.

Julian laughed. "Jealous, my love? I assure you, there's no need to be. My heart has always belonged to you."

"At this moment I should like to claim my property by cutting it out of your perfidious chest!" She leaped up and beat her fists against his hard muscles somewhere in the region of the offending organ.

"You know, Bryonny, when it comes to marrying the wrong person, you haven't got a leg to stand on," he said shaking with laughter. "No, now calm yourself, my love." He took her wrists and sat her back down. "There is an explanation, you know. I'm afraid it's a little indelicate, but I doubt it will surprise you. Cynthia told me she was having my child."

"Oh, Julian—no!" Bryonny's hand went to her mouth.

"So she claimed. I had no reason to doubt her, but Andrew discovered that she cannot bear a child. It was a lie designed to entrap me. Now do you understand?"

The breath went out of Bryonny in a long sigh. "Thank God." Then, as the meaning of Cynthia's lie set in, she said, "That's appalling! Even I can't believe she'd stoop so low! But surely she knew in only months you'd learn that—oh, of course. A conveniently staged miscarriage."

"Exactly. Not very nice. You should know that I considered marriage to Cynthia a fate worse than death, but Philip's letter saved me from that, too."

"Oh, Julian, look what terrible things happen because of lies and treachery."

"And now do you believe me when I tell you of the evil that lurks in man's chest?"

"You know I conceded the point months ago. Of course, that was when I thought you had proved out your own argument."

"Wicked girl. And do you also concede that I was right about choosing one's fate?"

Bryonny slipped her arms around him, pulling him close. "Yes, my lord. You were quite right."

Cook was in the kitchen garden when she heard the sound of a carriage pulling up the front drive. She poked her head out of the door curiously. "The master, no doubt, finally decided to return home. When will he ever learn to send notice? How am I supposed to know how many to prepare meals for! No one ever tells me anything, but they expect it all to be right there at the ready," she grumbled to herself, coming out to greet him.

Julian descended from the carriage. "Cook," he

said imperiously, his face wreathed in a grin, "I hope you and that woman, Mrs. Humphrey, have made adequate preparations for my bride as I requested?"

"Yes, my lord, all is in readiness, but you might have thought to give us some warning!" She looked horrified.

"Cook," he said, his grin growing even wider, "you should know by now that I do things in my own time and my own way. And if you've finished scolding, I would like to introduce you to my wife, the Marchioness of Hambledon, and our son Andrew."

Cook, probably for the first time in her life, was at a loss for words. She looked at Julian in complete amazement, her eyes as round as saucers. A familiar voice, long missed, came from behind her, bubbling with laughter.

"What is the trouble, Cook? Have I been away so long that you no longer know me?"

Cook spun around and threw her hands up in the air in a joyous exclamation. And then she smothered Bryonny and her child in her ample embrace. Recovering herself, she pulled away and looked at Bryonny severely.

"I might have known, Lady Bryonny, er, Lady Hambledon, that only you could unsettle the household in such a fashion." Tears streamed unbidden down her cheeks.

Bryonny grinned and casually handed her the baby. "Is there any poppy cake, Cook? I'm famished. Andrew gives me such an appetite."

About the Author

Katherine Kingsley was born in New York City and grew up there and in England. She is married to an Englishman and they live in the Colorado Mountains with their son.

A Signet Super Regency

"A tender and sensitive love story . . . an
exciting blend of romance and history"
—*Romantic Times*

The Guarded Heart
Barbara Hazard

Passion and danger embraced her—
but one man intoxicated her flesh
with love's irresistible promise . . .

Beautiful Erica Stone found her husband mysteriously mur-
dered in Vienna and herself alone and helpless in this city
of romance . . . until the handsome, cynical Owen Kingsley, Duke of Graves, promised her protection if she would
spy for England among the licentious lords of Europe.
Aside from the danger and intrigue, Erica found herself
wrestling with her passion, for the tantalizingly reserved
Duke, when their first achingly tender kiss sparked a
desire in her more powerfully exciting than her hesitant
heart had ever felt before. . . .
